George Gilfillan

Life of Sir Walter Scott

George Gilfillan

Life of Sir Walter Scott

ISBN/EAN: 9783337388744

Printed in Europe, USA, Canada, Australia, Japan

Cover: Foto ©Andreas Hilbeck / pixelio.de

More available books at **www.hansebooks.com**

LIFE

OF

SIR WALTER SCOTT,

BARONET.

BY THE

REV. GEORGE GILFILLAN,

DUNDEE.

EDINBURGH:

WILLIAM OLIPHANT & CO.

1870.

PREFACE.

THE purpose of the following work requires very little explanation. It was thought by its publishers—a view in which the author thoroughly coincided—that a popular life of Sir Walter Scott was a desideratum. There are indeed various lives of Sir Walter already. Lockhart's has long been the standard one, and continues to be justly regarded as a very able work, and as a mine of information on the subject. But it is too large, and, besides the personalities which abound in it and rather lessen its value, it contains a mass of correspondence and minute details which seem somewhat irrelevant and uninteresting now,—Scott's letters being the dullest of all his productions. There are many smaller lives; but they are in general meagre outlines.

The author has sought to produce something between the large work of Lockhart and the slighter biographies. He has not catered for gossip, and his book will be found to contain little, although there are not a few new facts sprinkled throughout. It aims rather at being an accurate summary of the leading events in Scott's life, and a candid, full, and genial criticism on his principal works. How far its aim has been successfully gained, the public must decide.

The book, whatever be its defects, may be thought a 'word in season,' as connected in time with that centenary celebration which is at hand, and which may be regarded not merely as a tribute to Scott's memory, but as at once an acknowledgment and outcome of that large and loving spirit which is abroad in the age, and which has been partly the result of the extensive diffusion of Sir Walter's writings.

Shakspeare says :

'The evil that men do lives after them ; the good
Is oft interred with their bones.'

It has been otherwise with Scott. Whatever was small and narrow in his history and opinions is forgotten. His real nature, which was as broad and catholic as the sun, remains with us, and is still powerfully affecting the world. Sitting the

other day under the shadow of his Edinburgh
monument, with the glory of a rich September
afternoon bathing the city which Scott loved so
well, we thought that we had too long regarded
him as a mirror of national manners and peculiarities, and that his true mission had been
misunderstood. That was of a cosmopolitan and
Christian character. And even as that splendid
monument is now pointing to the most magnificent
of landscapes, overhung by the most golden and
benignant of skies, united together into one grand
whole, his genius seemed to predict in its all-sided
character a nobler harmony, a more thorough re-
conciliation of the jarring elements in society and
human nature, than we can at present conceive of,
and leads us—undisturbed by the sad events of
the time—to anticipate, though faintly and far off,
that of which this beautiful day seems a prophecy
and a pledge :

'The bridal of the earth and sky.'

DUNDEE, *September* 1870.

CONTENTS.

CHAPTER XXIV.

CHAPTER XXV.

CHAPTER XXVI.

CHAPTER XXVII.

CONCLUSION.

CHAPTER I.

SCOTT IN BOYHOOD.

'THE child is father of the man;' and this is true of none more, or so much, as of Sir Walter Scott. Nay, in him, as in many great men, the man and the child refuse to be separated: they are always one. In his boyhood we find clear and full exemplification of all his noble qualities, his enthusiasm, warm-hearted affection, bold manly feelings, sense, honesty, and invincible perseverance. Afterwards these characteristics ripened and expanded, but they never changed; and hence a unity, amidst great breadth, in Scott as a man and as a writer, which has been rarely equalled, and perhaps never surpassed.

Walter Scott—the possessor of a name and fame only inferior in extent, and probably equal in duration, to those of Homer and Shakspeare— was born in Edinburgh on the 15th of August

1771, the same day of the month as had been sig-
nalized two years before by the birth of Napoleon
Bonaparte. He was the son of Walter Scott,
W.S., and Anne Rutherford, daughter of Dr. John
Rutherford, Professor of Medicine in the University of Edinburgh. Sir Walter, by his father, was
descended from a family on the Border, of old
extraction, which had branched off from the main
stem of the house of Buccleugh, and produced
some remarkable characters : such as Auld Wat
of Harden, famous in Border story and in the song
of his great descendant ; and Beardie (so called
from an enormous beard, which—as was also said
of Thomas Dalziel the Cavalier general—he never
cut, in token of his regret for the banished house
of Stuart), who was the great-grandfather of the
poet. Through his mother he was connected with
two other ancient families : the Bauld Rutherfords,
mentioned in the *Minstrelsy of the Scottish Border;* and the Swintons, one of whom (Sir John)
is extolled by Froissart as having unhorsed, at the
battle of Beaugé in France, the Duke of Clarence,
brother to Henry, and is the hero of Scott's own
poetic sketch, *Halidon Hill.* Through the Swintons Scott could also trace a connection between
himself and William Alexander Earl of Stirling,
the well-known poet and dramatist. Sir Walter

was proud of his lineage, proud of his connection with the Border, and almost looked on Harden as his birthplace. He for many years made regularly an autumnal excursion to the tower, picturesquely situated in a deep, dark, and narrow glen, through which a mountain brook discharges its waters into the Borthwick, a tributary of the Teviot. To this tower Auld Wat had brought home his beautiful bride Mary Scott, the 'Flower of Yarrow,'—the subject of many a Border ditty, and whose gentle disposition contrasted piquantly with the rough valour and masculine virtues of her lord. It was she who, when the last bullock stolen ('conveyed,' we will it call) from the English pastures was consumed, set before the assembled guests a pair of clean spurs, as a broad hint that they must work if they expected any more to eat. Beardie, too, he delights to commemorate for his devoted Jacobitism, his learning, and his intimacy with Dr. Pitcairn; although he admits that his political zeal, and the intrigues and scrapes it led him into withal, were the ruin of his fortunes, and nearly cost him his head. From his ancestors Scott derived some of his principal peculiarities—his ardent attachment to Scotland, his lingering love for the Pretender, his sympathy with martial enterprise and spirit, and a certain 'hairbrained sentimental trace' which took eccentric shapes in his predecessors, but in him became the fire of the great lyrical bard.

Beardie left three sons, and the second—Robert Scott—was the grandfather of the poet. He leased from Mr. Scott of Harden, his relative and chief, the farm of Sandyknowe. This is situated about a bowshot from the remarkable tower of Smailholm—a tower which figures in the poet's *Marmion* and *Eve of St. John.* It stands, a ruin, on the top of a rock of considerable height, surrounded by an amphitheatre of rugged hills, and commanding a most varied and magnificent prospect, including Dryburgh, where Scott himself now lies, 'not dead, but sleeping;' Melrose, on which his genius shed a light more magical than even the pale moonshine in which it shows so sweetly; Mertoun, with its deep groves—the seat of the Harden family; the Broom of the Cowden-knowes;

'Bonny Teviotdale, and Cheviot mountains blue;'

the Eildon Hills ('Yielding Hills' some call them, since at every step almost of view they change their aspect, like shifting clouds; 'Elden Hills' others, because there of old time blazed beacon-fires), with their three wizard peaks, belted by

Bowden (Thomas Aird's birthplace), Newtown, Melrose, and other haunted spots; the Merse, with the Lammermoors rising like an island in the midst, where the great novelist was to fix the scene of one of the grandest tragedies in any language; and relieved against the distant horizon, that storm of mountains which gathers around the wanderings of the Ettrick, Gala, and Yarrow. Over this landscape—where it has been said every field had its battle and every rivulet its song, we add every peak its watch-fire and every hillside its peel —Scott in boyhood often 'gazed himself away,' and would realize both the spectacle and the mood of the heroine whom he was afterwards to portray in the beautiful words :

> ' The lady looked in mournful mood,
>   Looked over hill and vale,
>   O'er Mertoun's wood and Tweed's fair flood,
>   And all down Teviotdale.'

Robert Chambers, in his interesting *Illustrations of the Waverley Novels*, will have it that Smailholm agrees in the leading features with Avenel Castle ; and there are certainly some points of resemblance, especially in the circumstance that the tower has once been surrounded by a lake, and that there are certain remains which still point to the existence of a drawbridge and a causeway crossing a moat. The view, however, as described by Scott in *The Abbot*, is not the same with that we have sought to portray above; and besides, in a note to *The Monastery*, Scott says: 'It were vain to search near Melrose for any such castle as is here described. But in Yetholm Loch there are the remains of a fortress called Lochside Tower, which, like the supposed Castle of Avenel, is built upon an island, and connected with the land by a causeway. It is much smaller than the Castle of Avenel is described.'

Robert Scott married a Miss Halyburton, a lady sprung from an ancient family in Berwickshire,—a family which enjoyed as portion of its patrimonial possessions a part of Dryburgh, including the ruins of the Abbey. This estate would have descended to Scott through his father, but was lost by the foolish speculations of a granduncle; and 'thus,' he says in his autobiography, 'we have nothing left of Dryburgh, although my father's maternal inheritance, but the right of stretching our bones, where mine may perhaps be laid ere any eye but my own glances over these pages,'—words written with a mixture of sadness, pride, and dignity very characteristic of the author. Robert Scott's eldest son was Walter, the poet's father. He was the first of the Scott family who ever adopted a town life. He was born in 1729, educated as a W.S., and although not much fitted naturally, either by astuteness or by temper, for the profession, yet rose to eminence in it by dint of probity and diligence. There is an epitaph in the Howff (burying-place) of Dundee :

> ' Here lies a writer and an honest man :
> Providence *works wonders nows and than.*'

Scott's father was one of these rare marvels of Divine Providence, being thoroughly honest. He was a man of somewhat distant and formal manners, but of singular kindness of heart, of sterling worth, and of deep-toned piety after the Calvinistic mode. He had a noble presence, handsome features, a sweet expression of countenance ; and, as Sir Walter says, ' he looked the mourner so well,' that he was often invited to funerals, and seems to have positively enjoyed those monotonous and melancholy formalities connected with Scottish interments, for which his son has expressed in his journal such disgust, and which he has limned in his *Guy Mannering* with such ludicrous fidelity. Old Fairford in *Redgauntlet* is unquestionably a graphic though slightly coloured sketch of the elder Scott by his son. His mother was well educated, as the times then went, not at all comely in aspect, short in stature, and somewhat stiff in manners. She lived to a great age. Their first six children (including a Walter) died in infancy. The first who survived was Robert. He became an officer in the East India Company's service, and fell a victim to the climate. The second, John, was a major in the army, and lived long on his half-pay in Edinburgh. The third was the poet. The fourth was a daughter, of a somewhat flighty temperament, Anne by name, who was cut off in 1801. The fifth was Thomas, a man of much humour and excellent parts, who went to Canada as paymaster to the 70th Regiment, and died there. He was at one time suspected of being author, in whole or part, of the Waverley Novels. The sixth was Daniel, the scapegrace of the family, whose conduct was in the last degree imprudent, and whose fate was disastrous: he had in the West Indies disgraced himself by coward-ice, and died on his return in 1806. Sir Walter disowned him, and put on no mourning at the news of his death,—conduct which he thought afterwards harsh and unfeeling, and bitterly re-gretted. Conachar, in the *Fair Maid of Perth,* has, Lockhart thinks, some traits of this poor unfortunate.

Walter Scott was born in a house belonging to

his father at the head of College Wynd, which was afterwards pulled down to make room for a part of the new College. He was an uncommonly healthy child till eighteen months old, when he was affected with a teething fever, at the close of which he was found to have lost the use of his right leg. Blisters and other topical remedies were applied to no purpose. He was at last, by the advice of his grandfather Dr. Rutherford, sent out to Sandyknowe, in the hope that air and exercise might remove his lameness. There he had the first consciousness of existence, and remembered himself, in conformity with some quack nostrum, wrapped up repeatedly in the skin of a sheep while still warm from the carcase of the animal, to encourage him to crawl, —a position in which he bears a certain ludicrous resemblance to his own hermit Brian, in the *Lady of the Lake*, enclosed in the skin of a white bull, and let down to the brink of a cataract to see visions and dream dreams of dreadful augury: it is the one step from the sublime to the ridiculous *inverted*. This strange expedient failed. Scott owed much, however, to his residence at Sandyknowe. He enjoyed the care of his venerable grandfather, now somewhat stricken in years. His grandmother, and his aunt Janet Scott, told him tales and sung him songs about the old Border

thieves, Wat of Harden, Wight Willie of Aik-
wood, Jamie Telfor of the fair Dodhead, the Deil
of Littledean, and their merry exploits; and thus
sowed in his mind the seeds of future Deloraines,
Clinthill Christies, and Robin Hoods. A neighbouring farmer had witnessed the execution of the
Jacobite rebels at Carlisle : he recounted it to Scott ;
and to this tale of horror, poured into the ear of the
boy poet, we are indebted for the trial and death
scenes at the close of *Waverley*,—perhaps the most
thrilling and powerful tragic matter, out of Shakspeare, in the language. The American war was
then raging ; and to the weekly bulletins about its
fluctuating progress, brought to Sandyknowe by his
uncle Thomas Scott, factor at Danesford, the little
lame child did seriously incline his ear, and his
cheek glowed and his eye kindled when he heard
of any success on the part of the British arms ;
so early did the Tory throb begin to beat within
him. Some old books, too, lay on the window seat
—*Antomathes* (a forgotten but ingenious fiction),
Ramsay's *Tea Table Miscellany*, and *Josephus*—
and were read to him during the dim days and the
long nights of winter. He learned, from hearing
the ballad of *Hardyknute* read, to recite it from
memory, and used to spout it aloud, to the annoy-
ance of the worthy parish minister, Dr. Duncan,

when he called. 'One may as well speak in the mouth of a cannon as where that child is,' exclaimed the testy divine. To this we probably owe Scott's life-long admiration and amiable overestimate of this ballad, which he recited to Byron with such effect, that the poet looked as if he had just received a challenge. With all deference to Scott, we have never been able to perceive any transcendent merit in' *Hardyknute:* we think it wordy and diffuse, and infinitely prefer *The Flowers of the Forest, The Dowie Dens of Yarrow,* and the ancient ballad of *Roncesvalles.* His Aunt Janet stood much in relation to Scott as Betty Davidson did to Burns —was his chief instructress, and the true nurse within him of the *poet.* He began, in spite of his lame limb, to stand, walk, and run, and his general health was confirmed by the pure mountain air. Previous to this, an old shepherd, Sandy Ormistoun, was accustomed to carry him to the hills, where he contracted a strong attachment to the woolly people, — an attachment which never forsook him. One Tibby Hunter described him as a sweet-tempered bairn, a darling with all about the house, and said that the young ewe-milkers delighted to carry him about on their backs among the crags. He had no greater pleasure than in rolling about all day long in the midst of the flocks, and he knew every sheep and lamb by head-mark.   On one occasion, it is said, he was forgotten among the knolls.   A thunder-storm came on.   In alarm, they sought for the boy, and found him, not weeping or crying out, like the Goblin Page, 'Lost! lost! lost!' but lying on his back looking at the lightning, clapping his hands at each suc-cessive flash, and exclaiming, 'Bonnie! bonnie!' It were a fine subject for a painter, 'The Minstrel Child lost in a Border thunder-storm;' and his attitude in the story reminds us of Gray's noble lines about Shakspeare in his *Progress of Poesy:*

> 'Far from the sun and summer gale,
>   In thy green lap was nature's darling laid.
> What time where lucid Avon strayed,
> To him the mighty mother did unveil
> Her awful face; the *dauntless child*
> Stretched forth his little arms, and smiled.'

When in his fourth year, Scott accompanied his Aunt Janet to Bath, where it was hoped the waters would benefit his lameness.   He journeyed from Leith to London in a smack called the *Duchess of Buccleugh*, Captain Beatson.   (A lady named Wright boasted long after waggishly to Joanna Baillie, that she had been once Walter Scott's bed-fellow; the irregularity, however, having taken place in the Leith smack, and the Eneas being only four years of age !) In London he saw the usual sights, which stamped themselves with uncommon vividness on his memory, so that when he visited the metropolis again he had hardly anything new to see. At Bath he lived a year, but derived little benefit from the waters. He attended, however, while there, a dame's school, and never, he says, had a 'more regular teacher of reading,' although he got a few lessons in Edinburgh afterwards. He met John Home, the author of *Douglas*, who, along with his lady, was residing there. His Uncle Robert, who joined the party afterwards, took his little nephew to most of the amusements in the city, including the theatre, where, at the sight of Orlando and Oliver, in *As You Like it*, quarrelling, he screamed out, 'Ar'n't they brothers ?'—a story reminding us of young Byron in the Aberdeen theatre, when Petruchio was trying to force down on Kate the paradox of the moon being the sun, roaring out, 'But I say it is the *meen*, sir !' Bath, too, which in all but the neighbourhood of the Grampians may be called the Perth, or Fair City, of England, he seems to have admired exceedingly.

From it he came back to Edinburgh, went thence to his beloved early haunt of Sandyknowe ; and we find him in his eighth year spending a few weeks

at Prestonpans, enjoying sea-bathing, and encountering an old military veteran named Dalgetty (a
significant name, as the readers of the *Legend of
Montrose* know full well), who became fond of
Scott, and, like the soldier in Goldsmith,

' Shouldered his crutch, and showed how fields were won.'

It is interesting to observe how not a few of the
familiar names known to him in his youth or boyhood have been preserved on his written page, and
are now classical. Thus Meg Dodds was the real
name of a woman, or 'Luckie,' in Howgate, 'who
brewed good ale for gentlemen.' In the account
of a Galloway trial, in which Scott was counsel,
occurs the name 'Mac-Guffog,' afterwards that of
the famous turnkey in *Guy Mannering*. The
name 'Durward' may still be seen on the signs of
Arbroath and Forfar, and Scott had doubtless met
it there ; as well as that of ' Prudfute, or Proudfoot,'
in or near Perth ; 'Morton,' in the lists of the western Whigs ; and 'Gilfillan,' in the catalogue of the
prisoners in Dunnottar Castle. Nothing, in fact,
that ever flashed on the eye or vibrated on the ear
of this extraordinary man but was in some form or
other reproduced in his writings. It was probably
the same with Shakspeare, although the most of
the data on the subject are lost ; and Mrs. Quickly,

Master Barnardine, Claudio, Shallow, Sir Andrew Aguecheek, and Falconbridge, seem all old acquaintances of the poet.

In 1778, Scott, having first got a few lessons from one Leechman and one French, was sent to the High School, under the charge of Luke Frazer, whom he describes as a worthy man and a capital scholar. Thence he passed to the rector's class, taught by the celebrated Dr. Adam. This remarkable person had not a little of his namesake Parson Adams, in Fielding, about him. He was a simple-minded, sincere, absent individual, as well as a profound scholar; just the kind of man, like the parson when regretting that he had lost his calf-skin Æschylus, to condole himself with the reflection, that as it was dark, it was impossible for him to have seen to read it. It was another kind of night which was descending on Alexander Adam when he uttered his memorable last saying, 'It is getting dark ; you may go home, boys.' His life, otherwise a useful, laborious, and happy one, was embittered first of all by the rude usage he met with from William Nicol, Burns' clever but coarse-minded associate, who was an under-teacher in the school, and who even on one occasion waylaid and assaulted the rector ; and secondly, by the obloquy to which his republican principles, which he avowed

on all occasions, and taught in his school, exposed
him. His works, *Roman Antiquities, Grammar
of Ancient Geography,* etc., show vast and very
exact learning, and were once popular schoolbooks.
Adam is said to have appreciated Scott's amazing
memory, and frequently called him up to answer
questions about dates; and although neither he nor
the other teachers had any suspicion of his genius,
he pronounced him better acquainted than any of
his contemporaries with the meaning, if not with
the words, of the classical authors. He encouraged
him also to make translations from Homer and
Virgil. One or two trifling pieces of verse by him
of this date have been discovered. But on the
whole, although not a dunce, Scott was, as he says,
an 'incorrigibly idle imp,' constantly glancing like
a meteor from the bottom to the top of the form,
and *vice versa,* and shone more in the *yards*—the
High School playgrounds—than in the class. Notwithstanding his infirmity, he was the bravest of
football players, the swiftest of racers, the strongest
of pugilists, the most persevering in snowball *bickers,*
the most daring climber of the *kittle nine steps* (a
pass of peril leading along the dark brow of the
Castle rock), and the most dexterous and strategic
commander in the mimic battles fought in the
Crosscauseway between the children of the mob

and those of the better citizens. Many poets, such as Cowper and Shelley, have been overborne and become broken-hearted amidst the rough play of a public school. But the Scott, the Byron, and the Wilson, find it their element ; and their early superiority in sports and pastimes is an augury of their future greatness, and a prelibation of the manhood of their character and the all-sidedness of their genius.

Previous to this, a lady in all points qualified to appreciate genius, the accomplished Mrs. Cockburn, the authoress of the modern version of *The Flowers o' the Forest*, had met Scott in his father's house in George Square, and thus describes him : 'I last night supped in Mr. Walter Scott's. He has the most extraordinary genius of a boy I ever saw. He was reading a poem to his mother when I went in. I made him read on : it was the description of a shipwreck. His passion rose with the storm. He lifted up his eyes and hands. "There's the mast gone," says he ; "crash it goes: they will all perish !" After his agitation he turns to me : "This is too melancholy," says he, "I must read you something more amusing." When taken to bed last night, he told his aunt that he liked that lady. "What lady?" says she. "Why, Mrs. Cockburn ; for I think she is a virtuoso, like myself."'

B

From Adam's tuition Scott would have instantly
gone to College, had it not been that his health
became delicate, and his father was induced to
send him to Kelso.   There, being once more
under the kind care of his Aunt Janet, he added
to the stores of his reading, which in Edinburgh had been very miscellaneous.   He became
acquainted with Percy's *Reliques of Ancient Poetry*,
which he read under the shade of a splendid
Platanus, or Oriental Plane, a huge hill of leaves
in his aunt's garden ; while attending the school
of one Lancelot he increased considerably his
stock of classical lore ; and he made the acquaintance of James Ballantyne, a man whose fortunes
were afterwards so closely linked with his own,
who seemed born to be his amanuensis and
literary factotum, and in whose company, now in
the school, and now when wandering along the
banks of the Tweed, he began to exercise his
unrivalled gift of telling stories.   At Kelso, too, a
spot distinguished by its combination of beauties,
the Tweed and Teviot beside it melting in music
into each other's arms, and with noble mansions and
ancient abbeys in the background, his eyes were
more fully opened to the beauties of that Scottish
nature of which he became the most ideal, yet
minute, the most lingering and loving depictor.

CHAPTER II.

AT COLLEGE, AND MAKING HIMSELF.

WHEN Byron felt that he had ceased to be a boy, it gave him, we are told, a pang of the most exquisite anguish. What Scott's feelings at this era were we are not particularly informed; but we suspect that it was with a deep sigh that he, too (in 1784), left the shade of his Platanus for that of his *Alma Mater*, and exchanged the delightful pages of Percy for the reading of the Latin and Greek classics under Professors Hill and Dalziel. In Latin he became a fair proficient; Greek he hated so intensely, that he was called by his fellow-students the 'Greek Blockhead.' Glorying in his shame, he wrote an essay, filled with all kinds of useless learning, in which he preferred Ariosto to Homer, and threw ignorant contempt on the fine old language of the latter. Had Sir Daniel Sandford been his professor, how his beautiful face would have rayed out wrath, 'as through his veins ran lightning,' at the presump- tuous lad, although his anger would have been short- lived, and he would have soon recognised his talent and independent spirit. Dalziel, whose sole claim to distinction lay in a collection of Greek extracts, told Scott that a dunce he was, and a dunce he would remain,—'a verdict,' says Scott, 'which he lived to revoke over a bottle of Burgundy at our literary club at Fortune's.' As it was, Scott forgot the very Greek alphabet, and afterwards bitterly regretted his early neglect of his Greek studies. We cannot say that we share much in this regret. Scott was naturally Gothic in his tastes. The only writer in Greek with whom his genius could ever have had much sympathy was Homer; and he was in many points a Homer himself: only, had he known more Greek, he might, in his ballad rhyme, have written the best conceivable transla- tion of the *Iliad*.

Besides the Latin and Greek, he attended the Ethical (Logic), the Mathematical, the Moral Philo- sophy, and the Historical Classes, as well as those of the Civil and Municipal Law. From Dugald Stewart's tuition he derived much benefit, and speaks of his striking and impressive eloquence as riveting the attention of the most volatile student. Most that now *read* Dugald Stewart vote him diffuse and languid, with much elegance, but little point or power; but all who *heard* him seem to have been profoundly impressed by his oratory, which probably owed much to his manner, his presence, and the excellence of his private character. Scott's real university was that library of strangest selection, and most miscellaneous variety, which he was piling up, partly on his shelves, and partly in the roomy chambers of his brain; and, like many other great men who have attended school and college, he was in reality a self-taught man. He read the romances and poetry of the South, he made himself an excellent French and Italian scholar, and subsequently became tolerably versed in German too. He ransacked the dusty shelves of old bookshops and circulating libraries; and in those repositories of forgotten lore he enjoyed occasional glimpses of the literary characters who frequented them.

Often, in the experience of a young man of letters, the real instructor is not a professor at all, but some student of his own standing, whom he has selected on a principle of natural affinity, with whom he reads favourite authors, goes to hear celebrated preachers, and, above all, communes with in those delicious private walks which in youth are so dear. Thus Hall and Mackintosh conversed as they wandered along the banks of the Dee and the Don, and were saluted by the inferior students as 'Plato and Herodotus.' Thus young Wordsworth and Coleridge talked to each other 'far above singing,' or schemed the *Anciente Marinere.* Thus Byron and Charles Skinner Matthews speculated and revelled at Newstead Abbey. These men were much about the same intellectual level, which was not the case with Scott and his associate, John Irving, W.S. Both, however, had some tastes in common. They were fond of repeating old legends, and began by and by to invent and recount stories of their own in imitation. And in weaving these pleasant yarns they spent many a holiday hour, by sunlight and by moonlight too, around Arthur's Seat and Salisbury Crags.

In conjunction with Mr Irving, too, he read much Italian, and even began to turn some of its treasures into English verse. One of these was *Guiscard and Matilda;* and Lockhart has preserved some verses, headed 'To Mr Walter Scott, on reading his poem of *Guiscard and Matilda,* inscribed to Miss Keith of Ravelston.' The writer, he thinks, was evidently a woman, and he thinks she was Scott's old admirer, Mrs. Cockburn.

On the 15th of May 1786, Scott was bound apprentice to his father as W.S., and from that day bade farewell to his academical studies. He wrote about this time a poem of 1600 lines, entitled *The Conquest of Granada*, which, so soon as it was finished, he committed to the flames. This and two or three love trifles, and the translation commended by Mrs. Cockburn, were, up to 1796, his only poetical productions. In 1786 there occurred the memorable meeting between Scott and Burns. Such momentary intersections of the orbits of literary stars, while the one is rising and the other beginning to set, are as uncommon as they are interesting. Thus met Ovid with Virgil, and Milton with Galileo, of which it has been said :

> ‘ With what comparison shall we compare
> The meeting of the matchless sage and bard ?
> Transit of Mercury across the Sun—
> Young Mercury across his father's brow ?
> Say rather, transit of that comet vast
> Which erst in autumn pierced our British skies
> And crossed Arcturus ; spectacle sublime !
> Which no gyration of the dancing heavens
> Shall e'er in grandeur or in grace surpass.
> Oh ! strange to see the wanderer advance,
> Fearless in courage, radiant with hope,
> Toward that ancient and serenest star,
> As if to look into the Eye of God.

Thus met the twain at Florence, soon to part :
The one to England bound, to fight the cause
Of Freedom, not with sword, but with a pen
Clear, bright, and piercing as Damascus blade ;
The other to remain in darkness pent,
Till to his eye the telescope of Death
His Lord applied, and lo ! not Night, but Day.'

Less singular in circumstances, and less august in aspect, the meeting of the two brightest geniuses of Caledonia. It was at a literary dinner party at Professor Fergusson's that Scott saw the boast, pride, and shame of Scotland—the truest and the worst used man our country ever produced. We all remember the effect produced on Burns' mind by the print of Bunbury, representing the soldier lying dead in the snow, his widow beside him, and a child in her arms ; and how the eyes of the hapless bard of Coila glowed with pity, passion, and enthusiasm as he read the line which Scott told him was Langhorne's—

' The child of misery baptized in tears.'

That look, and the tears through which it shone, haunted Scott's memory to the last; and those ardent eyes of the poet, which gleamed like dewy stars, to him never set. Nor did he forget the words of Burns to himself, ' You will be a man yet,' although he calls it an expression of mere civility. He pitied Burns' unhappy career, but his own in the long-run was not much more fortunate. He too, as well as Burns, was *ruined*, though in a different way. It is melancholy to remember that this is true of so many besides poets. How often do we hear it said, 'It is such and such a person's ruin,' almost every life being in some point or other a failure, and each vessel on the sad sea of time being more or less a wreck! Indeed, some may think that in all Burns' dark career there was nothing more dismal than the disastrous reversal of the fortunes, and the premature eclipse of the glorious mind, of Sir Walter Scott.

While serving his apprenticeship to his father, Scott commenced those yearly visits to the Highlands which were destined to exert such power on the development of his genius. He saw from the Wicks o' Baigley, a point to the south of Perth, that superb view of the winding Tay and its rich valley; the bold adjacent hills of Kinnoul, Kinfauns, and Moncreiff; the 'Fair City' and the distant Grampians, including Benvoirlich on the west, Schiehallion in the north, and Mounts Battock and Blair in the east, which struck his young fancy, and which he has described in one of the most eloquent pages of his *St. Valentine's Day.*

Stewart of Invernahyle, a client of his father's—an
old Jacobite, who had measured swords with Rob
Roy, and been out with Mar and with 'Charlie'—
invited the son to his Highland home, where his
experiences somewhat resembled those of Waverley with Fergus M'Ivor, and of Francis Osbaldistone in the M'Gregor's country. He found the
Highlands in a very primitive condition indeed :
the daughters of a laird loading a cart with manure
in the morning, and reappearing in the evening in
full dress, with radiant complexions, and display-
ing no little wit, intelligence, and good breeding ;
the principal dish in the first course of the dinner
being a gigantic *haggis*, borne into the hall in a
wicker basket by two half-naked Celts, while the
piper strutted fiercely behind them blowing a
tempest of dissonance ! Ever afterwards Scott's
heart and imagination were equally divided between the Border and the Perthshire Highlands.
It is remarkable that the scene of almost all his
Highland novels, certainly of his best ones—of
Waverley, of *Rob Roy*, the *Legend of Montrose*,
and of *The Fair Maid of Perth* (not to speak of
The Lady of the Lake)—is laid in the Yorkshire
of Scotland. There was one other region in our
country which had afterwards, as we shall see, a
still stronger interest for him, namely Kincardine-

shire, the birthplace of his first lost love ; but the painful recollections connected with the story perhaps repelled him, and he never does more than allude incidentally to some of its scenes—such as Cairna Mount and Clochmaben. But his associations with Perthshire were all delightful : *it* he visited in his fresh boyhood, his heart beating with enthusiasm, his brow throbbing with inspiration,— 'with hope,' as Lamb says of Coleridge, 'rising before him like a fiery column, *the dark side not yet turned.*' And while the inhabitants of the Border may be proud that Smailholm, Carterhaugh, and the Eildons attracted him about as strongly as his own romantic town, the Bass Rock, and Arthur's Seat, Perthshire men are quite as grateful for the new glory which he poured on the Trosachs, Loch Tay, Craighall, the 'hazel shade' of Glenartney, and the tall peak of Benvoirlich with the 'red beacon' of the morning burning upon its summit.

In the second year of his apprenticeship, according to Scott himself (Lockhart fixes it a little earlier), one of Scott's blood-vessels burst ; and he was put on a severe regimen and confined to bed, restricted, though it was in a cold spring, to a single blanket, bled, blistered, and fed on vegetables. His only resources were chess and reading. He plunged now into a wide sea of books, exhausting libraries, and driving their keepers to their wit's end to supply his cravings ; passing from novels, romances, and poems to voyages and travels, and thence to histories and to memoirs, and thus preparing himself for the future exigencies of his literary life as effectually on his quiet bed, where he was not suffered to speak above his breath, as when rambling through the mountains of Perthshire with Invernahyle, or 'making himself' with Shortreed among the traditionary wilds of Liddesdale. He illustrated the battles he read of by arranging shells, seeds, and pebbles to represent the movements of encountering armies, using mimic cross-bows and a small model fortress. By the assistance, too, of a combination of mirrors, he was enabled to look out at the Meadows, and see the troops marching to exercise, which must have been a great relief to his weary hours. After some months he recovered, resumed his labours in the office, and bade a long farewell to disease and medicine.

In 1788 he went to attend the class of Civil Law. Here, besides his old friends Irving and Fergusson, he met with some other young men who united literary tastes with legal aspirations. In later days we have seen at the bar chiefly two classes—literary

men who had no law, and plodding legalists who
had no genius. Before Scott's time, mere lawyers
constituted almost the whole tribe. But Scott,
Jeffrey, Cranstoun, and others, formed a conjunction
of the two characters, although perhaps in Jeffrey
alone were they thoroughly harmonized. Scott
was both a *littérateur* and a lawyer, but far more
a *littérateur;* Cranstoun and Cockburn were more
of the lawyer; while Jeffrey united both in nearly
equal proportions, being at once sharp as the
sharpest special pleader, and as acute and lively, if
not as genial or profound, a critic as Britain ever
produced. Along with William Clerk of Eldin,
Abercromby, and Cranstoun, Scott spent his mornings in the Law Class-room or in private study,
his evenings in the somewhat excessive convivialities of that time, and his holidays in rambles about
the surrounding country. Sometimes they strolled
too far for the contents of their purses, and had to
subsist on cold water and hips and haws in their
return. Such adventures are the romance and
magic of the early life of literary men and students.
We knew a youth, now a voluminous author, who
left Glasgow for Stirling with precisely one penny
in his pocket, which he.spent at Denny on a roll ;
and this with water from a running brook formed
his only refreshment for the twenty-eight miles of

road. Scott's father was rather annoyed at these
escapades, although he was so glad to see him
when he returned, that, like Kish with Saul, he
forgot the meditated rebuke. Scott's nickname
among his own set was Duns Scotus, or sometimes
by an *alias* of his own creation, Colonel Grogg.
His dress at this time was neglected : corduroy
breeches were his common attire ; and when re-
proached with their meanness, his reply was,
' They be good enough for drinking in : come, and
let us have some oysters in the Covenant Close.'
These convivialities, however, were afterwards re-
linquished. In his maturer years he was a strictly
temperate man ; and from grosser dissipation he
was kept almost entirely free, through means of a
pure and passionate attachment, of which we shall
speak in the sequel.

In 1792 (11th July) Scott was called to the bar.
He had joined previously the Speculative Society,
where Jeffrey first saw him, his *chafts* (Scottice)
wrapt up in a large woollen nightcap, the poet
being ill of toothache, and yet able to read a paper
on old ballads, which so interested Jeffrey, that he
got introduced to him, and they became great allies.
Like most young advocates, Scott had little business at first ; but he drank claret at Fortune's, and
ate oysters in St. John's Coffeehouse, dear to him

as erst the haunt of Dr. Pitcairn ; read now Stair's
Decisions, and now the last new novel ; and every
day might be seen sweeping with his gown the
boards of that Parliament House which seems the
Hall of Eblis to many a weary and briefless peri-
patetic.

In the autumn of this year he was introduced to
Mr. Robert Shortreed, the respected Sheriff-substi-
tute of Roxburghshire, and this led to a most important section of Scott's life.   He had felt a strong
desire, which was now gratified, to visit Liddesdale, and collect the ballads and traditions which
were floating there, especially those *riding ballads*
which he believed to be still preserved among the
descendants of the mosstroopers.   For seven successive years the twain persevered in making
autumnal excursions to that romantic region.   Liddesdale was then not much better known than the
interior of Africa is now.

> 'It lay like some unkenned of isle
> Ayont New Holland.'

But Scott and Shortreed were richly rewarded
for their daring exploration.   They saw fine
mountain scenes, drank in pure air, collected songs
and traditions, told stories, galloped long miles,
climbed hills, pursued foxes, speared salmon, lay in

Charlieshopes without number, kissed fraternally
the farmers' wives, fondled the children, floored if
possible at their own weapons of strong waters the
goodmen ; acted, in short, exactly as Captain Brown
did when residing with Dandie Dinmont, or as an
electioneering candidate is in the habit of doing,
but with a very different motive from the member ;
the one purchasing selfish popularity, and the other
laying in the materials of universal fame by con-
descension and kindness. The story, ' There's the
keg at last,' is too familiar to require to be recounted. ' He was *making himsel'* a' the time,' says
honest Shortreed, ' but he didna ken what he was
about till years had passed. At first he thought
o' little, I daresay, but the queerness and the fun.'

From these visits came in due time the *Minstrelsy
of the Scottish Border.* It has been said, absurdly
we think, that Scott had no pleasure while writing
his poems and novels. He had none, indeed, of
that half-inebriated ecstasy with which Burns wrote
his *Tam o' Shanter*, nor of that lingering, long
drawn out, concentrated pleasure with which
Wordsworth brooded over his thoughts while forming them into verse, saying, as it were, to each, ' I
will not let thee go except thou bless me.' Yet
surely, if he had neither the joy of inspiration nor
of incubation, he had a large measure of delight

while, amid the freshness of morning nature, with the sound of the Tweed in his ears, or the sun smiting the Castle rock before his eyes, he indited pages which he knew were as immortal and as pure as those waters or that sun-fire. But at all events he *had* enjoyment, the most exquisite and varied, while collecting their materials amongst the mosses or by the firesides of the Border : he was then luxuriating as well as ' making himself,' and probably looked back long afterwards to this as to the happiest period of his existence.

CHAPTER III.

EARLY LOVE, LITERATURE, MARRIAGE, AND POETRY.

ETTERCAIRN is a small estate in Kincardineshire, situated near the pleasant village of that name, on a rich level and stream-bisected spot, not far from the foot of the Grampians, which here somewhat stoop their mighty stature, and appear as it were kneeling before the German Ocean. Fettercairn is not only beautiful in itself, but surrounded on all sides by interesting scenes. The spot where Queen Finella's castle (a vitrified fort where Kenneth III. was murdered) is said to have stood is near it. The Burn, with all its marvellous woodland and water-side beauties, stands a few miles to the west ; and near it is the lovely Arnhall, with its fine old park, garden, and legendary memories. Fasque, the seat of the Gladstone family, is behind to the north, and in the same direction a steep hill-road conducts over the

Cairnamount to Banchory and Balmoral. The Castles of Edzell and Balbegno frown emulously westward; and a good way to the east, the proud ruin of Dunnottar Castle, with its huge structure and historical associations, links the mountains to the sea. Sir John Stuart of Fettercairn had a daughter named Williamina, who resided part of the year in Edinburgh. Sir Walter met this lady, it is said, in Greyfriars Churchyard after service, and during a shower of rain. The offer of an umbrella, which was graciously accepted, formed the commencement of an acquaintance, and the earnest of the offer of an heart; not, alas! so well received by the fair one. She is described as beautiful, a blue-eyed blonde, of very gentle manners and considerable literary accomplishments. Her mother had been an early companion of Scott's mother. His love was exceedingly ardent, and a recollection of her image colours his pictures of female heroines, particularly in the *Lay of the Last Minstrel, Rokeby,* and *Redgauntlet.* But not more hopeless was Dairsie Latimer's passion for Lilias Redgauntlet (his disguised sister) than Scott's for the fair Williamina. The different rank of the parties was an obstacle; and, besides, although she admired his genius, and corresponded with him on literary matters, her heart was given to another. In vain did he write original and translate German verses to please her, and carve out her name in Runic characters amidst the ruins of St. Andrews. In vain was he often attracted northwards by the spell of love, visiting Simprim, Dunnottar, Meigle, and Glamis ; at Dunnottar falling in by the way with ' Old Mortality,' and spending in Glamis an *eerie* night, under the hallucination that it was the castle where King Duncan was murdered by Macbeth. She continued inexorable, and at last, in October 1796, he received a point-blank refusal from her own lips at her own Grampian home. We see him mounting his horse, and bearing southwards through the bleak moors toward Montrose, perhaps in a wild, blustering autumn night, and with a face under the gruff, grim calmness of which one could have read strange matters, and caught glimpses of a wounded and well-nigh broken heart. Thence, in a kind of frenzy, he ' recoiled into the wilderness,' and reached first Perth, and then Edinburgh, by a circuitous and savage route, through ' moors and mosses mony O ;' dashing his steed, like his own Mowbray in *St. Ronan's Well*, over scaurs, and through forests and marshes, where in those days none but a desperate spirit could have preserved his life ; but in the course of his journey digesting his misery, and returning home a sadder and a wiser man. His friends, especially Miss Cranstoun, afterwards the Countess of Purgstall in Styria, a gifted female, who had taken a deep interest in this love affair, and who knew Scott's impetuous disposition, had expected some fearful explosion, and were glad to see him sitting down calmly to his books again. He says himself, however, that he was brokenhearted for two years, — a time we must surely restrict a little, since his disappointment happened in October 1796, and his marriage to Miss Carpenter took place in December the next year. Miss Stuart in 1797 married Sir. W. Forbes, son of the biographer of Beattie, who was afterwards of essential service to Scott in his misfortunes. The iron must have entered into his soul, although he contrived at first to conceal the wound ; since we find him not only often alluding to his loss, but in his latter days visiting the lady's mother, and spending a whole night of the joy of grief in talking over old stories, and mingling their tears, Lady Forbes being then dead. She was the first, and perhaps the last, person whom Scott, affectionate husband though he was, ever loved with his whole being. He passed afterwards Kincardineshire by sea, but we never hear of him visiting that part of Scotland again. One of the few points of resem-

blance (unless their infirmity of lameness) between
Scott and Byron lies in the early love disappointment which befell them both. But while Scott's
wound, though felt deeply and felt long, entirely
failed to poison his peace or to weaken his faith,
it was different with Byron. The image of Miss
Chaworth haunted him all his life afterwards—like
a spectre, stood between him and his bride—between him and

'Ada, sole daughter of his house and heart'—

between him, shall we say, and his happiness, his
heaven, and his God; and whenever he was at a
loss for a ground of quarrel with himself, with Providence, or with society, with the present, the past,
or the future, he came back to her, and her memory
became a sore that everlastingly ran—an *amari
aliquid* which always retained its taste of bitterness
and its hue of gloom. The resemblance between
Scott and Byron in this matter was simply acci-
dental; but the difference of the way in which each
managed his misery, measured all the distance
between one of the most morbid and one of the
healthiest and strongest of the children of men.

Scott had for some time previous been meditating an incursion into the realms of authorship.
He had written in a single sleepless night a trans-

lation of Bürger's famous ballad of *Leonore*, which
gained him much applause in his own coterie, and
which, if not perhaps quite equal to that of William Taylor of Norwich, is a piece of vigorous and
dashing verse. He had also translated *The Wild
Huntsman*, another ballad by the same poet. On
his return from the north in that spirit of *hardiesse*
and bravado which often follows disappointment,
and reveals the ferment of its remaining dregs, he
'rushed into print' with those two ballads. This
brochure, printed by Manners & Miller, was well
received in Edinburgh, and warmly commended
by honest William Taylor himself, but gained no
general acceptance in the south ; and let it be
consoling to incipient authors to know, that the
first production of the most popular of writers was
a complete failure and a dead loss.

In July 1797, Scott, disappointed at the failure
of his first poem, wearied with another campaign at
the bar, where his gains were as yet very moderate,
and with a little of his love-sickness still unmelted
about his heart, turned his thoughts toward his
favourite south of Scotland again. On this occasion, however, he extended his visit to England ;
and after a scamper through Peeblesshire, where
he had his first and only interview with David
Ritchie, the original of the *Black Dwarf*, in his

residence up Manor Water—a dreary spot, moss and mountains clustering all round the mud cottage where the misanthrope dwelt—and a rapid run through Carlisle, Penrith, Ulleswater, and Windermere, he reached the then sequestered little watering-place of Gilsland. His companions in this tour were his brother John, and Adam Fergusson. Scott had nearly fallen in love with a young lady residing at the Spa, when his real matrimonial Fate crossed his path. Riding one day near Gilsland, they met a lady on horseback whose appearance struck them so much, that they followed her, and found her to belong to the party at the Well, although they had not previously observed her. They became speedily acquainted. Her name was Charlotte Margaret Carpenter. She was the daughter of a French emigrant whose widow had fled from the horrors of the Revolution to England, where she and her children found an efficient protector and guardian in the Marquis of Downshire, who had previously known the family abroad.[1] The daughter and her governess were

---

[1] Since writing the above, we have been favoured with some additional particulars of this event, which we believe are authentic. The Marquis of Downshire, going on his travels, had a note of introduction from Mr. Bird, Dean of Carlisle, to Monsieur Carpenter of Paris. The unhappy result of the acquaintance was the elopement of Madame Carpenter, a

on a little excursion to some friends in the north of England, and had come for a few days to Gilsland. She was, as often happens with second loves as well as with second marriages, of exactly the opposite complexion, and perhaps also of disposition, to Scott's former flame,—having dark hair, deep brown eyes, and an olive complexion, very beautiful withal, and with an 'address hovering between the reserve of a pretty young Englishwoman who has not mingled widely with general

very beautiful woman, with his lordship. The husband did nothing in the matter except transmitting his two children, a boy and girl, to the care of his wife, and they lived for some years under her and Lord Downshire's protection. On her death he placed the girl in a French convent for her education, and sent out the boy to a lucrative situation in India, with the stipulation that £200 of his salary should go yearly to his sister. Miss Carpenter returned to London, and was placed under the charge of Miss Nicholson, a governess. The young lady formed an attachment to a young man, whose addresses were not agreeable to his lordship. He sent her and her governess down to Mr. Bird's at Carlisle, to keep her out of her lover's way. Mr. Bird had fixed previously to go to Gilsland, and he took Miss Carpenter and Miss Nicholson along with his family thither. They were placed, as usual with new-comers, at the foot of the table at the Spa ; and it so happened that a young Scotch gentleman, who had arrived later that day, was placed lower still, and thus brought into immediate contact with the Bird party. Mrs. Bird inquired at him if he knew a Scotch military man of her acquaintance, Major Riddell. Scott (for it was he) knew him well. This formed instantly a link of society, and a certain natural archness and gaiety that suited well with the accompaniment of a French accent.' She was a Protestant by faith. The courtship went off successfully. She had come, it is not uncharitable to suppose, to Gilsland like other specimens of the female 'Cœlebs in search of a husband ;' and here was an ardent youth, of great conversational powers and prepossessing appearance : a 'comely creature,' according to the testimony of a lady of the time. He,

connection, and the Birds invited him to tea with them in their own apartment ; and although his horse was ordered to the door to convey him on his journey, he at once consented. He had been struck at first sight with Miss Carpenter's appearance, and resolved to prosecute the acquaintance. He remained at the Spa, and was continually in her company. He even contrived to get himself invited to the Dean's country house ere he was compelled to return to Edinburgh. In a short time he reappeared in Mr. Bird's house, and enjoyed another fortnight of Miss Carpenter's society. His attentions became very marked, and Mrs. Bird at last wrote off to a friend in Edinburgh to make inquiries about this stranger. The answer was that he was a respectable young man, and rising at the bar. One of Scott's female acquaintances, however, perhaps chagrined at Scott's indifference to *her*, and having heard of some love adventure going on at Gilsland, wrote to Mrs. Bird inquiring about it, and wondering 'what kind of young lady it was who was to take Watty Scott.' The poet soon after found means to conciliate Lord Downshire to his views, and the marriage took place as related in the text. James Hogg insinuates that the Marquis was Charlotte Carpenter's father.

on the other hand, was precisely in that degree of
moderated love misery, and softened despair, his
heart a taper half-quenched, when a new object is
likely to surprise the man into a delight, in the
possibility of which he had almost forgotten to
believe. As an expatriated French loyalist, too,
there was something in her story to suit Scott's
political feelings, as well as to captivate his
romantic imagination. Then they met at a watering-place—a 'St. Ronan's Well'—where conventional barriers were broken down, and where
sudden and singular matches were the order of the
day. He fell, accordingly, or seemed to himself to
fall, into a violent love passion, which was returned
by the lady. Recalled from his romantic courtship to the Jedburgh Assizes, he astonished his
friend Shortreed by the ardour of his new affection.
The two worthy young lawyers sate till one in the
morning on the 30th September; Scott toasting
and raving about Miss Carpenter, and Shortreed
not daring to rebuke the madness of the poet.
After some little obstructions thrown in the way by
the parents and guardians had been surmounted,
and some agreeable nonsense had been talked
and written on both sides by the parties themselves, Walter Scott and the beautiful Charlotte
Carpenter were wedded at Carlisle on the 24th of

December 1797, about four months after they first met. She had, it may be mentioned, about £400 a year in her own right.

She went with him to Edinburgh, where, notwithstanding some foreign peculiarities of manners and tastes, she began her matrimonial career with considerable *éclat.* When summer arrived, Scott hired a beautiful cottage at Lasswade, on the banks of the Esk,—a river sweeping down through the richest woodlands and scenery of varied enchantment from Hawthornden, and thus uniting in a band of beauty the abodes of Drummond and Scott, two of Scotland's best and most patriotic children. It is pleasant to think of each period of Scott's literary history as linked with some spot of special natural loveliness. At Lasswade he commenced his real literary career, at Ashestiel his poetic genius culminated, and with Abbotsford is connected the memory of his matchless fictions. Ever to such nests of nature may the winged fledgelings of genius be traced. Wordsworth wrote best at Rydal Mount, Burns in Ellisland, and Byron among the giant pines of the forest of Ravenna.

The literary world has had at various periods the strangest autocrats, varying from King Stork to King Log, from men of the most exalted genius

to clever mediocrists, from a Dryden and a Pope
to a Pye and a Hayley; but we doubt if ever it
had such a scarecrow sovereign as Monk Lewis.
He was a man, no doubt, of considerable genius,
and of real warmth of heart, but vain, coxcombical,
and what is technically called 'gay' in his habits.
His novel *The Monk* has some convulsive power,
but is marred by a prurient licence which appalls
and disgusts modern readers. In poetry he is a
good imitator of the worst style of a very ingenious but fantastic school of Germans. To many
even then it was a matter of astonishment how a
ludicrously little and over-dressed mannikin (the
fac-simile of Lovel in *Evelina*), 'with eyes projecting like those of some insects, and flattish in the
orbits,' should be the lion of London literary
society, and how the Prince of Dandies should
have a taste for the weird and wonderful, and be
the first to transfer to English the spirit of some
of the early German bards. On Scott, such tales
as *Alonzo the Brave and the Fair Imogine*, extravagant and absurd as he deemed them afterwards,
exerted much influence. William Erskine had met
the Monk in London, and had shown him Scott's
version of Bürger's ballads. This led to a correspondence; and Lewis, shortly after visiting Edinburgh, invited Scott to his hotel,—an invitation

which 'elated' our hero more than anything that
had ever befallen him.   The two became speedily
intimate, although the intimacy now seems as dis-
proportionate as were that of a monkey with a
mammoth ; and in January 1799 Lewis negotiated
the publication of Scott's version of Goethe's *Goetz
von Berlichingen.*   One Bell bought it for twenty-
five guineas; and it appeared in February, but,
like his *Leonora,* failed to make much impression.
It swarms with verbal blunders, yet must ever
be interesting, not only as one of Scott's earliest
productions, but because it exhibits two of the
mightiest, and certainly the two most popular
writers of their period, in contact as mirrored and
mirroring.   The world has not yet fully made up
its mind about Goethe.   Admitting generally his
extraordinary powers, the greatness of his acquire-
ments, and the potent grasp with which he held
them—as Jupiter a sheaf of thunderbolts—his profound practical sagacity, and the splendour of three
or four of his poems, and of part of his novels,
it doubts of his taste, more than doubts of his
morale, and deplores the coldness of his temperament.   But it has no doubt of the powerful
influence he exerted on contemporary men of
genius, and others besides.   To *Faust* we owe
Manfred, The Deformed Transformed, and *Festus;*

and to his *Goetz of the Iron Hand* we trace much
of the chivalric spirit which breathes in Scott's
poetry and prose. Indeed, one of the scenes in
Goethe's poem has evidently suggested to Scott
the death-scene in *Marmion*, and the beautiful
picture of the storm, as seen from the turret by
Rebecca, and described to Ivanhoe. Nothing else,
before or afterwards written by Goethe, would have
attracted Scott so much as *Goetz*. He, we venture
to say, utterly loathed *Werther*, allowed some
passages in *Wilhelm Meister*, but characterized
the whole as fantastic and immoral ; and saw in
Faust, while ardently admiring, a production certainly above his powers to render into English,
but which perhaps might have been as well left
unwritten, even in German, the profanity and in-
completeness serving to neutralize the daring of
the thought and the marvellous luxuriance of the
fancy. A few of Goethe's minor poems and ballads,
and that almost Solomonic wealth of wisdom which
is scattered in so many nooks and interstices of his
writings, he admired, without envying or approving
of the personal experience through which much of
that wisdom was acquired.

In 1799, after the publication of *Goetz*, Scott
took his wife with him to London, where he had
not been since infancy, and was introduced by

Lewis to many literary and fashionable people. This, however, he enjoyed less than a visit to the Tower, Westminster Abbey, and the British Museum, where he at length was able to feed full his antiquarian enthusiasm. While he was in London, his worthy father—who, though not quite seventy, was entirely worn out by a series of protracted sufferings—died, and Thomas succeeded to the business. The property left was not great; but, besides enabling the widow to live in comfort for the remainder of her life, it formed a considerable addition to the fortunes of the rest of the family. His mother and sister came and spent the summer and autumn with him in Lasswade. About this time Scott wrote another Germanized drama, *The House of Aspen*, which was forwarded to London to be acted, but it did not please on rehearsal. The author printed it thirty years afterwards in one of the Annals. He spent a good deal of time, too, in contributing revised versions of *Leonora* and *The Wild Huntsman*, and some other pieces, to the 'hobgoblin repast' which Lewis was preparing in his *Tales of Wonder.*

It is worth noticing how Scott, with a native tendency to superstition, and who in his early productions dealt so much with the supernatural, has so little of it in his maturer writings; how he kept

his organ of wonder, which must have been enormous, in such severe and long-continued suppres-
sion. On the other hand, his bits of *diablerie*,
when they do occur, such as the apparition to
Fergus MacIvor in *Waverley*, the story of Martin
Walbeck in *The Antiquary*, and Wandering Willie's
Tale in *Redgauntlet*, are transcendent, and probably seem better from their rarity. The Wizard's
power of calling spirits from the vasty deep seems
to have been so absolute and so easy that he disdained to exercise it, and turned him to tasks from
which, being more difficult, greater glory was to be
gathered. In his premature dotage, however, we
find him, in *My Aunt Margaret's Mirror* and
other pieces, snatching eagerly at marvellous materials, which in the day of his power he would
have sternly waived aside. This summer (1799)
he wrote his ballads of *Glenfinlas*, *The Eve of St.
John*, *The Fire-king*, and others of similar merit ;
and toward the close of the year, James Ballantyne having now established his inimitable press in
Kelso, he printed with him a dozen copies of some
of these pieces, under the title of *Apology for Tales
of Wonder*, Mat Lewis' collection having been long
of appearing. The specimen of the printing pleased
Scott, and led him to project an issue from the
same press of the Border ballads which he had col-

lected; in other words, to form the idea of the
Minstrelsy of the Scottish Border, the publication
of which became an era in the history of James
Ballantyne, of Scott, of Scottish poetry, and of
modern literature in general. In December this
year, through the influence of the Earl of Dalkeith,
of Lord Montagu, and of the Dundases — Harry
Dundas being then the real king of Scotland—our
poet was appointed Sheriff-depute of Selkirkshire,
with £300 a year, little to do, and a still freer and
fuller access than before to the regions of Border
beauty and Border song, so peculiarly dear to his
imagination. In completing the design of the *Minstrelsy*, Scott found able coadjutors: the accomplished and learned Richard Heber; Dr. Jamieson,
the author of the *Scottish Dictionary*, himself a
mine of antique lore even richer than his book;
and the famous John Leyden. Of this man Scott
had a very high opinion. He says, in *The Lord
of the Isles*,

> ' A distant and a deadly shore
> Holds Leyden's cold remains.'

And in *St. Ronan's Well* he introduces Joseph
Cargill, when Leyden's name was mentioned, saying, 'I knew him; a lamp too early quenched.' He
was certainly the most determined of students, and

most eccentric of men, a Behemoth of capacity
and strong purpose, who took in a language ' like
Jordan' into his mouth ; who could master a whole
art like medicine in six months ; who once walked
forty miles and back again to procure a missing
ballad, and entered a company singing it with
enthusiastic gestures, and in the ' saw-tones ' of a
most energetic voice ; whose Border blood asserted
itself even amidst the languid atmosphere of India,
and on the sick-bed, whence he shouted out the old
chorus,

' Wha daur meddle wi' me ? '

and in whom a certain dash of charlatanerie, and
perhaps more than a dash of derangement, only
served as foils to the vigour of his mind, the solidity
of his learning, the freshness of his literary enthusiasm, and the fervour of his poetic genius : for
although not a great poet, a poet he was. We
shall not soon forget visiting the little room in a
poor cottage in the village of Denholm where this
prodigy of learning, diligence, and energy was
born—in the centre of those beautiful regions he
was afterwards to describe in his *Scenes of Infancy.*

Leyden and Thomas Campbell, both in Edinburgh at this time, never could agree. Campbell thought Leyden boastful and self-asserting ;

Leyden thought Campbell jealous and envious. We believe there was a modicum of truth in their estimates of each other. Campbell had been unfortunate and not over well conducted in his youth ; had been waylaid on his path to the pulpit by an unlucky circumstance ; and this, along with poverty, had soured him: and it is in the sour system that the malignant acid of envy is precipitated. Nor could all his after brilliant career entirely sweeten his spirit. Yet he was a fine-hearted man in the main, as well as a thoroughly true one. 'There was nothing false about him but his hair, which was a wig, and his whiskers, which were dyed.' Leyden had something of the self-glorification of a wild Indian chief, fond of showing his strings of scalps, and chanting fierce war-songs over his fallen foes ; but he, too, was sincere, warm-hearted, and guileless. When he read Campbell's *Hohenlinden*, he said to Scott, 'Dash it ! I hate the fellow, but he has written the best verses I have read for ever so long ;' to which Campbell replied, 'I detest Leyden with all my soul, but I know the value of his critical approbation.' Scott loved and was on friendly terms with both of them, and bore with their faults the more, as he had no envy, jealousy, or self-conceit in his own system.

In 1800 and 1801 he was busy with the *Min-*

strelsy, with the duties—not very burdensome—of
his Sheriffship, and with the bar, where he was
slowly increasing his business. In some of his professional visits to Selkirkshire he became acquainted
with William Laidlaw and James Hogg, both remarkable men. William Laidlaw possessed the
canine fidelity and fondness of Boswell, without the
meaner qualities, and with a sense, simplicity, and
poetic feeling which were denied to Jamie. His
Lucy's Flitting is an exquisitely true and pathetic
strain. James Hogg had a wild touch of the truest
genius, and an Alpine elevation and enthusiasm
of mind strangely co-existing with coarse tastes,
manners, and habits ; was one whom poetry had inspired without refining, and who had conceit, envy,
and spite enough to set up all Grub Street, blended
with a simplicity and rough kindness which partly
redeemed his failings, and partly served to render
the whole compound more intensely ridiculous.
Genius, like misery, has often dwelt with strange
bedfellows, but seldom with so many at once, and
seldom in such a monstrous *mesalliance*, as in the
idiosyncrasy and life of James Hogg. Yet, like
the bag of honey in the rough bee, there was in
him a singularly sweet vein of poetry, of which
Kilmeny was an outcome. His works, which are
very voluminous, show extraordinary versatility of

powers; and altogether, we may say of him, as Lockhart is compelled to do, that he was the most remarkable man that ever wore the *maud* of a Scottish shepherd.

Both these men adored Scott, both were pressed by him into the service of the *Minstrelsy*, and both materially aided him in his researches. At length, in January 1802, the first two volumes of the work appeared; and although they did not command a rapid sale, they made a great impression on the lovers of poetry. George Ellis, well known in those days for his collection of ancient English romances, and specimens of ancient English poetry, wrote of the book in terms of rapture, and was followed in a similar strain by Pinkerton, Chalmers, Ritson, and Miss Seward. Encouraged by their approbation, Scott began to prepare a third volume, and sent the old poetic romance of *Sir Tristram*, which he had found too long for the *Minstrelsy*, to the Border press, as it was now called, for separate publication. It did not, however, appear till after the third volume of the *Minstrelsy*, which was published in 1803, and contained an advertisement of *Sir Tristram*, and the *Lay of the Last Minstrel*, as speedily to be published. Ballantyne had now, at Scott's suggestion, removed to Edinburgh, and taken a printing-office near Holyrood.

CHAPTER IV.

THE BORDER MINSTRELSY, AND THE LAY OF
THE LAST MINSTREL.

THERE can be no doubt that the *Scottish Minstrelsy* exerted on poetry in general a most healthful influence. The book seemed a fresh well, a 'diamond of the desert' newly opened amid the dry sandy wastes and the brackish streams of a literary wilderness. Wordsworth's *Lyrical Ballads* had appeared a few years previously, but had hitherto made very little impression on the public mind. Lewis' *Tales of Terror*, and translations from the German, had been over-stimulating, and were beginning to pall. It was not surprising that, in such a dreary dearth, a few bunches of wild flowers, culled as it were from the walls of a ruined castle, but with the scent of free winds, and the freshness of the dew, and the tints of the sun upon the leaves, shot suddenly into the hands of men, should attract notice and awaken delight; that, while rejected by some of the fastidious, and the idolaters of Pope and Dryden, they should refresh the dispirited lovers of poetry; and that, while the vain and the worldly passed them by, if they did not tear and trample them under foot with fierce shouts of laughter, the simple-hearted on both sides of the Border took them up and folded them to their bosoms. Had the *Minstrelsy* appeared as an original work, we doubt if it would have met with such success. But, issued under the prestige of antiquity, criticism was disarmed: the prejudice men feel in favour of the old was enlisted in behalf of the new, and the book assumed the interest at once of a birth and a resurrection.

One main merit of these ballads lay in their relation to the period when they were sung, and in their thorough reflection of the manners, feelings, superstitions, and passions of a rude age. This, joined to the literary excellence possessed by most of its specimens, renders the old ballad by far the most interesting species of poetry. The interest springs from the primitive form of society described in it,— a society composed of a few simple elements, of the baron's ha', the peasant's cot; the feudal castle, the little dependent hamlet beside it; the sudden raids made by one hostile chief upon another; the wild

games, gatherings, and huntings which relieved ever
and anon the monotony of life ; the few travellers,
chiefly pilgrims or soldiers, moving through the
solitudes of the landscape ; the Monastery with its
cowled tenants, and the Minster with its commanding tower : from the glimpses given of an early
and uncultivated nature ; of dreary moors, with
jackmen spurring their horses across to seize a
prey ; of little patches of culture shining like spots
of arrested sunshine on the desolate hills; of evening
glens, down which are descending to their repose
long and lowing trains of cattle from the upland
pastures ; and of ancient forests of birch, or oak, or
pine, blackening along the ridges, half-choking the
cry of the cataracts, and furnishing a shelter for the
marauders of the time, if not also for the disem-
bodied dead, or evil spirits from the pit : from the
superstitions of that dark age,—ghosts standing
sheeted in blood by the bedside of their murderers ;
fairies footing it to the light of the moon, and the
music of the midnight wind ; witches dwelling in
caves communicating with hell ; and portents of the
sky—the *new moon in the old one's arms,* double suns,
and tearless rainbows : and from the view supplied
of fierce and stormy passions, boiling in hot abori-
ginal hearts, ever prompting to deeds of violence,
yet mingled with thrills of generous emotion, and

touches of chivalric grace. Then there was the *build* of the ballad, so simple yet striking, full even in its fragmentariness, bringing out all main events and master-strokes with complete success, often breaking off with an unconscious art at the very point where it was certain to produce the greatest effect ; its very splinters, like those of aromatic wood, smelling sweetest at the fracture ; its lyrical spirit, so changeful, gushing, bird-like ; and its language, so native, simple, graphic, yet in its simplicity powerful, and capable of the grandest occasional effects ; reminding you of an oak sapling, which in the hands of a strong yeoman has often turned aside the keen point of the rapier, dashed the claymore to the dust, and deadened the blow of the mighty descending mace. Not inferior, besides, to any of these elements of interest, is the figure projected on our vision of the Minstrel himself, wandering through the country like a breeze or a river at his own sweet will, with a harp, which is his passion, pride, and passport, in his hand ; now pausing on the rustic bridge, and watching the progress of the haunted stream, which had once ran red with gore in some ancient skirmish ; now seated on the mountain summit, and seeing in the castles, abbeys, and towers which dot the landscape on every side, as well as in the cottages, villages, braes, and woods,

a subject for his muse ; and now beheld in a tower
or castle, which even then had been for centuries a
ruin, silent in its age, like that solemn Kilchurn
Castle, standing at the base of Cruachan like a
hoary penitent before God, but soothed amidst remorse and anguish by the sympathetic murmur of
the dark Orchay and the silver ripple of the blue
Loch Awe, — meditating over other times, and
passing his hand across his lyre at intervals, with a
touch as casual and careless, yet music-stirring as
that of the breeze upon the nettles and the ivy
which in part adorn and in part insult the surrounding desolation,—or to view, in another aspect
still, the manifolded Minstrel, his figure seen now
entering a cottage at eventide, and drawing the
simple circle as if in a net around him, as he
sings

> ' Of old, unhappy, far-off things,
> And battles long ago,'

or as he touches the trembling chords of their
superstition by some weird tale of *diablerie ;* now
admitted, like Scott's famous hero, into the lordly
hall, and there surrounded by bright-eyed maidens,
and stimulated by the twofold flatteries of sugared
lips and generous wines, pouring out his high-
wrought, enthusiastic, yet measured and well-
modulated strains ; now meeting some brother

bard, and exchanging by the lonely mountain
wayside or in some rude hostelry their experience
and their songs ; now firing warriors on the morn
of battle by some Tyrtæan ode ; now soothing the
soul of the departing soldier, as did Allan Bane
Roderick Dhu, by some martial strain which seems
to the dying ear the last echo of the last of a
hundred fights ; now singing his dirge after his
death ; and now, in fine, himself expiring, with the
whole fire of the minstrel spirit mounting to his
eye, and with the harp and the cross meeting over
his dying pillow, as emblems of his joy on earth
and of his hope in heaven.   In addition to these
ideas, images, and associations, let us remember
the fact that ballads have been, as Fletcher said
long ago, the real laws of a country ; that they
have pervaded every rank of society ; mingled like
currents of air with men's loves, hatreds, enthu-
siasms, patriotic passions ; passed from the lips of
the Minstrel himself to those of the ploughman in
the field, the maid by the well (singing, perchance,
as in that exquisite scene in *Guy Mannering :*

> ' Are these the links of Forth, she said,
>   Or are they the crooks of Dee,
>   Or the bonnie woods of Warroch-head,
>   That I sae fain wad see ? '),

the reaper among the sheaves, the herdsman in the

noontide solitude of the hill or in the snow-buried shieling, the babe in the nursery, or the little maid in her solitude—how strange and holy !—with God for her only companion, while wandering to school through woods and wildernesses ; and the soldier resting after the fatigues of a day of blood, or returning to his mountain home when the wars are over, to the music of one of its own unforgotten songs. Who remembers not the ploughman in *Don Quixote*, who, as he goes forth to his morning labour, is singing the ancient ballad of 'Ronces Valles ?' And add still further, as an illustration of the power and charm of ballad poetry, that Homer, the earliest and all but the greatest of poets, was a ballad-maker ; that Shakspeare condescended to borrow stanzas, and plots, and hints from old English ballads ; and that many of our best modern poetic productions—Coleridge's *Christabel* and *Rime of the Anciente Marinere*, Wordsworth's *Lyrical Ballads*, Southey's *Old Woman of Berkeley*, Allan Cunningham's best lyrics, Macaulay's *Lays of Ancient Rome*, some of Tennyson's well-known verses, and innumerable more—are imitations in style, or in spirit, or in manner, or in all three, of those wild, early, spontaneous, immortal strains.

Specially did the *Lay of the Last Minstrel* and its successors spring naturally from the *Minstrelsy of the Scottish Border.* In this last Scott had been collecting the materials on which his genius was to feed, 'like fire to heather set.' He had been educating, too, the public taste to the pitch when such a poem as the *Lay* would likely be well received. No doubt he ran a certain risk by putting his own writings in competition with those exquisite old ballads. But he knew he was of kindred genius with their authors, and he hoped that by grafting the interest of a story on their beautifully simple structure, and connecting something like epic unity with their dramatic and lyrical spirit, he would not be entirely eclipsed in the comparison; and the event proved that he was right. To some incidents in Scott's life, intermediate between the *Border Minstrelsy* and the publication of the *Lay*, we shall advert in our next chapter. Let us now look as far forward as January 1805, when the first of his long and popular poems appeared. The *Lay of the Last Minstrel* was received with universal and unbounded applause. Thousands who had scarcely heard of the *Minstrelsy* read the *Lay*. Scott, like Byron afterwards, awoke one morning and found himself famous. The *Lay*, *Childe Harold*, the *Course of Time*, and Smith's *Life Drama*, have probably been the four most decided *hits* in the recent history of poetry. The *Lay* appeared in a splendid quarto form, a copy of which we were fortunate enough to find, some twenty-five years after its first publication, in a Glasgow library, not quite crumbled away ; and in it first began reading this enchanting poem on the street, amidst the glimmering lights of an April eve. The first edition of 750 copies was speedily exhausted ; others followed rapidly ; and before the author superintended the annotated edition in 1830, nearly 44,000 copies had been disposed of.

Amidst the general outburst of applause, some voices of special value and influence were soon distinguishable, such as those of Jeffrey in the *Edinburgh Review*, George Ellis, William Stewart Rose, Charles James Fox, and William Pitt. Pitt purposed Scott's professional promotion ; and after repeating some lines from the poem describing the old harper's embarrassment when asked to play, said, 'This is a sort of thing I might have expected in painting, but could never have fancied capable of being given in poetry.'

Looking at the *Lay* critically and calmly from our present point of view, we can hardly concur with the extremely high verdicts which the men of that time passed upon it. It is certainly not a great poem, and as certainly it is not in the main a piece of consummate art. But it has many very beautiful passages and spirit-stirring scenes. And these are set in a framework of the most exquisite construction, superior perhaps to anything of the kind in the compass of poetry,—that even of the *Queen's Wake*, which has been so much admired, not excepted. The whole has a gaiety and a gracefulness of movement, blended with a supernatural awe and weird grandeur about it which may be best imaged in its own lines:

> ' He knew by the streamers that shot so bright,
> *That spirits were riding the northern light.*'

The poem has more of lyrical fire, and unmitigated, elastic energy, than any of those which succeeded it. Scott's genius is throughout at the gallop, and it is that of a winged Pegasus careering over steeps

> ' Where mortal horseman ne'er might ride.'

Let it be remembered, too, as explaining the enthusiasm of the reception, that this was the opening of a new and fresh vein of national poetry. The harp of Caledonia had but just begun to sound to the master hand of Burns, when he was snatched prematurely away; and it had remained silent till Scott awoke it again into loftier if not tenderer vibrations. And then there were one or two passages which, in their sweetness and finish, as well

as in the patriotic feeling which breathed through
them, had seldom been surpassed.   Such was the
description of Melrose Abbey by moonlight, which
ranks with the moonlight scene in the *Iliad*, and
which, if not so grand, is more spiritual in its
beauty.   And such is that noble burst commencing,

> ' Breathes there a man with soul so dead,
> Who never to himself has said,
> This is my own, my native land ?'

Such passages have long had a hackneyed look,
from the frequency of quotation, and worse, the
vulgarity of recitation to which they have been sub-
jected ; but conceive their effect on Scotch and
Border blood when new.   Conceive them published
for the first time now : what a sensation they would
produce !   As it was, all Scotland instantly ranked
them with the close of the *Cottar's Saturday Night*,
and felt, and felt truly, that a kindred genius to
Burns had risen in their midst.   And as England's
own poets at that period were few and far between,
the greatest of them struggling with natal gloom
and envious mists, she, too, added her unanimous
voice to the acclamations amidst which Walter
Scott ascended the poetical throne.

E

CHAPTER V.

MINOR EVENTS AND EFFORTS.

AFTER closing his labours on the *Border Minstrelsy*, Scott took a trip to London, partly for the purpose of making some researches in reference to *Sir Tristram*, and partly to enjoy its literary society. His wife went with him, and they were domesticated under the roof of Mr. Charles Dumergne, an intimate acquaintance of Mrs. Scott's relatives the Carpenters, surgeon-dentist to the royal family, and a man of large-hearted hospitality. In London he had much intercourse with Heber, and with Mackintosh, then in the zenith of his conversational supremacy. These were old acquaintances; but he met now for the first time Samuel Rogers, William Stuart Rose, and some other men of great literary eminence. He spent a happy week at Sunninghill with his friends the Ellises, who had the luxury of hearing the first two or three cantos of the *Lay* read to them under one of the old oaks in Windsor Forest. Lockhart is careful to record that in this journey Scott was accompanied by a very large and fine bull-terrier called 'Camp,' one of the greatest favourites among the poet's many dear canine companions, whom he loved, however, not, like Byron, for their unlikeness to men, but for the human elements which they exhibited.

Thence they proceeded to Oxford, and here Scott saw for the first time Richard Heber's brother Reginald, afterwards the famous Bishop of Calcutta, who had just gained the poetical prize for the year, and read to Scott, at a breakfast-table where he met him, the MS. of his *Palestine.* Scott noticed that in the verses on Solomon's temple one remarkable circumstance had escaped him, namely, that no tool had been used in its erection ; when Reginald retired for a few minutes, and returned with the best lines in the poem :

> ' No hammer fell, no ponderous axes rung,
> *Like some tall palm the mystic fabric sprung.*
> Majestic silence !'

In October 1802 the *Edinburgh Review* began, and within a year of its commencement Scott became a contributor ; and in the course of 1803 and 1804 he reviewed Southey's *Amadis of Gaul,*

Sibbald's *Chronicle of Scottish Poetry*, Godwin's
Life of Chaucer, Ellis' *Specimens of Ancient English
Poetry*, and the *Life and Works of Chatterton*.
Scott's reviews in the *Edinburgh, Quarterly, Blackwood's Magazine*, and other periodicals, are all of a
pleasant, light, and gossiping kind. He nowhere
in them puts forth his whole strength, is nowhere
elaborate, never propounds principles, and his
critical *dicta* are often very questionable. But his
learning is great, his anecdotage exhaustless, his
style easy and conversational always, though careless often, his vein of humour now and then exceedingly rich, and, above all, his spirit genial and
kindly : he is never savage ; and one contrasts him
favourably in this point with the truculence and
malignity of Brougham, and even with the smart
and snappish severities in which Lord Jeffrey sometimes forgot his better nature. We may mention
here that Thomas Thomson, the Registrar-General
for Scotland, an intimate friend both of Scott's
and Jeffrey's, assured us that Brougham often *compelled* Jeffrey to insert some of the fiercest dia-
tribes, such as that on Walker's *Defence of Order*,
and on Byron's *Hours of Idleness*, against his will.
Jeffrey was naturally generous and amiable ;
Brougham, in those days at least, all that was the
reverse.

But Scott had other matters to occupy him besides literature and ballad poetry. Napoleon Bonaparte had 'accumulated all the materials of fury, havoc, and desolation into one black cloud,' which hung on the other side of the Channel like a menacing meteor. But, unlike the creditors of the Nabob of Arcot, the inhabitants of Britain did not regard it with 'idle stupefaction.' They rose as one man to encounter and roll it back. Our pulpits, from that of Robert Hall downwards, rang with anathemas on the usurper of France, and with appeals to the patriotic sentiments of Great Britain. Volunteer corps were formed all over the country. That

'Wall of fire around our much-loved isle,'

which Burns had anticipated in prophetic ecstasy, was now actually seen arising; and no bosom in the land beat with more heroic feelings than that of Scott. He became quartermaster of the Edinburgh Light Horse, and busied himself in military preparations. His blood rose with the prospect of danger; and there can be no doubt that, had the haughty threat of Gaul been fulfilled, the poet of the Border would have fought with all the courage of his ancestors. None but a man of the most dauntless bravery and martial enthusiasm could

have written either the poems or the novels of
Scott.

In the same year he for the first time met
Wordsworth, who was journeying in Scotland, and
they became fast friends. In many points they
differed, the objective and the subjective being
found in divers proportions in their nature ; Wordsworth being more of the philosophic poet, Scott of
the northern scald. But they resembled each other
in the sincerity of their enthusiasm, in their love
for the simple and primitive in nature and in character, in their attachment to mountain scenery
and to the antique—both traceable, phrenologists
would say, to their immense organ of *inhabitiveness*
—and in their domestic virtues. Wordsworth admired Scott as a man, without exactly believing in
him as a poet. Scott, while perhaps sagely smiling
at Wordsworth's *Alice Fells* and *Idiot Boys*, appreciated warmly his higher strains, and owned in him
the presence of one of the great original masters
of song, so sparsely sown in these later times.
When the Lake poet returned to England, he wrote
Scott a characteristic letter, closing thus : 'Your
sincere friend, for such I will call myself, though
*slow to use a word of such solemn meaning to any
one.* W. WORDSWORTH.'

This year (1803) also Scott published a small

edition of *Sir Tristram*, the chief interest in which
now is that it is said to be the work of Thomas of
Ercildoun, or Thomas the Rhymer, and was edited
by Sir Walter Scott. It obtained its sole circula-
tion among the antiquarians of that day.

In 1804 Scott left sweet Lasswade, the home of
his early wedded life, and the cradle of his nascent
fame, for Ashestiel, a place that shall always be
dear to the lovers of poetry. Never shall we at
least forget the scene of perfect peace it presented
in a calm though cloudy day of June 1844, with
the murmur of the Tweed hardly breaking the
serene silence which lay upon the green hills, the
woods, the plain, the brook, and the ever-honoured
mansion where the great minstrel dwelt. It seemed
to us then, and seems still, far more interesting
than Abbotsford. *That* turned out in the long-run
a foolish speculation, and was darkened by the
shadows of disaster and of death. With Ashestiel
the associations and memories are all delightful.
Scott passed there probably his serenest days. It
is a place of almost entire solitude, standing by the
side of a deep ravine covered with trees, down
which a brook finds its way to the Tweed, from
which river the mansion is separated by a narrow
strip of beautiful meadow. All around are the
silent hills ; not another house is in sight ; and the

nearest town, Selkirk, is seven miles away. 'Pastoral melancholy' is the pervading feeling of the spot, although it is a melancholy more akin to joy than to sorrow, and which one would not exchange for a millennium of coarse miscalled delights.

Here Scott set up for a season the staff of his rest. It suited him, as in the centre of Ettrick Forest, and near the scene of his duties as the Sheriff of Selkirkshire. He pleased himself, too, to think that Ashestiel belonged to the ancient division of the country called Reged. Here he took his well-known domestics Thomas Purdie and Peter Mathieson into his employment, the one as shepherd and the other as coachman. Purdie appeared before the Sheriff first as a poacher; but Scott became interested in his story, which he told with a mixture of pathos, simplicity, and pawky humour, and extended to him forgiveness and favour. Tom served him long and faithfully; and we have been told that Scott proposed for his epitaph the words, 'Here lies one who might have been trusted with untold gold, but not with unmeasured whisky.' Mathieson and Purdie adored Scott, he being one of the very few men who have been heroes to their valets. At Ashestiel, too, he became intimate with the famous Mungo Park, then newly returned from his first travels in Africa,

and practising as a surgeon in Selkirk. Park, as
all the world knows, was a brave, manly, and interesting character, thoroughly truthful too, and
who told Scott that he had suppressed certain
incidents in his travels, lest they should be thought
too marvellous to be real. He soon tired of the
life of a country surgeon, and said he would sooner
be broiling in Africa than riding over dirty roads
and wild moorlands, rewarded sometimes, after a
whole night's travel and work, by nothing better
than a roasted potato and a draught of butter-
milk. Scott came one day suddenly upon Park by
the side of the Yarrow, dropping in stones into the
waters. He asked what he meant, and the traveller
replied that this was the way he used to find out
the depths of the rivers in Africa, from the time
the bubbles took to rise to the surface. This little
incident convinced Scott that Park was revolving
the thought of a second journey, which he effected
accordingly the next year, perishing, all know, in
one of those African streams. Park spent a night
at Ashestiel before starting for his journey, and
next day the friends parted on the Williamhope
Bridge ; 'the autumnal mist, floating heavily and
slowly down the valley of the Yarrow,' presenting
to Scott's fancy a 'striking emblem of the troubled
and uncertain prospect which his undertaking

afforded.' In leaping a small ditch, Park's horse
stumbled. 'I am afraid, Mungo,' said the Sheriff,
'that is a bad omen.' 'Freits follow those who
follow them,' replied he, smiling, and setting spurs
to his horse galloped off, and Scott saw him no
more. Park's eldest brother remained in Scott's
neighbourhood for several years, and was his frequent companion in his sports and mountain rides.
He was himself a man of extraordinary strength
and of dauntless spirit. Yet he was often alarmed
by Scott's reckless riding, and once exclaimed,
'The deil's in ye, Sherra ; ye'll never halt till they
bring ye hame wi' your feet foremost.'

The triumphant success of the *Lay* decided
Scott's mind henceforth to apply himself mainly
to literature. The publishers of the first edition
were Longman & Co. of London, and Archibald
Constable & Co. of Edinburgh ; the latter house,
however, having only a small share in the adventure. Numerous offers were at this time made
to Scott by eminent booksellers. He was now a
popular author ; and to such, publishers are for a
season obedient humble servants. But Scott was
full of a project of his own, which offered fair at
first, but ultimately nearly ruined his rising fortunes. James Ballantyne had ere this, as we mentioned, removed to Edinburgh, and Scott entered

into a *sub rosa* partnership with him, embarking
in his concern almost the whole of his available
capital. He had fixed to quit the bar, where his
gains had been steadily though slowly increasing ;
he had no wish to attach himself exclusively to
any one of the many publishers who sought to
monopolize him ; and he determined to found,
under the name of Ballantyne, a gigantic publish-
ing business of his own. In this, had he been the
sole partner or the sole author, he might have
been successful. But from his connection with
men inferior to himself as publishers, and still
more from his connection with men inferior to
himself as authors, complications arose which
nearly strangled even the leonine man who alone
could, and who did afterwards, burst them asunder.

Meanwhile his mind was teeming with Brob-
dignagian projects. One of them was an edition
of the *British Poets.* And certainly never was
man so well qualified as he for this task, by
learning, enthusiasm, cautious judgment, wide
sympathies, and the powers of interesting narrative and genial criticism. His only danger had
been in overloading the text with superfluous
notes. But Scott's notes to his own poems are
like no other body's notes : their superfluity is
pardoned on account of their interest. It would

have been the same had he annotated the works of other bards. And his *Lives of the Poets,* if inferior to Johnson's in point, massive power, and sceptral majesty, would have far surpassed them in ease, variety, research, accurate knowledge, catholic taste, and fellow-feeling with genius. The plan, however, owing to rivalship among the book-sellers, came to nothing. He began then an edition of Dryden, to which he prefixed a very valuable memoir, written with more care and condensation than usual. He wrote, besides, several articles for the *Edinburgh Review;* one on Todd's edition of Spenser, another on Godwin's *Fleetwood* (in which he does justice to Caleb Williams, but very much underrates *St. Leon,* a romance almost 'equal to his own *Ivanhoe*), a third on the *Poems of Ossian,* a fourth on Frois-sart, a fifth on Thornton's *Sporting Tour,* etc. Ossian he on the whole admired, and has even imitated in his *Highland Widow* and some other of his tales; and of Macpherson he had formed a very different opinion from that which Macaulay has paraded so often, and expressed with a bitter-ness and *animus* altogether unaccountable.

He began *Waverley* this year; although, hav-ing read some of the opening scenes to William Erskine, who disapproved of them, he threw it aside. He was visited now by Southey, and they became friends, though never very warm or intimate ones. There were a certain strain and starch about Southey which Scott did not quite relish, highly as he admired his abilities and principles. He resumed his Volunteerism with redoubled energy. James Skene of Rubislaw spent a considerable portion of the autumn of 1805 at Ashestiel, and gives some very interesting sketches of Scott's occupations and amusements about this period of his life. He began now, for the first time, the habit he pursued ever afterwards, of rising very early, and, as he phrased it, 'breaking the neck of the day's work' before breakfast,—a practice to which some have ascribed in part the limpid clearness, temperate calm, freshness, and healthiness of his style. He plunged occasionally, with Mr Skene, amidst the wild moorlands of Moffatdale, St Mary's Loch, Loch Skene, the Grey Mare's Tail, and the neighbouring wildernesses, drinking in large draughts of inspiration, which *Marmion* was to prove had not been imbibed in vain. He visited Wordsworth, then resident on the banks of Grasmere ; and one day there rested on the brow of Helvellyn, shaming all its eagles, three of the mightiest spirits in Britain—Scott, Wordsworth, and Humphrey Davy.

From Grasmere he carried his wife to spend a few days at the old haunt of their loves, Gilsland ; and they were enjoying themselves much there when the news arrived that a French force was about to land in Scotland, and that all the leal-hearted volunteers of the Lothians and the Border must assemble themselves in Dalkeith. The poet instantly obeyed the summons ; and in twenty-four hours his noble horse, whom he had fortunately brought along with him, bore him in one fiery and unmitigated gallop for fully a hundred miles to the place of rendezvous. Here he found the scene in *The Antiquary* realized. It was a false alarm ; the beacon fires had been lit prematurely. But he met a goodly array of friends, who had come on the same April errand with himself; and as there was no fray toward, they feasted in lieu thereof, and great were the mirth and martial jollity that ensued.

Nor had his time on the road been lost. He had during his ride composed *The Bard's Incantation*, one of his most vigorous minor pieces, and assuredly it 'rings to boot and saddle.'

CHAPTER VI.

A RUN OF PERSONAL AND LITERARY SUCCESS.

EIGHTEEN HUNDRED AND SIX opened favourably for our poet. He was appointed one of the Principal Clerks of Session, with a salary of £800 a year and a few hours' labour, if labour it could be called, which amounted only to the duty of registering the decisions of the judges during the sitting of the Court. And there for a quarter of a century was Scott to sit, the observed of all observers, sometimes listening to the pleadings of the bar, and sometimes not ; occasionally writing poetry (as when moved by Jeffrey's eloquence he began *The Pibroch of Donnel Dhu*, his pen galloping to the tune of the pleader's voice), and often lost in the far-stretching reveries of his own spirit, wandering over the Highland hills, or carrying on imaginary conversations which were afterwards to

be wrought into his world-famous fictions. Lockhart, indeed, tries to find a matter of marvel in
reference to his hero, by magnifying the work he
had to do at the clerk's table. But we have conversed with lawyers of experience, who have
assured us that the situation was little other than
a sinecure. In order to gain this position he had
to repair to London, where Lord Spencer and Mr.
Fox favoured his claim, where he met for the first
time with Canning and Frere, and made, besides,
the acquaintance of two remarkable ladies of very
different character, and moving in very different
spheres—Joanna Baillie, and the unfortunate Caroline Princess of Wales. Joanna he ever afterwards
regarded with brotherly affection, as she most
assuredly deserved, at once on account of her
masculine genius and her feminine virtues, and
that blended simplicity and dignity which made
her the true spirit-sister of Scott. His opinion of
Caroline was at this time favourable. He calls
her 'an enchanting Princess, who dwells in an
enchanted palace, and I cannot help thinking that
her Prince must labour under some malignant spell
when he denies himself her society.' He afterwards, however, in common with all the Tory party
except Canning, altered his view, and spoke of her
in language unworthy of a gentleman or a man.

Lord Melville was at this time the leading power in Scotland. His character was complex. To high talent and much rough kindness he added many of the faults, and even vices, which characterized the statesmen of the olden time. Loved by his tenants at Dunira and his neighbours in Comrie,—who combined in building the handsome obelisk to his memory which stands on Dunmore, and looks down on one of the noblest prospects in Scotland: the massive mountains of Glenlednick behind; the Deil's Caldron sending up from below a voice of thunder, unsoftened by the muffling of its woods; the plain of Dalginross and the village of Comrie, washed by three mountain rivers to the south; Loch Earn; the Abruchill Hills and Benvoirlich on the west; and the Lomond Hills rounding off the prospect eastward—a prospect Scott must have seen when he visited his friend,— Lord Melville was hated by the Whigs, who were now the governing party; and they resolved to impeach him. He was acquitted, however, in spite of all the manly eloquence of Whitbread, his principal assailant; and his friends in Scotland held a dinner on the occasion. Though indebted for his recent promotion to the Whig party, Scott not only attended the dinner, but indited a song steeped in ferocious Toryism, and using the follow-

F

ing truculent language about Fox, who was then
known to be under a mortal illness:

> 'The brewer (Whitbread) we'll hoax,
> *Tallyho to the Fox,*
> And drink Melville for ever as long as we live.'

Nothing in all Scott's conduct gave such offence
as this allusion. Lord Cockburn tells us that
some of his warmest friends were cooled, and that
a few of his enemies never forgave him. The
amiable Countess of Rosslyn was one of the
former number; and so far down as the date of
the Queen's trial, the *Scotsman* reprinted the verses
to Scott's disadvantage. It was one of the few
errata of his life: he felt so himself very soon afterwards, and made in some measure the *amende
honorable* in the well-known lines on Fox in
Marmion.

He was all through the brief reign of the Whigs
in a very uneasy and irritable state of mind. On
one occasion, returning from a meeting where he
had been opposing some proposed innovations in
the legal courts, and displayed unusual freedom
and force of eloquence, and crossing the Mound
in company with Jeffrey and another reforming
friend, who were for treating the matter lightly,
he actually turned his head round, and in vain
sought to conceal his tears by resting it on the

wall of the Mound, as he said, 'No, no, gentlemen, 'tis no laughing matter. Little by little, whatever your wishes may be, you will destroy and undermine, till nothing that makes Scotland Scotland shall remain.'

In November 1806 he commenced *Marmion*, the second of his great poems in time, and in some respects the first in talent. And ere he had read a line of it Constable offered 1000 guineas,—a sum then thought enormous, but which Scott instantly accepted, the more eagerly as he needed money to help his brother Thomas. He studied for *Marmion* amidst the wilds of Ashestiel, often sitting by himself under some tall old ashes standing on a knoll in a neighbouring farm which still bears the name of the *Sheriff's Knowe;* sometimes to be seen under a huge oak by the brink of the Tweed ; sometimes wandering far from home, with no companion but his dog, 'in among those green and melancholy wildernesses where Yarrow creeps from her fountains,' returning not till the evening, and often, in his own language, 'having many a grand gallop among the braes' while revolving some of the more stirring scenes, or composing some of the more rapturous measures of the poem. Mr. Skene, however, informs us that the *Battle of Flodden* was composed by Scott during the

autumn of 1807, when at quarters with the cavalry
at Portobello, and that in the intervals of drilling
he used to walk his powerful black steed up and
down by himself upon the sands within the beating
of the surge, and now and then he would plunge in
his spurs and go off as if at the charge, with the
spray dashing about him. He often repeated to
Skene, as they rode back to Musselburgh, the
verses he had composed in the morning. In the
course of this year he visited London to find out
new materials for Dryden, and the Tories, now
in power, welcomed him with increased warmth,
since he had stuck to his colours, and even suffered
in their cause. In returning home he visited Lich-
field, and saw Miss Seward, who describes him
'coming like a sunbeam to her dwelling,' and gives
a very lady-like picture, or rather inventory, of his
'brown hair, flaxen eyebrows, long upper lip, and
light grey eyes.' She thought his recitation of
poetry, like Johnson's, too monotonous and violent.
When she showed him, in Carey's *Dante*, the passage where Michael Scott occurs (in the fourth
canto of the *Inferno*), he said that though he
admired the spirit and skill of the version, he could
find no pleasure in the *Divina Commedia*. The
plan appeared to him unhappy — the personal
malignity and strange mode of revenge presump-

tuous and uninteresting. Scott must have forgot all this, when we find him in Italy remarking to Mr. Cheney that it was mortifying to think how Dante thought none worth sending to hell except Italians; when Mr. C. remarked, that he of all men had no right to make this complaint, as his ancestor Michael Scott is introduced there!

Marmion appeared, amidst a hum of general expectation, on the 23d of February 1808. It was received by the public at large with an enthusiasm only second to that which had welcomed the *Lay*, but it was rather roughly handled by the *Edinburgh Review*. Jeffrey had been engaged to dine with Scott on the day the review appeared ; but feeling a little apprehensive of the consequences, wrote an explanatory note along with the copy of the number. Scott replied in a good spirit. Jeffrey, although with manifest reluctance, came, and the poet received him with his usual bland courtesy. But conceive the critic's feelings when, as he was leaving, the hostess of the house said, ' Well, good night, Mr. Jeffrey : dey tell me you have abused Scott in the *Review*, and I hope Mr. Constable has paid you very well for writing it.' She never spoke to him again. The critique in some points was unfair. It asserted, for example, that Scott throughout neglected Scottish feelings and Scottish characters,—a charge which to name is to stamp with absurdity, and which Jeffrey could hardly have himself seriously entertained.   The faults of *Marmion* were obvious, but they were venial, and the critic brought down on them a weight of disapprobation entirely disproportioned to their guilt.   It was as though the vagrant courses of a truant boy had been punished by death.   But justice was done to the genius of the author, and the *Battle of Flodden* especially was praised as more Homeric than even Homer's best.

The general impression about *Marmion* now is, that while in plan imperfect, in the choice of hero unfortunate, and in composition very unequal, it is in parts and passages superior to his other poems, and shows a power which, had it been systematically exerted on a worthier subject, and had not the age of epics been over, would have achieved a Scottish *Iliad*, or, at the least, an *Orlando Furioso*. But Scott, industrious though he was, wanted the true epic patience, ' the long choosing and beginning late,' the calm and cumulative workmanship, and the majestic serenity of the heroic poet.   His best things were dashed off at a heat.   Like the tiger, if his first spring failed, he never tried a second, but retired grumbling to his jungle ; and if he could not go through his subject at the pace of the

whirlwind, he was motionless. The preliminary
epistles were read with as much pleasure as any
other parts of the book, although entirely uncon-
nected with it. They were beautiful excrescences,
and indeed had been at first intended for separate
publication.

Marmion was much admired by Scott's special
friends as well as by the public, although Wordsworth's severe and peculiar taste was unsatisfied.
In his letter, after giving the new poem some equivocal and scanty praise, with what gusto he turns
to a more favourite theme—the beautiful nature
around him! 'The spring has burst out upon us
all at once, and the vale is now in exquisite beauty.
A gentle shower has fallen this morning, and I
hear the thrush who has built in my orchard
singing amain.' How characteristic! What were
Tantallon Castle, 'Edinburgh throned on crags,'
or Flodden Field, to Grasmere in spring? what
Scott's powerful though unequal and heated strains
to the voice of the thrush,

> 'Pouring her full heart
> In profuse strains of unpremeditated art?'

Jeffrey's critique produced important consequences. It cut, although at first silently, the tie
between Scott and the *Edinburgh Review*, and

combined, along with circumstances of a later date, to cool the poet with Constable. Shortly after its appearance we find Scott moving heaven and earth to establish in London the *Quarterly Review* as a counterweight to the *Edinburgh* both in literary criticism and in politics,—a project in which, ere the end of the year, he was successful.

Meanwhile his *Dryden* appeared in eighteen volumes; he aided Henry Weber, a poor German hack, who ultimately went deranged in Scott's house, in his *Ancient Metrical Romances;* began a laborious edition of *Swift;* edited Strutt's *Queen Hoo Hall,* Carleton's *War of the Spanish Succession,* the *Memoirs of Cary Duke of Monmouth;* and projected a general edition of the *Novelists of Britain,* with notes. He took, besides, a lively interest in the affairs, always involved and unlucky, of James Hogg, and gave effectual patronage to John Struthers of Glasgow, the author of *The Poor Man's Sabbath,* a man of remarkable ability, at first a shoemaker by trade, and to the end a 'poor man,' but who wrote good poetry and powerful prose, and has always been reckoned an honour to his native city. Scott got his poem published for him, and we find Struthers afterwards making a pilgrimage of gratitude to Abbotsford.

Toward the close of 1808 the breach between

Constable and Scott widened to its utmost. It was precipitated by the appearance in the 26th number of the *Edinburgh Review* of an article on *Don Pedro Cevallos.* ' This paper was written by Lord Brougham, and forms perhaps the best specimen extant of his style, which had not then got so involved, parenthetical, and cumbrous as it became afterwards. It is a most powerful and eloquent diatribe, and told like a bombshell in the Tory camp. It irritàted Scott's political prejudices ; and he, in common with many of the Edinburgh citizens, withdrew their subscriptions. (In Constable's list of subscribers to the *Edinburgh Review* there appears, opposite Scott's name, an indignant dash of Constable's pen — ' Stopt !!! ') He set himself immediately to take vengeance on his adversaries : first, by establishing John Ballantyne as a publisher in opposition to Constable ; and secondly, by completing the arrangements for the *Quarterly Review.* In the former he after a season failed, but in the latter he succeeded. The *Quarterly Review* soon came out under Gifford in great force.

In the spring of 1809 Scott again visited London to prosecute his gigantic plans. There, along with Canning, Croker, and Ellis, he concocted the new *Review.* Coleridge, at that time unfortunate as an

author, depressed in spirits, and straitened in circumstances, was nevertheless forcing his way into
fame by his matchless conversational and lecturing
powers, and had become, next to Scott himself,
the lion of the season, and the great orator of the
dining-tables in the metropolis. Scott met him at
Sotheby's, and was much struck by his talk, although probably he did not understand it all, any
more than his other auditors, or sometimes the
lecturer himself.

On his return he commenced the *Lady of the
Lake.* While writing it he was subject to fits of
absence. His mind was in the Trosachs; and
once he mistook another house in Castle Street for
his own, but cried out, when he discovered the
blunder, ' Ah! there are too many bairns' bannets
here for this hoose to be mine!' He went with his
wife in autumn to revisit the well-known localities
of his new poem, and satisfied himself in his own
person that a good horseman might gallop from
Loch Venachar to Stirling within the space he was
to allot to Fitz-James. He then visited Ross
Priory and Buchanan House, and read there to the
assembled guests the description of the stag-chase
which he had not long before composed,—read it
almost in the shadow of Ben Ledi.

At Buchanan House he saw, for the first time,

Byron's *English Bards and Scotch Reviewers*, and
was not at all annoyed by the young poet's attack
on himself. He had read the *Hours of Idleness*,
and even from it had predicted the future fame of
the poet—had deprecated the article in the *Edinburgh Review*, and once thought of remonstrating
with Jeffrey on the subject.

He issued this year an edition of *Sir Ralph
Sadler's State Papers*, in three quarto volumes.
John Kemble visited him in the autumn, and
'seduced him somewhat into the old compotatory
habits of "Colonel Grogg."' It was on this occasion that the twain were pursued by a furious
bull. They tried to escape by crossing a stream,
but found it in *spate*, when Kemble exclaimed, in
all the pomp of stage declamation (as Scott used
to relate with exquisite mimicry), 'The flood is
angry, Sheriff; methinks I'll get me up into a
tree!' But no tree was at hand; and had not
the dogs succeeded in diverting the animal, King
John's days had been numbered. This year Miss
Seward died; but her loss was more than supplied
to Scott by his becoming acquainted with Daniel
Terry, who afterwards adapted so many of his
novels for the stage, and was, besides, a warm,
intelligent, and amusing friend.

1810 was one of Scott's brightest years. Early

in May appeared the *Lady of the Lake*, and was
received with boundless enthusiasm. The critics
and the public were for once of the same opinion
to an iota. On all the roads leading to the
Trosachs was suddenly heard the rushing of
many horses and chariots. Old inns were crowded
to suffocation; bad dinners and breakfasts, and
enormous charges, were endured with exemplary
patience; and new inns sprung up like mushrooms.
Post-hire permanently rose. Every corner of that
fine gorge was explored, and every foot of that
beautiful loch was traversed, by travellers carrying
copies of the book in their hands; and as they
sailed toward Glengyle, or climbed the grey scalp
of Ben An, or sate in the shady hollow of Coir-
nan-Uriskin, or leaned over the still waters of Loch
Achray, repeating passages from it with unfeigned
rapture. It was as if a ray from another sphere
had fallen on and revealed a nook of matchless
loveliness, and all rejoiced in the gleam and its
revelation.

The *Lady of the Lake* has always been, as a
whole, our favourite among Scott's poems. We
love it for the delicious naturalness and interest
of the story,—the breathless rapidity of the verse,
reminding you of the gallop of the gallant grey
which bore its hero in the storm of chase till he

sank in death; the freshness of its spirit, like
morning dew sparkling on the heath flowers of
Ellen's Isle; its exquisitely assorted and contrasted characters,—and because we have known
from boyhood so well the scenery of the poem:
Glenartney's hazel shade; the wild heights of
Uamvar; lone Glenfinlas; Ben Ledi's heaving sides
and hoary summit; the down-rushing masses of
Ben Venue; Loch Achray, as sweet, if not so solitary still, as when Allan Bane uttered his thrilling
farewell; and the gnarled defile of the Trosachs,
in which to fancy's ear the horn of Fitz-James is
heard 'still sounding for evermore.' In the un-
mixed delight afforded by this poem there is no
parallel in literature, save in two or three of the
author's own novels, or in a few of Shakspeare's
plays; and he that has given that to all readers
may well defy carping criticism. Walter Savage
Landor justly magnifies its closing verses as unequalled in princely dignity and gracefulness.

In the same propitious year Scott recommenced
Waverley, but threw it again aside upon a cold
criticism from James Ballantyne.

CHAPTER VII

ASHESTIEL TO ABBOTSFORD—GLIMPSE OF FAMILY,
DOMESTIC CIRCUMSTANCES, AND HOME LIFE.

IN the *Lady of the Lake* Scott's poetical career had come to its height. He had come to the first 'Rest and be Thankful' in his upward course. Even then, indeed, as usually happens, the chariot of his triumph had a slave riding behind it. But before speaking of the business entanglements which were beginning slowly to gather round him, we shall now look at his domestic circumstances, growing family, and his change of residence, and what it implied.

Scott's married life, as we saw, commenced under auspices on the whole favourable. We are aware that rumours affecting Mrs. Scott's prudence, education, economy, and other still more indispensable virtues in the female charac-

ter, were long and are still afloat, and that many
did not hesitate to say that the match was unhappy, and that she was by no means a fitting
life-companion for Scott. But, in the first place,
we wonder where a lady exactly adapted to and
on the level of a man like Scott could at that time
be found. Would Miss Stuart of Fettercairn have
been the person? She was never tried, and we
have our doubts on the matter. Joanna Baillie
we have called his 'soul's sister,' but a soul's sister
may be sometimes a poor heart and home wife.
(We shall quote immediately what Miss Baillie
herself says of Mrs. Scott.) The marriage, no
doubt, was a hasty one; but hasty marriages have
often been happy,—the difference only being, that
the disenchantment which takes place in all marriages to a certain extent may, in these 'love at
first sight' matches, begin a little sooner, and
contrast somewhat more strongly with the first
effervescence of feeling. But in them, as well
as in the others, the re-reaction, so beautifully
described by Emerson in his paper on 'Love,'
usually takes place, and the object of ardent first
passion becomes

    'A gentle wife—though fairy none ;'

and a 'thorough good understanding' established

between them makes up for the once wild and tumultuous love of espousals. We think this was the case with Scott. If his wife did not come up to the high-strung expectations he had formed when courting her at Gilsland, or toasting her all that September night with Shortrede, she was nevertheless an affectionate partner, a kind mother ; and her faults, whatever they were, did not compromise her status in society, and bore hardest on herself. Scott, when he met Byron in London in 1815, spoke to him warmly of his domestic comfort, and the unhappy poet (then himself married) envied his friend's lot. Henry Crabb Robinson records the following in his journal : ' Mrs. Walter Scott was spoken of rather disparagingly, when Miss Baillie gave her this good word : " When I visited her, I saw a great deal to like. She seemed to admire and look up to her husband. She was very kind to her guests. Her children were well bred, and the house was in excellent order. And she had some smart roses in her cap, and I did not like her the less for that."' Scott, as we shall see, sincerely and deeply mourned her loss. Altogether, Mrs., latterly Lady Scott, although neither a Minerva nor a Venus, neither a Miss Baillie, Mrs. Hemans, or Madame de Stael, neither a Rebecca, Jeanie Deans, or Die Vernon, was a very fair speci-

men of a poet's wife, and so Scott accordingly
rated her.

Scott had in all four children, two boys and two
girls. Charlotte Sophia, afterwards Mrs. Lockhart,
was born on the 15th November 1799. She is
described as by far the best of the family,
the likest her father, was his special favourite,
and devoted to him, amiable, full of a gentle
enthusiasm, and a beautiful singer of the 'auld
Scottish sangs' and Border ballads. Walter, also
a great favourite of the father, was born 28th
October 1801. Scott, in his later days, doted on
his son's personal appearance and athletic accomplishments, and used to say, 'Isn't he a fine fellow?'
The intellect of the sire, however, like Hamlet
in the mutilated play, was, we fear, omitted by
special desire; nor was the paternal prudence conspicuous in the character. Ann, born 2d February
1803, was the wag of the family, with a good deal
of tart, sardonic humour in her composition, as well
as warm attachment to her father. Charles, the
youngest, was born on the 24th December 1805,
studied at Lampeter and Oxford, became a clerk
in the Foreign Office, was attached to the Embassy
at Naples, and accompanied his father part of his
last melancholy journey.

Scott warmly loved children, his own and others.

G

We may refer our readers, in proof of this, to Dr.
John Brown's delightful little paper entitled *Pet
Marjorie*, a paper intensely interesting in itself,
as descriptive of a young girl of promise early removed — lest we might imagine she should ever
become less than 'a little lower than the angels' —
and one of the sweetest of those 'child cherubs'
whom so many memories cherish as having sparkled,
been exhaled, and gone to heaven ; and interesting,
as revealing a secret flowery nook in the history of
a great and good man, which otherwise would have
been unsuspected. What finer spectacle than that
of Scott with sweet Marjory on his knee, or in a
corner of his plaid, or reciting poetry to him till
he blubbered and shook with emotion — the lion
dandling the kid ! To his own children Scott was
less a sire than a companion—a playmate called
'Papa.' He rollicked, laughed, tumbled with them,
told them stories ; and all the while was insinuat-
ing instruction into their minds. He allowed them
to read no Pinnock's Catechisms, and other rubbish
pretending to teach children science, and set old
heads upon young shoulders by some premature
and preposterous process ; but he let them loose, as
he had been in his early time let loose, on *Blue-
beard, Jack the Giant-killer, Ali Baba,* and *Aladdin
with the Wonderful Lamp.* And as they read to-

gether, one could hardly distinguish the glee of the parent from that of the children, so merry and ringing was the laughter which rose around and enveloped them all. He taught them history, and particularly that of their own country, with special care; and on Sundays he often, after morning service, took them with him to the braeside, and told them scriptural narratives, with all the fascinating power which distinguished his fictions, adding new interest to the most interesting stories in the world. The Lambs have given us *Tales from Shakspeare*, and they are admirable; but what 'Tales from Scripture' could Scott have produced! He did not send his daughters to boarding-schools to be 'finished' (a word with two edges!), but he had a private governess of approved character for them; and he took care, above all, that they should be well instructed in Scottish music and song, which he loved, as he did everything that was Scottish, with his whole heart, and soul, and mind, and strength.

Strange, after such training, that his family did not make a greater figure, some one will say. There might have been counteracting elements. On the whole, however, they were a comfort and a blessing to Scott: cheered him when his great calamities came upon him; stood round his death-

bed and received his last breath.   And what more
would we have, the rather as Scott has left hundreds of 'dream children,' and men have *them* to
solace and to inspire them for evermore?

At home, Scott was not only happy himself, but
a spring of pleasure to all that knew him.   No one
worked harder, no one enjoyed life more.   This is
almost always the case : even the galley-slave is in
heaven compared to the idle man ; his labour by
practice becomes light, his moments of leisure are
divine, and his sleep is Elysium.   We are never weary
of seeing Scott, as Lockhart describes him, having
finished his task in the morning, coming down
stairs rubbing his hands for glee ; and having laid
in the amplest stores a Scotch breakfast-table could
supply, sallying forth to his well-won recreation,—
his walk with 'Camp' or 'Maida,' his gallop o'er
the hills, or his picnic party with friends to Melrose,
Cauldshields Loch, or his old haunt of Smailholm
Tower.   This was while he spent his vacations in
the country ; but scarcely less delightful were his
dinner parties or evening reunions in Castle Street,
when, surrounded by his family and selected friends,
he poured out the full riches of his knowledge, of
his sense, of his fun, of his feeling : at one time
repeating poetry, such as Wordsworth's *Kilchurn
Castle*, 'with a trumpet voice, while his grey eyes

now glowed and now gloomed, and alternate
fires and clouds seemed to flicker and float over
that pile of forehead;' and anon telling ludicrous
stories, 'while his lungs did crow like chanticleer,
his syllables in the struggle growing more em-
phatic, his accent more strongly Scotch, and his
voice *plaintive with excess of merriment.'* Some
consequential people thought his conversation not
very logical or consecutive; but Henry Cockburn
rebuked them by saying, 'I beg your pardon,
gentlemen; but Scott's *sense* has always appeared
to me more wonderful than even his genius.'

His dinner-table was, on the whole, a catholic
one; 'Tullochgorum' being then and there his
gathering march. Jeffrey came to it with his sharp
features, dark flashing eyes, *frightened*-seeming
hair, and brisk, melodious, endless talk; Cockburn, with his beautiful oval face, and rich Scotch
brogue; Constable, with his distinguished bearing
and crafty eye; James Ballantyne, with his *ore
rotundo*, black beard, bull neck, turned up upper
lip, and great gloating eyes; John his brother,
with his theatrical airs, frowns, starts, twistings of
features, and floods of merriment; Washington
Irving, with his mild, dreaming countenance; James
Hogg, with his Calibanic manners, strong shepherd
sense, grotesque humour, and inordinate self-esteem,

calling, as the cups circulated, his host 'Wattie,' and his hostess Charlotte, till both screamed with laughter; and latterly Lockhart, with his fine Italian features, haughty sneer, high, thin, shrill, scornful laugh, and keen, cutting, sententious conversation; and Professor Wilson, with his 'storm of golden hair,' glowing cheek, stately stature, wild, tameless eye, and talk wilder and more tameless still, although often in the presence of the Mighty Minstrel he was silent as are the mountains at the rising of the morning sun.

Others of less note *now* were there, although *then* thought men of much mark and likelihood. Such were his old friends William Erskine and William Clerk of Eldin,—the one more a woman, and a woman of a very sensitive nature, than a man, the other of a more masculine type; George Cranstoun, afterwards Lord Corehouse, a most accomplished person in taste, eloquence, and manners; Scott's colleagues in the clerk's office,—David Hume, nephew of the historian, Hector MacDonald Buchanan of Drummakiln, Sir Robert Dundas of Beechwood, and Colin Mackenzie of Portmore; the humorists Charles Matthews and Daniel Terry; Adam Fergusson, and Thomas Thomson, and his brother the preacher and painter of Duddingston; and last, not least, Mr. Morritt of

Rokeby, one of Scott's steadiest correspondents
and warmest friends, whose mansion he has im-
mortalized, although at less expenditure of power
than might have been desired. These, after all,
are only a few of the *élite* of the Scotland of that
day who sate often at Scott's hospitable board,
and were privileged to hear his conversation while
still in the prime of his early manhood.

Ashestiel had been a favourite residence of
Scott's, and never lost its charm for his mind.
But the lease expired ; and besides, he began to
hanker after a wider if not a more congenial
sphere. The aspiration to be a landed proprietor, a
feudal baron, arose in an evil hour in his mind. He
was a baron already by nature. His tastes, habits,
opinions, all proved it. Round his large, lord-like
being gathered dependants, like the Ballantynes,
Hogg, Laidlaw, and the rest, as if by inevitable
instinct. His very dogs and horses—Camp, Maida,
Lenore (his first charger), Captain, Lieutenant, and
Brown Adam, who in succession bore him—seemed
all to recognise in him, what he had playfully
called himself, an 'Earl Walter,' and some of them
would not allow themselves to be backed by any
other rider. But 'Earl Walter' was 'landless,
landless,' like his own Gregarach, and he could
not fulfil his dream of feudal power till he had

broad acres as well as a large following. He set himself therefore to add field to field, and to build for himself a mansion worthy of a Norman, if not rather copied after some piece of aerial architecture—some castle in the clouds,

‘ For ever flushing round a summer's sky.’

The result was Abbotsford.

In 1811 his salary had, through a new arrangement of Court of Session matters, been increased from £800 to £1300. The *Lady of the Lake* had been a triumphant mercantile success. Flushed with this, Scott fixed his eyes on a small farm which lay a few miles from Ashestiel, and was soon to be in the market. It included a spot where a battle had taken place in 1526 between the Earls of Angus and Home and the two chiefs of the race of Kerr on the one side, and Buccleugh on the other ; the possession of King James the Fifth being the object, and that prince himself a spectator, of the contest,—a rude stone still marking the spot

‘ Where gallant Cessford's life-blood dear
   Reeked on dark Elliot's Border spear.’

This interested Scott ; and the place, though only then a strip of meadow land along the river, with some undulating country above, was in the centre of the Melrose district, so dear to the poet's mind, and had indeed once belonged to the Abbey, as the word *Abbotsford* itself indicated. At all events, the purchase was made, and Scott proceeded to improve, to plant, to annex, to build, and, in fine, to *flit*, in the end of May 1812, leaving Ashestiel with much regret, in which we think all his admirers must share. Yet Abbotsford, if it was to be the grave of Scott's towering worldly hopes, was to be the cradle of the Waverley Novels.

In 1812 he was occupied with minor matters: he read Byron's *Childe Harold*, and frankly admitted its transcendent power; began the poem *Rokeby*, and visited the place Rokeby; passed by Hexham, near which he met the famous blacksmith John Lundie, turned doctor, whose specifics were '*laudamy* and *calamy*,' and who consoled himself with the thought that if he did accidentally kill a few Southrons by his drugs, it would be long ere he made up for Flodden! corresponded with and cheered the heart of worthy George Crabbe, the poet; and, in fine, published *Rokeby;* and when that poem had appeared, returned to his ' Patmos of Abbotsford, as blithe as bird on tree.'

Rokeby was pronounced the first decided failure among his poems. The *Vision of Don Roderick*, indeed, which appeared a year or two before, was not a great success; but then it was not a great effort. It claimed to be only an improvise, published for a benevolent purpose. *Rokeby* was a serious trial of strength. But although its sale was rapid and large, its reception was not nearly so favourable as even *Roderick*. It had less power than any of his previous poems, and consisted of more commonplace and Minerva press-like materials. It sprung, too, less from impulse than from a desire to gratify Mr. Morritt, by 'doing' his beautiful seat for him in song.

CHAPTER VIII.

VICISSITUDES IN LIFE, LITERATURE, AND BUSINESS—'WAVERLEY' LAUNCHED.

IT was sympathy with the Portuguese, at that time trampled under the iron hoof of the French armies, which had led Scott in 1811 to write his *Vision of Don Roderick*, the profits of which he gave to the distressed patriots. There were in it two or three noble passages. Who has forgot the description of the landing of the three nations, English, Scotch, and Irish, on the shores of Portugal? and who that ever heard can forget Professor Wilson's recitation of that description in his class-room, in the deepest of his deep and lingering tones, with the fieriest of his soul-quelling glances, and with the most impassioned of his natural and commanding gestures? The book, however, was less admired than its review in the *Edinburgh*, where Jeffrey in his best style rebuked the author for his silence in reference to the good, gallant, and unfortunate Sir John Moore,—an omission as inexcusable in a Scotchman, as if one writing an epic on Bruce were to take no notice at all of the name of Wallace.

With a certain falling off in the power of his poetry there coincided the uprise of Byron, who, after some elegant trifling in his first production, and some adroit grinning in his second, began fairly to exert his force in the third. *Childe Harold's Pilgrimage* had come like a comet across the literary sky, and the poems of Scott seemed tame as lunar rainbows in the comparison. The victory of the English bard needed but one or two fiery fragments like the *Giaour* on his part, and one more splendid failure on Scott's (the *Lord of the Isles*), to make it complete, and, so far as verse was concerned, final. Lockhart, indeed, says that the success of Byron's first pieces arose chiefly from their resemblance to, and unconscious imitation of, Scott's poetry. But this is the criticism of a son-in-law. Had these poems been mere imitations of Scott, they would have fallen powerless, as all echoes do, on the public ear. And whatever resemblance they bore to Scott's, it was not the similitude, it was the *difference*, between the English and the Scottish poet, and their respective styles, which secured Byron's success. The public saw intensity substituted for slipshod ease, the passionate for the picturesque, the thoughtful for the lively,—the scenery, the manners, and the suns of Spain and Greece, for those of Scotland ; and the change was grateful and stimulating at the time. In short, as Scott confessed long after, Byron *bett* (beat) him, although, by happily shifting his ground, and, like his own *Ivanhoe*, disguising himself, he more than recovered his laurels. Immediately after *Rokeby*, appeared anonymously his *Bridal of Triermain*, which he meant as a trap for the critics, Jeffrey particularly, but which was instantly discovered to be a second or third rate effusion of his own master mind. It was the same afterwards with *Harold the Dauntless*, another anonymous production of his pen.

While writing the *Vision*, Scott lost two of his friends very suddenly—President Blair and Lord Melville. He tells a curious story about a dentist called Dubisson, who met the President the day before his death, and he used a particular expression to him. He met Lord Melville the day before *his* death, who, to the man's surprise, used the same expression. Dubisson, after the second death, jocularly remarked that he himself would be the third to die. He was taken ill, and expired in an hour's space! Lord Melville had been hurried from his seat of Dunira in Perthshire to Edinburgh by the news of Blair's death. While driving through the village of Comrie, two boys, one of them an elder brother of ours, were playing on the street. They caught a glimpse of him in his carriage, and the one said to the other, 'That's a dying man!' The boy himself could not account for the impulse which led him to the exclamation; but perhaps, though Melville was thought in his usual health, there might have been some pallid and ghastly expression on his face. Scott felt the loss of these two men keenly. Blair was a man of colossal understanding, the son of Robert Blair of Athelstaneford, the author of *The Grave.* With Melville the head of the Tory *régime* in Scotland dropped off, and its palmy and pristine health was never to recover. We find Scott repeatedly saying afterwards, 'Ah, honest Hal Dundas! such things would not have been permitted in *thy* day.'

Bookselling matters were beginning to assume rather a serious aspect with the firm of which Scott was a veiled partner. Even while the *Lady of the Lake* was careering on in its unrivalled success, the shelves of John Ballantyne & Co. were groaning under unsold thousands of *Histories of Culdees* (a very learned book by Dr. Jamieson, of the *Dic-*

tionary), *Tixall Poetry*, and *Edinburgh Annual Registers*, all printed at the instance and under the patronage of the most popular of poets and most reckless of publishers.

In May 1813 things came to a crisis with the Ballantynes ; and Scott, dissolving partnership with them, opened up negotiations with Constable, who was again to be his publisher, on the condition of his taking off a great part of the unsaleable rubbish which had accumulated on the shelves of the unfortunate firm. We shall recur to the subject of Scott's connection with the Ballantynes when we come to speak of his failure. Scarce had his good terms with Constable been resumed, than we find Scott offering to sell him the copyright of a poem, as yet unwritten, entitled *The Nameless Glen.* He was prompted to this by a desire to acquire a hilly tract behind Abbotsford, leading up to Cauldshields Loch. He gained his object by and by, although not till the *Nameless Glen* yielded to the *Lord of the Isles*, the last of Scott's serious efforts in poetry.

At this time the Prince Regent, in a very handsome manner, gave Scott the offer of the Laureateship, vacant by the death of Pye. He declined it, however, 'unwilling,' he says, 'to incur the censure of engrossing the emolument attached to one of the few appointments which seems proper to be

filled by a man of literature who has no other views
in life.'   He bethought him of Southey, and gave
Croker, then omnipotent with the Prince, the hint
to offer the vacant office to him, which was done,
and accepted ; Scott cordially congratulating him
on his new dignity : 'Long may you live, as Paddy
says, to rule over us, and to redeem the crown of
Spenser and Dryden to its pristine dignity.   I
know no man so welcome to Xeres sack as your-
self, though many bards would make a better figure
at drinking it.'

He was at this time deep in an edition of Swift,
after the fashion of his edition of Dryden, and spent
the autumn months of 1813 in annotating its closing volumes, and writing a long and very interesting life of the Dean.   He was all the while harassed
excessively by the affairs of the Ballantynes, and
by their applications for his aid, alike in money and
in literary work, and says in a postscript to one of
his letters to James B. : 'For God's sake, treat me
as a man, and not as a milch cow.'

He began to mature in his own mind the plan of
the *Lord of the Isles*, and wrote a portion of the
first canto so much to his own satisfaction, that he
renewed negotiations with Constable for the sale of
the whole or part of its copyright.

Looking, as he describes himself, one day into

an old cabinet in search of some fishing tackle, he happened to light upon the old fragment of *Waverley*, which had been twice condemned by friends. He read it over again, thought it had been underrated, and resolved to continue the story.

Two lessons from the facts connected with the early history of *Waverley* may be taught us. First, let friends beware of their critical advices. Two of the best novels ever written had nearly been strangled in this way. Godwin gave his *Caleb Williams* to be read by a friend, who returned it, telling him 'that, if published, it would be the grave of his literary reputation.' And how it fared with *Waverley* we know. Probably hundreds of similar instances might be quoted from D'Israeli the elder, and other collectors of literary *Ana*. The second lesson is, that authors should never allow the severe criticisms of friends to drive them in rash disgust to burn or otherwise destroy the children of their brains. Let them put them under as many locks and keys as they like ; let them observe Horace's precept, ' Premat ad nonum annum,' as religiously as they please ; but let them spare their lives. Nay, let them keep them as carefully as the Mohammedans do the least scrap of paper they find, lest peradventure it contains the name of Mohammed or Allah. Depend on it,

H

their day may come. Clergymen have often re-
gretted that they did not preserve their early sermons, their students' discourses and all, however
poor or juvenile. And for this there are two good
reasons : first, such discourses, rewritten and cor-
rected, may serve them in good stead amidst their
pressing labours in after life ; and secondly, they
would form a silent history of their intellectual
progress. And so with literary men when they
are wise. Godwin dared the risk, and his novel
is now the principal pillar of his reputation.
Scott serenely shut up the 'trash' of *Waverley;*
and returning after many days, found it to be a
priceless treasure. Wordsworth murmured to himself, while writing down his every line, ' Scribo in
æternitatem.' *If* the preserved MSS. be worthless,
all we need grudge is the *room* they occupy ! And
if they be too bad ever to be printed, they at least
are interesting to the author himself as landmarks
of memory ; and one old leaf may tell us what
heart histories ! and, like Painting in Campbell's
fine verses,

> ' May give us back the dead,
> Even in the loveliest looks they wore.'

1814 may be regarded as one of the most important years in Scott's career. In it appeared his
valuable edition of Swift. His life of that strange,

strong, and most unhappy man was able, but, like his *Roderick*, was eclipsed in the splendour of the review it obtained in the *Edinburgh*,—a review in which, in power of writing, Jeffrey surpassed himself. We think, however, especially since a recent perusal of Swift's *Journal to Stella*, that the critic's view of Swift's *morale* is far too harsh and sweeping. Swift, with all his faults, which the public now knows passing well, and with all his madness, which, as in the case of poor Byron, none can know, was altogether a noble spirit, loved, and deserving to be loved, by the most gifted men and the most accomplished women of his time ; the idol, and most justly the idol, of the people of Ireland ; and in point of mental power and original genius, ranking with Edmund Burke and Daniel O'Connell, as the first three men that country has hitherto produced. 'We shall never have such a Rector of Laracor ;' no, nor ever such a creator of new worlds as the author of *Gulliver's Travels*, or such a daring humorist as the author of the *Tale of a Tub*. Besides writing some papers on chivalry and the drama for the supplement to the *Edinburgh Encyclopædia*, Scott completed *Waverley*, which appeared in July, and became instantly popular. And so soon as it was off his hands, he, as we shall see in the next chapter, proceeded on a sea voyage round Scotland.

Here let us linger for a moment on the fact of the publication of *Waverley*. With what emotion do we see the first welling out of one of the great rivers of the earth from its far desert or mountain spring! Surely with deeper feeling may the lover of literature turn back to the day when there began a series of the finest creations of the human mind, combining lifelike reality with ideal beauty, full of simplicity, essentially Christian feeling, pathos and humanity, as well as of the highest eloquence, interest, and imagination,—a series which has bettered and blessed, as well as cheered and electrified, myriads and myriads more of mankind, and which, so far from having exhausted its artistic or beneficent power, is likely to increase in widespread influence as man advances and as ages roll on. And if Bruce was not blamed when, as he stood by the fountain whence he deemed the 'Great Father of Egypt's waters' took his rise, he swelled that fountain by his tears, let our emotion now not be counted false or factitious, while standing beside a well whence streams of intellectual life, as bountiful and copious as the Nile, have flowed out to gladden, to instruct, and to elevate the human race. To effect this, let it be remembered, was the purpose, the pride, and the joy, and that he had effected it was ultimately the consolation, of our noble Scottish novelist.

CHAPTER IX.

AT SEA.

COTT was now culminating, if not exactly culminated. His prestige as a poet had, indeed, in some measure declined; but he had established his name, and had newly opened up a mine of virgin richness in *Waverley*. He was still young, only forty-three; and there was as yet no indication of those complicated maladies which were destined first to shake, and then prematurely to destroy, one of the most robust constitutions, both in body and mind, that ever existed. Having propelled *Waverley* to the point of publication, he joyfully threw down the oar, and started on a long delightful excursion round the northern coast of Scotland. He writes, ere starting, to Morritt: ' I have accepted an invitation from the Commissioners of the Northern Lights (I don't mean the Edinburgh reviewers, but the *bona fide* Commissioners for the beacons) to accompany them upon a nautical tour round Scotland, visiting all that is curious in continent and isle. The party are three gentlemen.' Those gentlemen were: Robert Hamilton, Sheriff of Lanarkshire; Adam Duff, Sheriff of Forfarshire; and William Erskine, Sheriff of Orkney and Shetland; besides a few others, with Mr. Stevenson as surveyor-viceroy over the Commissioners,—all more or less kindred spirits to Scott, and all pleasant, gentlemanly persons.

There is something peculiarly exhilarating in a tour undertaken immediately after some strenuous and successful literary effort. The mind continues cheerfully to chew the cud of its recent felicitous endeavour, and is at the same time, having shaken off a load, free to welcome every new impression, and ready to feel that idleness is a duty as well as an exquisite delight. Scott, too, had so much enthusiasm for the scenery of the North, that he must have looked forward to this excursion as to a long gala-day. And so it proved. Surrounded by such sympathetic friends as William Erskine, every new morning lighting in some new spot of loveliness, grandeur, or romantic interest, their time and the vessel at the entire disposal of the party, Scott was thoroughly in his element, as his journal kept during the voyage proves. Then he was not

altogether idle, since he was traversing scenes
which he designed to turn to account at a future
and not a very remote day, in the *Lord of the Isles*,
a poem already begun, as well as afterwards in
The Pirate.

His Edinburgh friends saw him embark with
pleasure more than regret, knowing that he would
return with many spoils, as well as greatly enjoy
himself during the journey. James Hogg, indeed,
wrote a curious letter to Lord Byron on the subject, which his Lordship thus quizzically notices
in one of his epistles to Moore: 'Oh! I have had
the most amusing letter from Hogg, the Ettrick
minstrel and shepherd. Scott, he says, is gone to
the Orkneys in a gale of wind ; during which wind,
he affirms, the said Scott, "he is sure, is not at his
ease, to say the least of it." Lord! Lord! if these
home-keeping minstrels had crossed your Atlantic
or my Mediterranean, and tasted a little open
boating in a white squall, or a gale in the "Gut,"
or the Bay of Biscay with no gale at all, how it
would enliven and introduce them to a few of the
sensations!'

On the 29th of July 1814, Scott started on his
norland tour ; and he had scarcely cleared the
Firth when the gale of wind did overtake him,
and blew him on to Arbroath, where, after having

been very sick at sea, he landed and spent some hours. He says: 'I visited the Abbey Church for the third time,—the first being, *eheu!* the second with T. Thomson.' 'There is here an allusion, without doubt,' says Lockhart, 'to some happy day's excursion, when his *first love* was of the party.' Poor fellow! he had not forgotten her yet; and probably the next day, when with a fair wind he 'glided enchantingly' along the coast of Kincardineshire, part of the enchantment resulted from the recollections which steeped that country in the joy of grief, and he would heave some of these delicious sighs, in which regret and pleasure are so beautifully blended, beyond all chymical solution. He saw Dunnottar Castle, with its massive ruins, rise and sink on his left, and that also would waken old memories of joy and sorrow; he admired the view of the 'Granite City' from the sea; he admired Slaines Castle, standing sheer on its sea-beat rock, and circled by the everlasting clang of the wings of sea-birds; he landed at the Bullars of Buchan, entered the dark cavern in which boils the caldron, and probably thought, with Dr. Johnson, that there was no more suitable place for the confinement of a demon; he passed the Reef of Rattray, afterwards commemorated in *The Antiquary.* Leav-

ing Fraserburgh and the Moray Firth behind, he
stretched across for Shetland, which at first, he
says, seemed *in meditatione fugæ* from him and
his companion the Sheriff of these isles, whom
he urged to issue a warrant accordingly; but the
weather cleared up, and they made the harbour of
Lerwick,—a town the situation of which, 'screened
on all sides from the wind by hills of a gentle elevation,' Scott admired exceedingly. He spent some
time in studying the manners of this primitive
country; in exploring its savage scenery, its stony
moorlands, its silent voes, its bold and beetling
headlands, the Cradle of Noss, Sumburgh Head,
etc.; and in gleaning those picturesque particulars
of character and superstition which he was afterwards to work into *The Pirate.* He visited then
Orkney, touching with much interest on the Fair
Isle in his way; he examined with great care the
Cathedral of St. Magnus; he saw, but did *not*
climb, Whiteford Hill, to the north of Kirkwall,—
whence perhaps it is, that, according to Orcadians,
his description of the view from it in the novel is
not so accurate or felicitous as his wont; felt the
eternal rocking of the Pentland Firth, Scotland's
Bay of Biscay; landed on the bold Hill of Hoy,
with its three peaks rising sheer up from the wave,
—its Dwarfie stone,—its mysterious Carbuncle,

seen, it is said, on the breast of a mountain from
below, but which, when the hill is climbed, can
nowhere be found,—with the magnificent view of
the Atlantic from its steep western side,—and
with the midnight sun, if you can believe the
natives, seen in summer from its summit; visited
Stromness, and those old grey spectres the
Stones of Stennis, where in ancient days human
victims were sacrificed to demon-gods, and where,
in his own novel, a nobler sacrifice — that of
Minna laying her misplaced love for Cleveland
on the stormy altar—was consummated; made
Cape Wrath, the weather being in keeping with
the stormy name; and entered the marvellous
Cave of Smowe, with its rocky ledges, inky waters,
dark cavern-sides sparkling with ten thousand
times ten thousand stalactites, and slippery preci-
pices hanging over bottomless gulfs, where it
occurred to his imagination that a Water Kelpie,
or some spirit lonelier and fiercer still, might find
a fitting abode. Scott compares this cave to that
of Montesinos in *Don Quixote*, describes it with
great eloquence, and it had manifestly impressed
his imagination very deeply.

After rounding Cape Wrath, he passed, and
very much admired, the wild mountains of Assynt
in Ross-shire, as exhibiting the true Highland

character—torn, serrated, and tempestuous in outline. He went on shore at Coruisk in Skye, the
darkest and most terrific of Scotland's lochs, liker
the 'Last Lake of God's Wrath' in Aird's magnificent *Devil's Dream* than an earthly scene, and
which he was afterwards thus to describe:

'Rarely human eye has known
A scene so stern as that dread lake,
    With its dark ledge of barren stone.
Seems that primeval earthquake's sway
Hath rent a strange and shattered way
    Through the rude bosom of the hill,
And that each naked precipice,
Sable ravine, and dark abyss,
    Tells of the outrage still.
The wildest glen, but this, can show
Some touch of Nature's genial glow;
On high Benmore green mosses grow,
And heath-bells bud in deep Glencroe,
    And copse on Cruchan-Ben;
But here, above, around, below,
    On mountain or in glen,
Nor tree, nor shrub, nor plant, nor flower,
Nor aught of vegetative power,
    The weary eye may ken.
For all is rocks at random thrown,
Black waves, bare crags, and banks of stone,
    As if were here denied
The summer sun, the spring's sweet dew,
That clothe with many a varied hue
    The bleakest mountain side.'

LORD OF THE ISLES, *Canto* III.

He visited also MacAlister's Cave, and a cave in Egg ; revisited Iona and Staffa, and felt, like Johnson, his piety grow warmer amidst the ruins of the former, and his poetic genius touched with the deepest sense of the sublime in the Fingal's Cave of the latter. He had more congenial society when there, than it was our fortune to enjoy when visiting it. Conceive, in the heart of that cathedral of nature, that great Sanctuary of the Sea, a proposition made in a large boatful of people, for *three cheers !* It seemed to us as absurd as though one should ruff the thunder, or encore the earthquake. And yet it was carried, and perhaps not three in the company felt the profanation. At Torloisk, in Mull, he and his companions went on shore, and called on their old acquaintances the family of the Clephanes, in whom, and especially in the eldest daughter, afterwards Marchioness of Northampton, Scott took a great interest, giving her away in marriage, and watching sedulously over her career, which was, we believe, a chequeredly brilliant one. He and the rest of them felt it quite a luxury to find themselves in the most refined female society, regaled by music and intellectual conversation, in the centre of these lonely and desolate Hebrides,

' Placed far amidst the melancholy main ;'

and it was with no little reluctance that they
proceeded on their journey. They admired that
noble prospect in the Sound of Mull, of the wall of
mountains stretching between Ben Cruachan and
Ben Nevis, as between two mighty watch-towers.
They touched at the beautiful little town of Oban,
and examined the ruins of Dunolly and Dun-
staffnage Castles; the latter commanding a grand'
view of Loch Etive, Ben Cruachan, and the supposed site of the ancient Caledonian city of Bere-
genium. Thence they crossed over to the Giant's
Causeway, watching the Paps of Jura, and listening to the roar of the whirlpool of Corrievreckan
on their way. When they reached Port Rush, '
Scott learned the news of the death of the
Duchess of Buccleugh, a most admirable woman,
and one of his warmest friends. And, in fine, he
returned to Edinburgh, 'having enjoyed as much
pleasure as in any six weeks of his life.' He had
left, as we saw, on the 29th of July, and returned
on the 9th of September—six weeks, to a day.
This tour did not merely tend to strengthen his
body and to exhilarate his mind, but had an
important influence on his genius. It brought
him in contact with scenery and manners of a
new and very peculiar kind, and qualified him
for writing his *Lord of the Isles* and *The Pirate*,

which, if not the best of his works, are yet valuable for their pictures of the wildest and most
romantic Scottish scenes, and because one of
them at least preserves the memory of interesting customs and characters which have now
passed away. During the journey he was often
in a truly bardic state of inspiration, sometimes
'pacing the deck rapidly, muttering to himself,'
and at Loch Corriskin quite overwhelmed with
his feelings as he roamed and gazed about by
himself.

On his return, to balance the sadness produced
by the death of the good Duchess, he found
that during his abence two editions of *Waverley*
had gone off,—that the applause was universal,
and that equally so was the curiosity about the
name of the author. It was surmised by many
that it was Scott—such acute judges as Jeffrey
and Mat Lewis knew at a glance the fine Roman
hand; but the secret had been entrusted to only
a few, including, besides the Ballantynes and
Constable, Erskine and Morritt. He had scarcely
reached home till he resumed the *Lord of the Isles*,
which he meant as a trial of strength—in order to
determine the question whether he should retire
or not from the poetical arena. He wrote the last
three cantos with fiery rapidity, finished them in

December 1814, and started for Abbotsford to 'refresh the machine,' which might well be worn out with the labours of the year. These included the *Life of Swift, Waverley*, the *Lord of the Isles*, two essays in the *Encyclopædia* supplement, several annotated reprints of old treatises and memoirs, and a vast mass of correspondence, besides the journal kept during his six weeks' tour. Probably no man has ever, unless Scott at another time, compressed so much valuable literary work into twelve months before or since. And ere the bells rung in the year of Waterloo, he had commenced another and one of the very happiest efforts of his genius.

CHAPTER X.

THE FIRST THREE WAVERLEY NOVELS.

WE have often envied those who lived while the great battles of Napoleon were succeeding each other; heard safely on this side of the Channel, like successive peals of distant thunder, by those basking in sunshine, — serving to enhance the sense of security, and to deepen the feeling of repose, and yet starting the sublimest emotions. How many eyes must have kindled, and hearts beat high, when the news of Austerlitz arrived! And so have we envied those who had reached their full consciousness when the first Waverley Novels came forth in softer music, like sweet and lofty melodies succeeding each other from the harp of some great minstrel, who was himself unseen! Ere we were capable of appreciating them, their prestige was in some measure lessened, and their power in some measure gone. *Guy Mannering* or *Old Mortality* read fresh from the press! what a luxury there is in the mere idea; how much more in the reality!

The publication of *Waverley*, strange to say, had been preceded by considerable misgivings on the part of Constable and his house. To test its merits, and secure for it friends, proof-sheets of some of its chapters were put by James Ballantyne into the hands of Henry Mackenzie, Dr. Thomas Brown, Mrs. Hamilton (the authoress of *The Cottagers of Glenburnie*), and others, who were unanimous in its favour. Then Constable came to terms. When it appeared, these critics were of course ready to take its part openly, as they had done in private; and the result was, after a little hesitation on the part of the public, triumphant success. One smiles at all this now, but it has not been uncommon in the history of popular works. With *Childe Harold*, for instance, a similar tentative process took place. With *Vanity Fair*, again, it was worse, as it had to go the round of the trade before it was accepted. It is quite possible that some real masterpieces have been strangled in the effort to be born, and that Mr. Horne in his *False Medium* was right after all.

I

Waverley, the first, is also with many still the chief favourite among these fine productions. It is less finished in composition than some of them, and less probable in story. Its hero, as Scott says himself, is a 'sneaking piece of imbecility;' and the first five or six chapters are heavy and lumbering. But from the moment that he catches a glimpse of the 'Highlands of Perthshire, which at first had appeared a blue outline on the horizon, but now swelled into gigantic masses which frowned defiance on the more level country,' Scott goes on with unmitigated energy and unwearying interest. The manners are painted with a bold pencil. The style has an elastic movement, as if it trode on heather. The characters, which are fresh, varied, and admirably contrasted, are seen to vivid advantage against the magnificent background of Highland scenery. Many of the separate passages are written with great elegance as well as power. Some of the incidents are of the most thrilling character; and the scenes in Carlisle, for example, have never been surpassed in manly pathos.

Meanwhile the *Lord of the Isles* had appeared, and turned out a disappointment. It read more like an imitation of Scott by an inferior hand, than a new work of the author. It had the rush without the force, the sound and fury but not the strength, the eloquence but not the inspiration, of his former poems. In only one or two passages, such as the pictures of Staffa and Loch Coriskin, did the old minstrel genius display itself; for, although Lockhart says the contrary, the public has never put the battle-piece of Bannockburn on the same level with that of Flodden : the former seems a faint pencil sketch, while the latter is painted in colours of fire. The comparative failure of this poem determined the author to devote himself to prose.

Scott, we saw, had gone down to Abbotsford at Christmas 1814, to 'refresh the machine.' And this he did by writing another novel in six weeks! This was *Guy Mannering.* Let us, in passing, notice one rather curious circumstance. This novel was written in the depth of winter, and all the scenes in *Guy Mannering* occur in the winter season, which may partly explain their exceeding verisimilitude.

Scott had previously to this become acquainted with Mr. Joseph Train, supervisor of Excise in Newton-Stewart. This ingenious and estimable man had been occupied in collecting materials for a history of Galloway, and had communicated to Scott a number of anecdotes concerning the Galloway gipsies, and a story of an astrologer who had called at a farm-house when the good-wife was in travail, and had spaed the child's fortune much as the novel describes it. , On these hints, and on an imperfect recollection of a Durham ballad, containing the same tale at greater length, , was *Guy Mannering* founded. Scott, the great lion, had several lion's providers; but to none is the public more indebted than to the modest and worthy Joseph Train.

This novel appeared on the 24th of February 1815. We question if the feat implied in its rapid writing was ever equalled in the annals of improvisation. Byron's writing the *Corsair* in a fortnight is hardly equal to it. It is not merely at the size, but at the exquisite and varied quality, of a work written in so short a space, that we are called to wonder. It is to us at least the most *delightful* of Scott's novels. It reads like one sentence. The interest never flags for a moment, not even in Julia's letters, and, as Lockhart remarks, continues increasing till almost the last page. Critics have justly magnified the admirable ease, unity, and thorough fusion of materials which distinguish *Tam o' Shanter;* but to find the same qualities in a work a thousand times as large is proportionably more marvellous. *Guy Mannering* is by far the most Scott-like of Scott's tales, if it does not contain his very highest flights of genius. Its hearty homeliness, as exhibited in the Dandie Dinmont and Charlieshope scenes ; the wild flavour of romance and enthusiasm manifested in the astrological and gipsy departments of the book ; the passionate love for Scottish scenery, for rocks, woods, and waves ; and its sympathy with the old mirthful life of the Edinburgh lawyers, are all characteristic of the composite genius and broad, manifold nature of the author, who united intense interest in simple country manners, and enjoyment of every-day existence, with feelings of the loftiest poetry.

The reception of this novel was as rapturous as that of *Waverley*, perhaps more so ; although the *Quarterly Review* gave it a cold and captious notice, quite unworthy of the book, although quite worthy of a journal which was soon after to abuse and insult such writers as Shelley, Hazlitt, Lamb, and Keats, which had previously damned Wordsworth with faint praise, and ignored Coleridge entirely. The *Edinburgh Review* neither noticed *Guy Mannering* nor *The Antiquary* at the time of their publication, although this seems to have arisen from anything but indifference. Immediately after *Guy Mannering* appeared, Scott, his wife, and their eldest daughter, visited London. During this visit a long expected interview took

place with Lord Byron, then in the morning splendour of a career soon to be clouded by heavy
shadows, and to go down in premature night.
Scott had, with a half-humorous, half-earnest interest, eagerly anticipated a meeting with his
brother bard, telling James Ballantyne that they
should accost each other when they encountered
in the language of the farce of *Tom Thumb.*

‘Art thou the man whom men famed Grizzle call?

    .   .   .   .   ▪   .   .   .

Art thou the still more famed Tom Thumb the small?’

It was, we think, John Murray’s drawing-room
that first witnessed the meeting of these two poets.
They became instantly intimate : their very diver-
sity of character serving to weld their attachment.
Byron reposed his weary and racking self-conscious-
ness on the wide and genial temperament of Scott
as on a pillow ; and Scott was deeply moved with
admiration for the fervent genius, and with sympathy for the unhappy disposition and unsettled
opinions of Byron, of whose natural goodness of
heart he formed a better opinion than the rest of
the world.   Scott told Byron he would alter, if he
lived, his religious views, not by turning Methodist,
but Catholic devotee.   He thought him a Whig
by accident, and a patrician by principle.   Byron
envied Scott’s domestic felicity, and said he would

give all fame, and the other advantages of his position, to be happy at home. They met often and exchanged gifts ; Scott conferring on Byron a beautiful Turkish dagger mounted with gold. Byron reciprocated by the present of a large vase of silver full of Grecian bones ; and they rallied each other about the gloomy and ominous nature of their mutual gifts. Byron, by the way, had a singular superstition about the ill omen connected with sharp-pointed objects as presents, and once returned a splendid pin given him by Lady Blessington ; and it is almost a wonder he retained Scott's present, which might afterwards have seemed, like that fatal air-drawn dagger in *Macbeth*, to marshal the way to the disastrous catastrophe of the poet's separation from his wife and exile from his country, which occurred a few months afterwards. On Scott's return from Paris he had a parting interview with Byron at Long's, where the latter was as playful as a kitten, full of gaiety and good humour. So he seemed to Scott. But his namesake, Scott of Gala, who was present, says that Byron's pale face had a miserable expression, and that his conversation was 'bitter, bitter,' strongly contrasting with that of the author of *Guy Mannering*. Speaking of some one at Waterloo who had lost his head by a cannon-ball, Byron remarked, 'No great loss ;

it was never of much use to him.' Scott was just starting for the north, and he and Byron never met again. They continued, however, friends and occasional correspondents to the close of the unhappy poet's life. Scott watched with deep interest the fluctuating but splendid career of his friend. He did him good service in the darkest hour of his life, by defending him in the *Quarterly Review* against the howl of the whole world; and he anticipated much from his matured and sobered genius, and from his expedition to Greece. Scott is one of the few men of whom Byron speaks uniformly well, and he was never weary of devouring his novels. It is singular that the two men of genius in the age most opposite in temperament to Scott, seem to have read him with the greatest avidity, and to have found in his works the best anodyne for their habitual gloom — Foster and Byron. In a future chapter we intend some more remarks on Scott's relation to Byron, and to his other eminent contemporaries.

At this period, too, Scott dined twice with the Prince Regent, and narrowly escaped betraying his connection with the Scotch Novels in reply to a toast proposed by the Prince. When asked what he thought of the Prince's intellect, he said he could hardly judge of the mind of a man who introduced whatever subject he liked, talked of it as long as he liked, and dropped it whenever he liked. He thought highly of his manners, but was too acute a judge of human nature to be blind to that selfish heartlessness which a fine address decorated but could not disguise, although far too thorough a Tory to acknowledge it. He returned to Edinburgh on the 22d of May.

A month afterwards, the cannon of Waterloo startled every ear, and the Empire of the Hundred Days and its founder sunk with a shock which echoed through the world. While Robert Hall was saying in England that this event had put the clock of the world several degrees backward, our poet in Scotland was exulting and straining on the slip to visit the memorable field. In company with some friends and neighbours, he started for the Continent in July, having made a previous arrangement with Constable to describe his tour in a series of letters. He visited Brussels, Waterloo, Paris, and met a flattering reception from Wellington, Blucher, the Emperor Alexander, and other of the magnates of the earth, who were then dancing their giddy and guilty dance over what Shelley calls 'the last hopes of trampled France.' It was both here and on the Continent a time of joy, amounting to foolish and wicked delirium, in which

Scott participated to a degree which seems to have weakened his powers; for although his *Paul's Letters to his Kinsfolk* are graphic and interesting, his poem on Waterloo, which appeared in October, is not up to the mark. Scott at that period was too happy and triumphant a man to write well on the gloomier and sublimer aspects of war. The Spirit of the spot where

'That red rain had made the harvest grow,'

was to lead Byron to it next year, and to tell him to limn it in the everlasting chiaroscuro of *Childe Harold.* Scott returned to Abbotsford in September, passing by and examining the old castles of Warwick and Kenilworth on his homeward way. Toward the close of the year he seems to have written a few pages of *The Antiquary.*

Early in 1816 appeared *Paul's Letters to his Kinsfolk*, which was well but not rapturously received. Some other books on the subject, such as *John Scott's Visit to Paris in* 1815, had got the start of it. In May appeared *The Antiquary.* It sold rapidly, 6000 copies going off in six days; but otherwise at first received a frigid welcome. Some even said the author's vein was manifestly exhausted! It by and by, however, rose to, and has ever since kept, its level. It had not the high historic character of *Waverley*, nor the unique yet varied charm of *Guy Mannering;* but in certain scenes and characters surpassed them both, nay, surpassed perhaps aught else the author ever wrote. The storm scene has seldom been equalled in power of language and thrilling interest of incident. It is curious, however, that he has marred an otherwise magnificent passage by the gross blunder of making the sun set in the German Ocean; and more curious still, that not even the 'inevitable eye' of James Ballantyne, who looked over all the sheets of his tales, seems to have detected the oversight. Scott no doubt practised, in his descriptions, the art of *composition*, as painters call it; but that art has its limits, and he might as well have introduced palms into Glencoe or bananas into Balquhidder, as describe the sun seen from the eastern coasts of Scotland sinking in the sea. Edie Ochiltree is one of the very happiest of its author's creations, in his combination of humour, kindliness, and *auldfarrand* sense, of pawkiness and poetry. But by far the most original and Shaksperean portions of the book are the scenes in the fisherman's cottage. The funeral is a masterpiece of pathos and picturesque effect; and Elspeth Mucklebackit is a character resembling the style of Crabbe, but tinged with an imagination and shown in a weird light which that poet could not command. She is more fearful in the fell passions which lurk in the blood of old age, and inspire the lips of dotage, than the witches of *Macbeth;* and, although with no supernaturalism about her, has a wild sublimity of thought and language more impressive still. And what exquisite humour and knowledge of Scotch character in the Post Office scene, and in the story of 'Little Davie and his pony!' Altogether, *The Antiquary* is a mine of the purest and richest ore. It never disappoints, and it can never be exhausted.

CHAPTER XI.

SCOTT AND THE COVENANTERS.

SCARCELY had *The Antiquary* left its author's hands, than he planned the *Tales of my Landlord*, projected a series of *Letters on the History of Scotland*, which were never completed, and undertook to write the historical department of the *Edinburgh Annual Register*. Not willing that Constable should monopolize the publication of his novels, and for certain personal reasons besides, Scott offered his new work to Murray and Blackwood. Discouraged a little by the coldness with which *The Antiquary* was at first received, he once thought of bringing out the *Tales of my Landlord* without the words 'by the Author of *Waverley*,' although in this he changed his mind. William Blackwood, a man of rare penetration and rough vigour of speech, found fault with the closing part of the *Black Dwarf*, and even suggested another way in which he thought the story should terminate. Scott got very indignant, and wrote, saying, ' Confound his impudence! Tell him I belong to the Black Hussars of literature, who neither give nor take quarter.' This being out of Scott's usual measured style, had a proportionate effect, and told like thunder from a cloudless sky. The *Tales* appeared in December 1816, and the reception of the first of them showed the sagacious bibliopole was right. The *Black Dwarf* was thought to begin delightfully, but to come to a lame and impotent conclusion. But *Old Mortality*, while bearing up its weaker brother, challenged a place instantly among Scott's proudest works. In the upper literary circles of London especially its reception was rapturous. The lion and the lamb, Gifford and Lord Holland, here lay down together. The latter distinguished nobleman sate up all night to read it; 'nothing slept but his gout.'

In Scotland, too, its power was felt, but speedily a storm arose against it for its treatment of the Covenanters; a storm swelled, if not originally stirred, by Dr. M'Crie, who, in a succession of able and eloquent papers in the *Edinburgh Christian Instructor*, then edited by Dr. Andrew Thomson of St. George's, assailed its statements, and went nigh to impugn the integrity of its author's motives.

Scott at first resolved to remain silent; but finding
the impression strong and general, he wrote a reply
to the Doctor in the somewhat equivocal form of a
review of his own book in the *Quarterly*. M'Crie's
work was published separately, ran through various
editions, and was in 1846 re-issued under the patronage of the Free Church General Assembly. We
are disposed, looking back at the controversy, to
think that the whole truth lay with neither of the
contending parties; and it is our wish to steer
between the Charybdis of the *Quarterly Review* on
the one side, and the Scylla of Dr. M'Crie on the
other. We do not think that Scott was animated
by any intense and virulent hatred against the
Covenanters, as has been supposed. All Claverhouse was not slumbering in his breast. He was a
good hater, but incapable of deliberate and long-
drawn malice. He had strong prejudices and passions; but neither against individuals nor parties
can we conceive him cherishing slow, burning,
vindictive resentment. He was attracted to the
subject by its historic interest, and the opportunity
it afforded him of exercising his favourite powers;
and he sate down to *Old Mortality*, as he did to
his other novels, with little definite plan or purpose,
and least of all with the intention of systematically
blackening the memory of any party. But, on the

other hand, it is certain that he had imbibed strong prejudices against the Covenanters, which, finding this channel open, ran too readily and recklessly along it. Scott had been brought up in the atmosphere partly of Edinburgh *persiflage* and scepticism, and partly of Border enthusiasm. The mixture of something of the Jeffrey and something of the Leyden element in him, with a dash besides of Highland superstition and Jacobite prejudice, rendered his own character a singular compound, and accounts for his unfitness fully to sympathize with the narrow, intense current of genuine earnestness which ran in the Presbyterian veins. Yet his enthusiasm, though very different from that of the Covenanters (being more that of personal genius, *class*, and country, than of *cause*), prevented him, along with his sense of justice, from treating them as mere subjects of scorn. His early Edinburgh training might have suggested unmitigated ridicule ; but his Border blood and poetic fire interposed, and compelled him to blend with it a certain respect and admiration. Hence his novel veers to and fro in feeling. Like Balaam, he comes to curse, and remains to bless. He is, like many men of genius, overruled by the power behind him. He awakens a demon, to whom he is compelled to be obedient. The fine instinct in him works out of his original atmosphere, casts it off as the sun a ring of clouds, and pours undesigned and therefore more precious light upon his subject. Moreover, the people of Scotland were not fair judges. Taught and trained in unbounded reverence for their forefathers, they were prepared to fasten on every word and syllable that told against them ; to find the blame outrageous, and the praise null. They judged of the work from particular scenes, from what they thought its apparent purpose, and from the general result it produced. It was otherwise, on the whole, with the men of the South. Take Hazlitt as a specimen. This celebrated critic always speaks of *Old Mortality* as Scott's noblest work ; and, in verifying his criticism, uniformly appeals, not to the passages in which it caricatures, but to those in which it honours the Covenanters ; not to Mause Headrigg or Habakkuk Mucklewrath, but to MacBriar preaching on the evening of Drumclog, or to Bessie MacLure in her disinterested heroism, now sitting in her red cloak by the wayside to warn a friend, and now exposing her life to danger to save a foe of the Covenanting cause. The book, in fact, had produced in his mind, which on that subject was on the whole unprejudiced, an impression most favourable to the Covenanters ; and he, we believe, is the type of southland thousands.

K

No doubt Scott has caricatured Covenanting manners. His picture of the coarseness and vulgarity of their lowest rank, of the cant of their ministers, of the fierceness, the rancour, and the bigotry of the Cameronians, of the selfishness, revenge, and cruelty, which blend with nobler elements in Burley, is undoubtedly overdrawn. Such a being as Mucklewrath never existed. Wild as some of the hillmen were, the wildest of them was sobriety personified compared to that monstrous mixture of monomania, fanaticism, and fury. Old Mause is a more credible character, and is drawn with exquisite humour, but is also highly caricatured. MacBriar's conduct to Morton in the farmhouse, where they are about to put him to death, totally belies all the finer traits the novelist had given him before, and jars on the memory as we witness his heroic and sublime appearance in the trial scene. It is gratifying to see Poundtext made ridiculous as one of the indulged parsons of the period, those 'dumb dogs that could not bark,' keeping by their comfortable cribs, and munching their bones, while their brave brethren were chased like wolves upon the mountains. But Kettledrummle is a clumsy caricature of the more rigid divine. All the wit connected with him, indeed, lies in his name. To Burley we have just alluded.

His whole conduct in reference to Basil Olifant, to Edith Bellenden, and to Lord Evandale, is a libel alike on the Covenanters and on human nature. His killing of Sharpe at Magus Muir rises to an act of virtue when compared to the mean, cold-blooded, and long-winded atrocities which are gratuitously transferred to his character. But Sir Walter has sinned more deeply when he seeks to whitewash the persecutors, than when he blackens their victims. A good character aspersed soon rights itself; the dirt dries and disappears by a sure and swift process. A bad character defended and deified is often allowed without opposition to slip into the Pantheon. Men are more interested—and it says something for them—in defending the unjustly assailed than in pulling down the graven images of the guilty. Scott was too favourable to the cavalier character. Hence, in his picture of the persecutors, their every dragoon is half a hero; Sergeant Bothwell a whole one, made so in spite of his admitted faults; and Lord Evandale is something higher, a kind of link between the soldier and the seraph. Claverhouse is marred by gross inconsistency of conception, and is much more melodramatic than natural. He is not represented as a mere brutal butcher, nor yet as a perfect model of chivalry, but as an awkward compound of the fierce, careless warrior, and the refined and gallant knight. Few readers, we suspect, lay down *Old Mortality* without a deeper detestation for the dancing bear, the educated tiger, the handsome and accomplished murderer, which is all, in reality, the author makes him out to be.

Yet if in some parts of this novel no one has caricatured the Covenanters more severely, none has brought out their picturesque aspects with such felicity and force. None but Scott could have described that scene in the inn, where Burley overthrows Bothwell; or that profounder scene in the barn, where, on the old sleeping homicide's brow, the sweat-drops of a great agony are standing like 'bubbles on the late disturbed stream,' as the tragedy of Magus Muir is being re-enacted in his soul; or the skirmish of Drumclog; or the tent-preaching which succeeded; or the rout of Bothwell; or the torture scene; or the shaggy mountain solitude where Burley found his last desperate retreat, retiring from the company of men to that of devils, and who can match, in the fierce passions of his own breast, that 'hell of waters' which is perpetually thundering around him. It sometimes happens that a caricature is more forcible, more life-like, more characteristic than a picture, especially if the countenance be strongly marked. And so, probably, Scott has to many given an impression of the rough energy, the honesty, the daring, and the zeal of the Covenanters, which a tamer and more friendly portraiture could never have produced. These concessions of an enemy are confessedly more valuable than the *ex parte* statements of a friend. And still more, when an enemy is transcendently powerful, may his reluctant testimony, and the rude, careless grandeur of his touch, be more effectual than all the pleadings and reclamations of weaker advocates on the other side.

A modified sentence is that, therefore, of wisdom. Few can think *Old Mortality* a strictly accurate or fair account of its age ; and few, on the other hand, would be disposed to erase it as a blot from the list of its author's works. It is a great partisan production, like the histories of Clarendon and Hume. Like them, it must always be read, but like them, too, should be read with great caution, and with the addition of not a few grains of salt.

M'Crie's reply was also partisan. He would scarcely admit that the Covenanters committed an error, or, if he did yield an inch of ground, it was after a struggle like that of Morton and Burley when they kept Bothwell Brigg. He weakened the effect, too, by commencing with an underestimate of the genius and works of his opponent,—

in this case a signal error. He speaks, for instance, rather coldly of *Guy Mannering*, contemptuously of *The Antiquary*, and admits little literary merit in the book he was answering. Still his reply was vigorous and eloquent. He carried the war, too, with triumphant success into the enemy's camp; and, by way of counterpoise to Scott's caricatures of Presbyterian preaching, quoted from Episcopalian divines of the same period specimens of bathos profounder still, of a more adventurous nonsense, of silliness and stupidity more unique, and of prejudice, bigotry, and blindness far more total and hopeless.

Old Mortality was and yet was not answered. Where it grossly offended against truth and fact, its errors were now exposed; but its powerful pictures of an enthusiasm which sometimes erred, and of a zeal and energy which often mistook or missed their mark, remained intact, and are as immortal as the memory of the Covenant itself. The controversy on the subject did much good. It attracted attention to a topic and a time which had been allowed, in a great measure, to drop from the minds of men, and it poured a flood of light upon a field over which thick mists were beginning to gather, and yet which had been one of the noblest in the history of Scotland or of the Church of Christ.

CHAPTER XII.

CONTINUED SUCCESS, WITH PRELIMINARY SHADOWS.

SCOTT, to a mind of gigantic power united a tall and massive bodily framework. When the first Napoleon met Goethe, he was prodigiously struck with his personal appearance,—his majestic stature, stately gait, noble forehead, and great flashing eyes,—his whole aspect combining the fire of a poet with the dignity of a prince. The conqueror of Italy, the hero of Marengo, Lodi, and Austerlitz, felt himself small in the presence of the author of *Werter* and *Faust,* and exclaimed, 'Vous êtes homme!'—You are a man. And although Scott had not the ideal physiognomy or the perfect figure of the great German, yet there was something in his pile of forehead, the curtained lightning of his eye, and the gruff sagacity of his lower face, in which Napoleon, who was a great observer, and looked quite through the deeds of men, would have owned a true type of manhood, and granted that, if there were more splendour and subtlety in Goethe, there was in Scott quite as much strength, and a vast deal more simplicity. There was enough about him, at least, soul and body combined, to awaken (if the pagan poets are to be believed) in the gods the envy they feel at the superior mortals, and to start Apollonic shafts against a mark so conspicuous and so broad. It was on the body that the arrow was first to alight ; the mind was for more than another decade to be spared.

He had made himself the easier prey by the incessant labours in which he had been occupied, alternating with many social engagements. Against the effects of all this, while in the country, air and exercise hardened him ; but it was otherwise in the town. And in the town, accordingly, the first blow fell. On the 5th March 1817, at the close of a joyous party in Castle Street, he was seized with severe cramp in the stomach, and had to retire from the room, as he himself describes it, 'roaring like a bull-calf.' Such attacks yielded readily enough to medicine at first, but they recurred at intervals for more than two years, and terribly shattered his constitution, although they served to reveal new resources in his marvellous genius. During the convalescence succeeding the first attack, he commenced his dramatic sketch of the *Doom of Devorgoil,* one of that set of third-rate poetic productions with which he continued to the close to amuse his leisure, and to tantalize rather than gratify the public. Some smaller things also dropped from his pen, such as a 'Farewell Address,' recited by John Kemble on leaving the Edinburgh stage, and some anecdotes of the Scotch gipsies, containing the crude germ of *Guy Mannering,* inserted in *Constable's Magazine.* William Laidlaw, his faithful ally, came to live at Kaeside, and to be his amanuensis. Scott began to project *Rob Roy* as the subject of his next novel, and sent in to Edinburgh for Constable and John Ballantyne to arrange the publication. The three dined joyously; and Scott, though he had had a severe attack of cramp the day before, got into high spirits, and told Constable that he believed he would make a great hit in a Glasgow weaver, whom he would *ravel* up with Rob; and he proceeded to extemporize a dialogue between the two, something like that which he afterwards described as taking place in the Tolbooth. Hence came in due time the immortal Bailie Nicol Jarvie. Ere commencing the tale, he paid a visit to Loch Lomond and Glasgow to study the scenery, and gather up the *disjecta membra* of the Bailie.

At this time his friend Captain Fergusson, relieved by the peace from campaigning, took a house at Huntly Burn, in his vicinity. Scott had newly purchased much adjacent land there, and was now master of all the haunts of 'True Thomas' the Rhymer, and of the whole ground of the battle of Melrose. The dreary cramp, however, poisoned all his pleasures; and we find him writing verses at this time as sweet and sad as ever came from the broken heart of Byron, or from the lyre which Shelley flung aside, to lie down on the Bay of Naples, seeking,

> ' Like a tired child,
> To weep away this life of care.'

STANZAS.

> ' The sun upon the Weirdlaw Hill,
> In Ettrick Vale, is sinking sweet,
> The westland wind is hush and still,
> The lake lies sleeping at my feet.

> ' Yet not the landscape to mine eye
> Bears those bright hues that once it bore,
> Though evening with her richest dye
> Flames o'er the hills of Ettrick's shore.

'With listless look along the plain
    I see Tweed's silver current glide,
And coldly mark the holy fane
    Of Melrose rise in ruined pride.

'The quiet lake, the balmy air,
    The hill, the stream, the tower, the tree,
Are they still such as once they were,
    Or is the dreary change in me?

'Alas! the warped and broken board,
    How can it bear the painter's dye?
The harp of strained and tuneless chord,
    How to the minstrel's skill reply?

'To aching eyes each landscape lowers,
    To feverish pulse each gale blows chill,
And Araby's or Eden bowers .
    Were barren as this moorland hill.'

The house of Abbotsford was meanwhile increasing in size and splendour, and assuming its castellated form. It had become a resort for distinguished strangers from every part of the world; and this summer it was visited by such welcome guests as Washington Irving (who has gracefully recorded the particulars of his visit), Lady Byron, of whom Scott speaks highly, wondering why Byron could have failed to love her, and Sir David Wilkie. In the end of the year he completed *Rob Roy*, which was written amidst many obstructions, springing from his severe attacks of

cramp, and the dullifying effects of the opium he
was obliged to use, and which gave him

    ' All the wild trash of sleep without the rest.'

William Laidlaw took down the most of it from
his lips. Sometimes he wrote at it himself. On
one occasion James Ballantyne, calling on him for
copy, found him sitting with a clean pen and a
blank sheet before him. He expressed his surprise. 'Ay, ay, Jemmy,' said he, 'it is easy for
you to tell me to get on; but how the mischief can
I make Rob Roy's wife speak with such a curmur-
ring in my guts?'

It became very popular. In no novel has he
been less happy in the construction of his plot,
and, some think, in the adjustment to each other
of the very different materials; but in no novel
has he surpassed the individual portraitures of
character, or more beautifully described the
scenery of his country. The Bailie is the general
favourite; but we think quite as much, in his way,
of Andrew Fairservice, the ideal of a Scottish
serving-man of the last century; nay, we are
mistaken if he has not been met in this too,—
impudent, greedy, conceited, pragmatical, and yet
attached to his master, and overflowing with
mother-wit. Nothing can be better than the

'Dougal Cratur,' or than Rob Roy, especially among his own rocks, 'his foot on his native heath, and his name MacGregor.' Diana Vernon is the first of his heroines who has much *character*, and ranks in interest with the Rebeccas, Lucy Ashtons, Margaret Ramsays, and Clara Mowbrays who followed. His common run of heroines, as well as heroes, is singularly insipid. The most unpleasing characters are Rashleigh and Helen MacGregor; but both are used to much, though melodramatic purpose. Among the descriptions, those of the preaching in the High Church of Glasgow, the midnight scene at the bridge there, and the Clachan of Aberfoyle on a harvest morning, were exceedingly admired.

Stimulated by its success, Scott began another and a higher effort of his genius. This was the *Heart of Midlothian*, which appeared in June 1818. In Edinburgh, owing to the choice of the *locale*, its reception was enthusiastic beyond precedent. Some thirteen years ago we saw a MS. letter, in which Walter Savage Landor declared that if 'Scott had written nothing else, it would have stamped him the most illustrious author of the age.' The power lay in the pathetic interest of the story (a story which the authoress of *Adam Bede* has imitated unsuccessfully); in the simpli-

city of Jeanie Deans,—a simplicity which soars up
by a quick yet natural gradation into sublime
heroism, and returns as easily into simplicity
again ; in the romantic interest attaching to the
subordinate characters, especially to Madge Wild-
fire, whom Coleridge pronounces the most original
of all Scott's characters ; in the admirably drawn
portrait of David Deans, who looks like an *amende
honorable* to the insulted Covenanters ; and in the
purely historical part of the narrative, the description of the fate of Porteous, which shows
what an historian of Scotland Sir Walter might
have been, had he sought the smiles of Clio at
an earlier period of his life.   The last volume,
notwithstanding all the humour of Duncan Knock-
dunder, should not have been written.   It is
hastily and carelessly composed.   Roseneath is
called an island again and again ; and the incident
of the father falling by the hand of his illegiti-
mate son is unpleasing.   Effie, too, in her trans-
formation into the fine lady, has left all that was
interesting and natural behind her with her short-
gown and her snood.

Lockhart marks the completion of this novel
as the climax of Scott's career.   He was apparently realizing £10,000 a year by his writings ;
his house was expanding into a castle ; a fine

family were growing up around him; his popularity as a man and as a poet was unbounded; and he was still sheltered by the shield of the Anonymous from some of the pains and penalties of authorship. We would rather fix it a little later, when his illness had been mastered, and *Ivanhoe*, his most brilliantly successful tale, was speedily succeeded by a baronetcy. At present there were dark spots on his sun. His constitution had received a dreadful shock; and he felt, along with this, that hard toil was now essential to him. He was annoyed, too, although he bore this better than we believe any other man of his day could have done, by the intrusion of endless visitants on the precincts of Abbotsford, and by an incessant shower of MSS. and letters from every quarter under heaven. What might have been the case under the penny postage we can only conjecture. As it was, he was pressed beyond measure and strength, although he seldom complained, and attended to every request.

Lockhart at this time made the acquaintance of his future father-in-law. One of the very best bits in all his biography is where he describes himself dining with William Menzies, afterwards a supreme judge at the Cape. They were carousing in a room looking northwards to Castle

Street, when suddenly a shade came over Menzies'
face, who was seated opposite Lockhart. 'Are
you well enough?'—'Yes; at least when I change
places with you I shall. But the fact is, there is
a confounded *hand* in sight of me here, which
has often bothered me before, and it won't let me
fill my glass with right good-will. It never stops.
Page after page it throws upon the pile of MS.,
and still it goes on.'—'Poh!' said Lockhart, glancing across and seeing the hand; 'it is that of some
stupid engrossing, everlasting clerk.'—'No,' replied
the other; 'it is that of Walter Scott!' And it
was at that moment writing *Waverley!*

This was in 1814. In 1818 Lockhart met Scott
for the first time; and we must refer our readers
to his graphic description of his habits of unwearied labour,—his private manners, so manly yet
bland; his amusing symposia with his publishers
on occasion of a new tale; and his daily life in
Abbotsford, where, while the caressed of princes,
men of letters, and the nobility of the land, he
was also the administrator of justice, and a common good to the whole country-side. 'I have
neighbours beside me,' writes to us this year a
gentleman residing near Melrose, 'old men who,
when they are started, will talk for any length of
time about the memory of their kind-hearted, un-

selfish master,—for I find this is the universal feeling ; and Sir Walter's large-hearted charity to the labouring poor about Darnick is the great feature in his character ; and it, independent of his works, causes his memory to be cherished round Abbotsford.'

During all the close of 1818, and the beginning of 1819, he continued to be assaulted by cramp, and was reduced to a skeleton. His hair became white as snow, his cheek faded, and the last days of the Last Minstrel seemed to have come. He laboured on, however, dictating to William Laidlaw and John Ballantyne (his dictation often interrupted by shouts of agony) *The Bride of Lammermoor, The Legend of Montrose,* and the most of *Ivanhoe.* The first two of these appeared in June 1819, and were read with intenser interest that they were thought the last creations of his mind. One day Scott thought himself dying, summoned his family around him, bade them a pathetic and Christian farewell, expressing confidence in his Redeemer, turned then his face to the wall, but fell into a deep sleep, and from that hour began slowly to recover. His disease, which had resisted opiates, heated salt, etc., at last yielded to small doses, composed chiefly of calomel. It is doubtful, however, if he ever became so strong as he had been.

L

He was forty-six when first assailed by the malady, but, ere three years had elapsed, his constitution was at least a decade older. And, while yet the die of his life span doubtful, his aged mother expired on the 24th of December.

CHAPTER XIII.

CULMINATION OF FAME AND FORTUNE—
'IVANHOE' AND BARONETCY.

N the same month that his mother died, and his own life hung trembling in the balance, *Ivanhoe* appeared. Never in the literary world had there been, perhaps, such a tumult of applause, particularly in England.

> ' Men met each other with erected look,
> The steps were higher that they took;
> Friends to congratulate their friends made haste,
> And long estranged foes saluted as they passed.'

It seemed an event of national triumph when Ivanhoe rode with his vizor down into the lists, Rebecca by his side, and the Black Knight hovering on the skirts of the scene. As Dr. Johnson says of Gray's *Odes*, ' Criticism was lost in wonder.' But it was not, as Johnson would imply in reference to Gray, a wonder blended with doubt

and a spice of scorn, but wonder mixed with unbounded delight, the very feeling of the Queen of
Sheba : 'The half had not been told us. We were
prepared for much, but never for aught like this.'
We shall inquire as to the justice of these sentiments in a little ; at present we record the
unquestionable fact. The two tales which preceded it had been welcomed warmly too. There
is a fine romantic spirit hovering over the *Legend
of Montrose.* It has a smell of heather, wears a
coronet of mist, and a deep autumnal charm
breathes in every page. Byron says of it, indeed
justly, ' He don't make enough of Montrose.' That
hero is dwindled beside three other characters,
all admirable and all eccentric,—Sir Dugald Dalgetty, a mixture in equal proportions of trooper,
pedant, and picaroon ; Ranald MacEagh, the grey-
haired Son of the Mist, with his inimitable dying
speech to his grandson ; and Allan MacAulay,
parcel hero, *parcel* homicide, *parcel* maniac, and
parcel poet. Annot Lyle, whose song comes over
his dark soul like a ' sunbeam on a sullen sea,' is
a sweet creation. And no episode in all Scott's
novels surpasses in stirring adventure, blended with
humour, Dalgetty's tour to Inveraray.

Coleridge says that there is an exaggeration in
the third series of the *Tales of my Landlord* and

in *Ivanhoe* not to be found in any other of Scott's stories. Perhaps the cause of this lay partly in his disease, and partly in the enormous quantity of laudanum he was compelled, contrary to his taste and habits, to swallow to relieve it. Caleb Balderstone, in some of his exhibitions, is precisely such an extravaganza as you might expect from a brain under a twofold morbific influence. Yet what must have been the strength of the mind which could in such an unfavourable state retain so much of its balance? Scott, it will be remembered, when he recovered, had no recollection of having written these novels. Perhaps a morbid mood was the appropriate chiaroscuro through which to show us the dark tragedy of Lucy Ashton,—a tragedy which may be compared to those stern adumbrations of Fate contained in the Grecian plays, and the pathos of which is so heart-rending. There is no point of interest in all literature superior to that in which, as Ravenswood bursts on the assembled marriage party, Lucy exclaims, ' He is come, he is come ;' and out of Shakspeare there are no dialogues superior to those of the two old witch women at the bridal and at the burial of the hapless victim.

Ivanhoe is certainly less natural, less probable, less life-like than his first novels. And so are *The*

Tempest and the *Midsummer Night's Dream* less
life-like and probable than the *Julius Cæsar* or
King Henry the Fourth of Shakspeare. But they
show more invention and more fancy. Much of
the best matter in *Waverley, Guy Mannering*, and
The Antiquary is borrowed from real incidents and
characters, while in *Ivanhoe* he is compelled to
make many of his materials. It introduces us into
a world almost as distinctly new as that of *The
Tempest*, full of characters for which there exists
no real historical type ; knights breathing a more
than mortal spirit of chivalry ; Saxons with a
plusquam Saxonic boldness and independence ;
banditti, 'minions of the moon' not only in their
clandestine calling, but in the poetic light which
colours them ; and, above all, a Jewess, who, amidst
the depths of her nation's degeneracy, exhibits
more than the grandeur of Deborah, more than
the tenderness of Rachel, and more than the loveliness of Solomon's spouse, and sings a song of
Zion almost equal to those old strains which
marched with the ark, or trembled out a more subdued and solemn music of adoration, while Jahveh
was thundering on Sinai's summit. Nowhere, too,
does Scott display more of the master's power
than in his management of these strange materials : the adjustment of each to each, and all to all ;

the happy cross lights of contrast which he throws in ever and anon, and the perfect oneness of the dream which they combine to form.   There is another point, too, in which *Ivanhoe* is very remarkable.   It has three climaxes, each rising above the other like mountain stairs,—the first at the close of the tournament, the second at the completion of the storm of Torquilstone, and the third at the final deliverance of Rebecca.   He gains a height on which inferior writers would have paused, and makes that the mere basis from which he takes a bolder and yet a bolder step.   Thrice in the course of the novel is that exquisite pang, which the close of a good story always inflicts, felt in our bosoms, and each pang is more exquisite and more intense than that which went before.   And what can be imagined superior to the parting interview between Rowena and Rebecca?   It reads almost like the book of Ruth.

Scott's eldest son Walter had ere this joined the 4th Regiment of Hussars.   In the beginning of 1820 he published some papers entitled *The Visionary*, in order to calm down the political agitation of the times, and bolster up the reign of Toryism, then beginning to totter to its fall.   Like Professor Wilson, Scott's power always deserted him when he wrote on political subjects.   Wilson foamed and screamed like a maniac ; Scott maundered like an old doting woman.

In March appeared *The Monastery.* It was commonly thought the first failure in the splendid series ; yet it succeeded the *Black Dwarf,* which assuredly was much worse. It cannot be denied, in reference to the Waverley Novels, that they are not only, like most works, unequal, but that from the date of the *Black Dwarf* there ever and anon appears in them a layer of utterly inferior and unworthy matter. Previous to Scott's acknowledgment of the sole authorship, many accounted for this on the supposition of another and inferior hand being sometimes employed on the work ; and certainly this surmise was rendered probable at the time by the immense contrast between the two stories in the first *Tales of my Landlord,* in one of which the author drivels like James Hogg in his worst novels, while in the other he writes like a man inspired. We have sometimes thought that the disease, softening of the brain, of which he ultimately died, began to affect him, although fitfully, at an earlier period than is usually thought.

With all its faults, we love *The Monastery,*— partly, indeed, because it was the first of the series we read. The White Lady is a failure,—rather, however, as Scott himself maintains, in execution than

in design. The witching scenes connected with
her are, for the most part, exceedingly poor. She
is far inferior to Undine, that fairy of the waters ;
yet we love to haunt her well, in the depths of
Corrinanshian,—love to see her holly-tree

> ' Startling the bewildered hind,
> Who sees it wave without a wind ;'

and love to hear her soft, sad voice from the sky
exclaiming,—

> ' The breeze that brought me hither now must sweep Egyptian
>   ground ;
> The fleecy cloud on which I ride for Araby is bound.
> The fleecy cloud is drifting by, the breeze sighs for my stay,
> And I must sail a thousand miles before the close of day.'

Piercy Shaften is a fool, but a generous, brave,
and warm-hearted fool ; and Mysie Happer is one
of the most interesting of all Scott's female characters,—incomparably more so than Mary Avenel,
who is pale and cold as the secondary cloud which
rises from a cataract, and seems the spirit of spray.
The scenes in Avenel Castle are written with power
and pathos. Murray and Morton are painted to the
life. And when the Last Minstrel hears, like Job's
horse, the sound of the trumpet and the shouting,
he becomes all himself ; and the death of Julian
Avenel, the cry from his paramour, ' Christie of

the Clinthill, Rowley, Hutcheon, ye were constant at the feast, but ye fled from him at the fray,
false villains that ye are!' and Christie's exclamation ere he dies, ' Not I, by heaven!' are worthy
of him who described Brian De Bois Guilbert in his
last and noblest moments, dying in his steel harness
full knightly. Yet *The Monastery* WAS a failure;
but this was little more regarded than is one stumble
in the walk of a stately and stalwart man. While
the public were reading it with mingled feelings,
swallowing it eagerly, but disputing about the
taste it left behind, Scott was off to London, to
receive an honour which, cheap as it now appears
to the admirers of his genius, was very gratifying
at the time to him and to his family,—a baronetcy.
This should have been conferred in the spring of
the previous year, but for his illness; and at Christmas, had it not been for family afflictions. He had
scarcely reached town till Sir Thomas Lawrence
called on, and got him to sit as a figure in a great
gallery of distinguished men for Windsor Castle;
and the painter has, according to Lockhart, ' fixed
with admirable skill one of the loftiest expressions
of Scott's face at the proudest period of his life.'
Lawrence said afterwards, that, in his judgment,
the two greatest men he ever drew were the Duke
of Wellington and Scott; and, curiously, both

selected the same hour for sitting,—seven in the morning. The only way to catch Scott's best and highest look was to get him to repeat a piece of poetry, and then the fire of the Makkar looked out from his eye in almost stormy grandeur. To Chantrey, too, he sat for a bust, and on this occasion made the personal acquaintance of Allan Cunningham. This gifted and admirable man had long admired Scott with all the enthusiasm of a self-taught genius. He describes himself, in a letter to Hogg, reading *The Lay of the Last Minstrel* along with the shepherd on Queensberry Hill ' under the sunny rain ;' and he had on one occasion, when a stone-mason in Nithsdale, walked all the way to Edinburgh simply to see the author of *Marmion* passing along the street. Scott heartily responded, and spoke of him afterwards as Honest Allan, and being a credit to Caledonia.

This was altogether a happy as well as a proud and *eclatant* visit. Scott met lords many, including Lords Melville and Huntly ; some gifted and noble women, especially Lady Huntly, who ' sang Scotch tunes like a Highland angel,' and whose variations of ' Kenmure's on and awa ' were, he told her, enough to raise a whole country-side ; saw the Duke of York, and others of the great of the hour. But he had far more true pleasure when going

out and spending a Sabbath-day quietly with
Joanna Baillie and John Richardson at Hampstead.
Nor did he allow ' champagne and plovers' eggs,'
the blandishments of lords, ladies, or literati, to
hinder him from using his influence, while in
London, in behalf of his friend John Wilson, who
was then, against much opposition, canvassing the
Edinburgh Town Council for the Moral Philosophy
chair.   In a letter to Lockhart on this subject, he
says, ' You are aware that the only point of exception to Wilson may be that, with the fire of genius,
he has possessed some of its eccentricities ; but did
he ever approach to those of Henry Brougham,
who is the god of Whiggish idolatry ?   If the high
and rare qualities with which he is invested are to
be thrown aside as useless, because they may be
clouded by a few grains of dust which he can blow
aside at pleasure, it is less a punishment on Mr.
Wilson than on the country.'   Wilson, every one
knows, got the chair, did not become a model
Metaphysical or Moral Philosophy professor either,
but filled his class-room with the strong breath
of genius, and left such impressions on the minds
of the successive students, who for thirty-one years
attended his prelections, as more than justified
Scott's canvassing eagerness and prognosticating
foresight.

When the King in person conferred on Scott the baronetcy, he said, as the poet kissed his hand, 'I shall always reflect with pleasure on Sir Walter Scott's having been the first creation of my reign.' *The Gazette* announcing this event was dated the 30th March, and published on the 2d of April; and soon afterwards his native land again welcomed back her most distinguished son as SIR WALTER SCOTT.

CHAPTER XIV.

SCOTT AT HOME, AND AGAIN IN LONDON.

HE came home a little earlier, that he might be present at a marriage,—the marriage of his eldest daughter Sophia to J. G. Lockhart. This took place on the 29th of April, Scott having arranged that it should not be deferred to the unlucky month of May. He liked to cherish all these old superstitions, which, though only venerable cobwebs, he treated as if they were antique tapestry. We have already characterized the bride in this fair marriage. The bridegroom was of a more composite character. Possessed of a robust intellect, powerful though limited imagination, keen and savage sarcasm, and of a varied and catholic culture, he seemed destined to take the very highest place in the world of letters. But there was a cross-grained element in his nature. He was rather strong than genial ; his humour often coarse and poisoned with personalities ; and he now appears in the eye

174

of the public a 'secondary Scottish novelist,' a translator, not a poet, and an admirable biographer, as his *Lives of Scott, Burns,* and *Napoleon* prove. With culture about equal, and a more masculine style of thought and language, he has not nearly now such acceptance as Professor Wilson with the Scottish people. What a different destiny might have been expected for the man who in youth could write *Valerius !*

As it is, his immortality now rests almost entirely on his connection with Sir Walter Scott. His pictures of the great novelist's private life and habits, —his companions, amusements, and methods of study,—combine breadth and minute accuracy, are written with a rare vigour and felicity of style, and for them all after time must be grateful. Lockhart has done for Castle Street and Abbotsford what Boswell did for Bolt Court ; for Scott what Boswell did for Johnson ; and yet has not much compromised his dignity, or at all sacrificed his individuality. And if he has not recorded so many pithy sayings and *bon mots* of his hero, he has given a general view of his everyday life quite as vivid ; and, while bringing him out as the centre of the literary scene, has not omitted faithfully and fully to depict the surrounding and subordinate figures, some of whom were among the first men of their time. Well might he say to William Allan, when standing before the porch of Abbotsford house after breakfast, and when a brilliant party were about to start on a day's coursing match, 'A faithful sketch of what you at this moment see, would be more interesting a hundred years hence than the grandest so-called historical picture that you will ever exhibit in Somerset House;' and Allan might well grant that he was right.

In defect of Allan's sketch, we have Lockhart's own most masterly picture of Sir Humphrey Davy in his fisherman's costume,—a brown hat with flexible brim, surrounded with line upon line and innumerable fly-hooks, jack-boots worthy of a Dutch smuggler, and a fustian surtout dabbled with the blood of salmon; Dr. Wollaston in black, with his noble and dignified countenance, like a sporting archbishop; Mackenzie, the Man of Feeling, in the seventy-sixth year of his age, with a white hat turned up with green, green spectacles, green jacket, long brown leathern gaiters, and a dog-whistle round his neck; and Sir Walter himself, mounted on Sybil Grey, the giant Maida gambolling about and barking for joy, and Scott's *pet*, a little black pig, frisking around the pony, and evidently ambitious to join the party, while her master exclaims,—

'What will I do gin my hoggie die,
   My joy, my pride, my hoggie ;
My only beast, I had na mae,
   And vow but I was vogie !'

Davy especially enjoyed Scott. He had much
of the poet in his own composition, and has written
some splendid lines on the doctrine of Spinoza.
Scott and he served to draw each other out, partly
by their points of resemblance and partly of contrast, and the effects were electrical. Both talked
their best, Scott becoming less anecdotical and more
impassioned ; Davy impregnating his science with
imagination till it shone and burned ; and William
Laidlaw standing by, the happiest of the sons of
men, and whispering to Lockhart, with his eye
cocked like a bird's, 'Gude preserve us, this is a
very superior occasion. Eh, sirs ! I wonder if Shakspeare and Bacon ever met to screw ilk ither up !'

These were gala days, and *noctes cœnæque Deûm.*
But there were others which, though homelier,
were quite as happy. Such, each 28th of October,
young Walter's birthday, was the Abbotsford
Hunt, with all its glee and glory, which made
farmers wish that they could sleep all the year
through till it came again ; 'for there's only ae
thing in this warld worth living for, and that's the
Abbotsford Hunt !' And such was his annual bout

M

of salmon-fishing, closing sometimes with such a spearing of the water as is described in *Guy Mannering*,—the Sherra himself often appearing on the boat, wielding, if not a spear, a torch, the more poetical of the two, and seeming a premature morn risen on the midnight. Let us not forget the regale on the newly-caught prey, boiled or grilled or roasted, with a great old ash bending over the heads of the party, the Tweed murmuring like a happy bee beside, and the harvest moon rising on the scene ere it was closed, and adding to it her weird light and nameless ecstasy. We fancy Scott exclaiming, 'Burke might be a great man, but he was absurdly wrong when he said the age of chivalry and romance is gone: it is here. Bear witness, that rejoicing river, those grey hills, that lovely moon, and those hearts as young and blithe as can be found in " Christendie !" '

In September 1820 appeared *The Abbot*, the sequel to *The Monastery*, and usually thought the stronger of the two. Appearing as it did at the time when the miserable business of George IV. and his Queen was agitating the country, many thought that there must be some allusion, open or covert, in the novel to the times. As Scott's *animus* in favour of the King was well known, and as the tale might be construed into an apology for

the Queen, some wiseacres (including, as Moore's
Memoirs inform us, one or two of the Holland
House circle) came to the conclusion that Green-
field, a man of accomplishments, who had been
forced to flee from Edinburgh on account of a
frightful scandal, and was in hiding somewhere on
the other side of the Border, was its author, as
well as of two or three of the other novels. This
was a mere falsehood, although it continued long
afterwards to be repeated in periodicals, one writer
in the *Eclectic Review* renewing it almost every
year; and the resemblance on which it principally
rested, of Mary's case to Caroline's, was quite
arbitrary and absurd. A 'Queen,' however, this
autumn was triumphant in fiction as well as in
reality. Caroline was acquitted; and Mary, in
The Abbot, was welcomed with universal applause.
The beginning of that novel, though full of a certain melancholy beauty, is rather tedious. But
the scenes in Edinburgh, when Roland Graeme
enters it, are spirited; and those in Lochleven,
circling round the Queen, are equal to anything in
Scott's historical fictions for grace, vraisemblance,
and romantic interest. The battle at Langside,
and Mary's retreat to England, are most tenderly
pictured. Among the characters, Roland and Catherine, the lovers, are lively and natural; Dryfes-

dale, a gloomy spirit, starts from the canvas ; Queen
Mary is every inch a queen ; and what pathos in
George of Douglas, and power and character in
his words, when the Queen fancies herself on the
back of Rosabelle, her favourite palfrey : 'Mary
needed Rosabelle, and Rosabelle is here !' Most
touching, too, the character of the noble abbot,
Edward Glendinning, to whom, devoted to duty
as he is in the watches of the night, memories
of his happier period of life at Glendearg, and
the pale face of Mary Avenel, still unutterably
beloved, are often recurring ; and the conversation
between the Queen, Lords Ruthven and Lindsay of
the Byres, is one of the most delicately beautiful
and profoundly heart-searching in all the Novels.
Scott knew he had recovered his ground, and wrote
to Lockhart (on a slip of paper inserted in the first
volume) two lines from a forgotten *jeu d'esprit*
entitled ' Tom Cribb's Memorial to Congress,'

> ' Up he rose in a funk, lapped a toothful of brandy,
>   And *to it* again ! any odds upon Sandy.'

Scott had picked up some of the materials of
The Abbot in the course of the annual visits he
had been in the habit of paying to Blair Adam, in
the neighbourhood of Kinross, where the Right
Honourable William Adam fixed his summer
residence. In midsummer 1816 he was visited

there by some of his friends, William Clark, Adam Fergusson, and Scott. They enjoyed each other so much that they determined to hold a similar meeting every year at the same season and at the same place, along with a few additions to the party. Thus was formed the Blair Adam Club, where Scott never failed to attend from 1816 to 1831. To it, besides those mentioned before, and some near relations of Chief Commissioner Adam, there belonged Thomson of Duddingston, his brother the Registrar-General, and Sir Samuel Shepherd, the Chief Baron of Exchequer. They usually met on a Friday, spent the Saturday on a visit to some scene of historical or picturesque interest in the neighbourhood, on Sunday attended duly and devoutly the parish church of Cleish, devoted Monday to another excursion, and returned to Edinburgh on Tuesday in time for the Courts. In this way they visited St. Andrews, Magus Muir, Castle Campbell, Falkland, and Dunfermline; and what a picnic in Scott's company would be, we may gather from its picture on the written page of *The Antiquary*. On one occasion the Chief Commissioner and Scott were waiting for the boat at the Hawes Inn near Queensferry. The seals were sporting in the glassy bay, and Sir Walter exclaimed, ' What fine fellows they are ! I have the greatest

respect for them. I would as soon kill a man as a
Phoca.' The scene on the beach in the novel
instantly flashed in the Chief Commissioner's mind,
and he saw the author of *Waverley* and the father
of Jonathan Oldbuck standing by his side. In his
Abbot he had mentioned the Kiery Craggs, a
placé of romantic scenery enclosed in the grounds
of Blair Adam, and the name of which was not
generally known. Soon after its publication the
party had met on the top of this rocky ridge, when
the Chief Baron Shepherd, looking Scott full in
the face, and stamping his staff on the ground,
exclaimed, ' Now, Sir Walter, I think we be on the
top of the Kiery Craggs ?' Sir Walter said nothing,
but looked down as if conscious he was 'found,
found,' like his own Goblin Page. Constable, since
Mary had fared so well, insisted on his bringing
her great rival Elizabeth on the stage in his next
tale ; and, with his usual sagacity, he proposed as
subject 'The Armada.' What a pity Scott had
not taken the hint! How the mere words, 'The
Armada, by the author of *Ivanhoe*,' would at that
time have startled the public imagination! It
may be said that he could not bear to write up to
a title, and that he might have failed. One is
reminded of Sir Thomas Vaux's whisper to Richard
Cœur de Lion when he was about to cut the mass

of steel with his two-handed sword in the company of Saladin, ' Take care ; your majesty is not fully recovered.'—' Fool !' replied the monarch ; ' do you think I could fail in *his* presence ?' So it is difficult to conceive of Scott failing in the presence of a subject so great as the Armada,—a subject swelled, as it were, by so many elements of grandeur—danger, battle, shipwreck, the war of elements, patriotic passion, defiance, defeat, and glorious deliverance. Elizabeth's medal ran, ' HE˙ blew with His wind, and they were scattered ;' and *that* would have been a sublime motto, and have ministered inspiration to the great novelist, in the wind of whose awakened spirit the whole mar- vellous story would have begun to live and move, to breathe and burn again, not an atom of the life lost, nor quenched one spark of the heaven- kindled fire ! Scott, however, chose *Kenilworth* instead ; and in January 1821 appeared that most interesting, varied, pathetic, and sparkling tale. In the word ' sparkling' we allude to its dialogue, which equals that of the Elizabethan drama in wit and elastic brilliance. Queen Elizabeth, if not a portrait true to *her*, is true to Scott's *idea* of her, and is executed with wonderful power and skill. Amy Robsart is one of his most natural and woman-like females. Scott *calls* some of his other heroines lovely, but he *makes* her so, both in body and mind. Dickie Sludge escapes from criticism as he does from pursuit, by his dexterity and mother-wit. And Lambourne, Varney, and Alasco constitute a famous cluster of villains,—three dark stars, with their different shades of gloom most accurately discriminated. The interest, too, of the story never flags, and becomes near the close unendurably thrilling. Immediately after the publication of this novel Scott hied to London on legal business ; heard while there of the birth of his grandchild, John Hugh Lockhart, to whom he afterwards addressed his *Tales of a Grandfather ;* and was consulted about the establishment of a Society of Literature,—a project which bore fruit by and by. In June died his old and most devoted friend, John Ballantyne, after a long and lingering illness. While committing poor Rigdum Funnidos' remains to the Calton Burying-ground, the heavens, which had been dark, cleared up, and the mid-day sun shone forth. Scott glanced his eye along the gleaming Calton Hill, and then, turning to the grave, said in a whisper to Lockhart, 'I feel as if there would be less sunshine for me from this day forth.' 'Garrick's death eclipsed the gaiety of nations.' Ballantyne's, in shading that of Scott, shaded that of Scotland and of the world.

On the 19th of July we find him again in London, present at what one calls the 'contemptible mummery of a coronation,' never so contemptible in the eyes of the public as when George IV. was the king crowned, although to Scott it seemed a personal triumph. He met, indeed, there with what was equivalent. Returning home on foot after the banquet, he got locked in the crowd about three in the morning, and his friend with him became apprehensive of some accident to his lame limb. Scott, observing an open space in the middle of the street, asked a sergeant of the Scots Greys on guard to allow him to pass. He replied it was impossible, his orders were strict. At this moment a wild wave of the multitude came rolling behind, and his companion exclaimed, 'Sir Walter Scott, take care!' The soldier cried out, 'What! Sir Walter Scott! *he* shall pass at all events. Make room, men, for our illustrious countryman.' And amidst shouts of 'Walter Scott, God bless him!' he gained the place of safety.

During this visit he called again on Allan Cunningham, and talked with him about Crechope Linn, where he had been when a boy, and other Scottish matters; and in returning home he visited Stratford-on-Avon, and wrote on the wall of the room a name only second among British authors to that of its original tenant.

CHAPTER XV.

SCOTT'S RELATION TO HIS CONTEMPORARIES, GOETHE, BYRON, WORDSWORTH, SOUTHEY, AND THE REST.

NO literary man in Britain since Johnson, and before him, Pope, and before him, Dryden, had such a good title to the name autocrat as Sir Walter Scott. But while Dryden and Pope were tyrants, and active tyrants too, constantly warring with their rebel subjects, writing MacFlecknoes and Dunciads ; and Johnson, a lazy despot, who would only take the trouble to growl at those who would not kiss his ferula for a sceptre ; Scott was a wise, calm, and moderate monarch. He had few who did not bow to his supremacy, none who hated his rule, none who envied him, and none whom he hated or envied. Hazlitt abhorred his politics, bitterly assailed them, misunderstood the man, and depreciated

the Poet; but Hazlitt admired the novelist and
the novels to enthusiasm. Byron, when most
powerful as a writer, on the publication, namely,
of his 4th Canto of *Childe Harold*, was most unpopular as a man ; and when he produced his *Don
Juan*, he lost his poetical prestige too. It was, he
says,

> 'His Leipsic, Fahero,
> His Moscow and his Waterloo was Cain ;'

and it was not merely the satiated voluptuary but
the dethroned king of song who took refuge in
Greece. But such was the love felt universally for
Scott, that, as in his heyday of power, all rejoiced
in his great light, when it sank prematurely, everybody mourned as at a personal calamity, and
tried to catch warmth even from the feeble beams
of his setting sun. Some authors, while generally
popular with the public, are not so with their contemporaries and rivals in fame. To this Shakspeare and Scott were happy exceptions. All accounts show this to have been the case with the first
of these, the 'Gentle Willy.' His contemporaries,
though they had to look up such a vast height,
looked up with love as well as wonder. Wordsworth was said by Coleridge to stride so far before
other men as to dwindle in the distance. Shakspeare, like Mont Blanc, though exceedingly remote

in his altitude, looked close at hand : his distance seemed annihilated by his dazzling splendour. Goethe alone, in his age, was counted as great or greater than Scott ; yet how delightful the relation which subsisted between these two sovereigns of literature ! Scott, who had commenced his career as a translator from the German Bard, was always ready to acknowledge his admiration of him, speaks in a letter to Goethe himself of ' the obligations which he owed to ONE to whom all the authors of this generation have been so much obliged that they are bound to look up to him with filial reverence,' and felt the news of his death very deeply. Goethe, on the other hand, in writing Scott, acknowledges ' the lively interest he had long taken in his wonderful pictures of human life.' When he read *The Fair Maid of Perth,* he expressed his intense appreciation of the masterly genius which that novel exhibited ; and even the *Life of Napoleon* he valued, not historically, nor artistically, but as a true record of the impressions made on such a mind as Scott's, by the marvellous revolutions which were in progress during his own time. To find two men of their order so far *en rapport* was the more pleasing, as in taste, certain points of morale, and religious views, they differed very widely, and as Scott was compelled to severely censure the spirit of some of Goethe's works.

His friendship with Byron was still more remarkable. No two poets were ever more unlike in most respects,—their chief resemblance lying in the fact that their unbounded popularity during life passed with little pause, and as certainly as the crescent becomes the full moon, into permanent fame. The one was the least, the other the most self-conscious of men. The one was constitutionally happy, though subject to temporary depressions ; the other constitutionally melancholy to wretchedness, though often surprised into strange excesses of boyish mirth. The one was theoretically a Tory, but, in sympathy with the lower orders, a Liberal ; the other theoretically a Whig, but in feeling as proud an aristocrat as ever admired the Norman blood seen and scarcely seen to flow in his delicate white hands. Byron was dissipated in life ; Scott a domestic, regular, yet genial man. Byron was a sceptic more from pride and passion than from conviction ; Scott a Christian more from the accidents of a Scotch training and constitutional veneration than from personal experience. Scott was intensely healthy in thought, temperament, and style ; Byron was a strong disease, embodied with weaknesses equal to, and which almost seemed to support and beautify his strength. Both resembled each other in their lameness; but this, while it constituted to Byron a constant source of torment, and inspirited some insane utterances of discontent, was to Scott a gentle, ever-living lesson, a constant hint, 'Thou also art mortal.' Sir Walter imagined that the link connecting him with Byron (as well as afterwards with Moore) was that they were both men of the world rather than authors. But this name, applied to them, did not signify the same thing as when used to others, nor were they men of the world at all in the strict sense of that term. Both, indeed, were *up* to the manners and usages of the world; both mingled at ease in all circles; both loved the world too well,—the one the position, the other the fame and pleasure, it gave them; but neither must be confounded with that heartless, soulless slave of form and fashion, that prostrate worshipper of success and *eclât*, which the ordinary 'man of the world' too often becomes. And, latterly, both seceded in a great measure from society,—Byron in disgust and disappointment; Scott because, while he perhaps still loved, he had failed in it, and knew that even in his case it had exacted a certain penalty, and fixed a certain brand on his brow.

In point of genius, taking Scott in the entire

sphere of his achievements, he was undoubtedly the larger orb of the two. He was simpler and sincerer; his sympathies were much wider, his dramatic power greater, his knowledge immensely larger, his touches of nature making the whole world kin were far more numerous. As Shakspeare to Marlowe, as Goethe to Schiller, so was Scott to Byron. But as a poet Byron was unquestionably superior. Scott has produced no such compact and consummate masterpiece as *The Corsair;* no such long and splendid gush of high-wrought enthusiasm as the 4th Canto of *Childe Harold;* no such exquisite poetical drama as *Manfred;* no such daring flight of imagination as *Cain;* and no amalgam in a similar compass, of wit, sarcasm, poetry, passion, knowledge of human nature, inimitable ease of writing, interesting adventure, terse sentiment, concentred power of description, and melting pathos, as *Don Juan.* In sobriety, sweetness, health, and breadth, he is as far superior to Byron as he is in moral sentiment; but he is inferior in strength of muscle, in intensity, eloquence, and eagle-winged genius. It must be remembered, too, that Byron had performed all his marvellous achievements and was dead, at an age when Scott had only written the first of his larger poems.

In his relation to the Lakers, and particularly to

Wordsworth and Coleridge, Scott had ample room
at once for his generosity and for his wisdom.   He
knew that these men were much underrated in
their own time, and that before them lay a great
empire in the future,—an empire which, though
it could not overturn, yet might divide dominion
with his own.   Men of less kindly and manly
nature might have felt prospective jealousy toward
these poets who, though struggling, were secure
of triumph, and whose influence might probably
become profounder, if not so wide as his.   Instead,
however, of seeking to repress or damn them with
faint praise, Scott is never weary, in his correspondence and conversation, of praising them ; and in
his Novels, now by quotations from their works in
the text, and now by allusions in footnotes to their
talents, he writes them up with all his might.   He
procured, we have seen, the poet-laureateship for
Southey.   He listened to Coleridge, 'that extraordinary man who, during a very hearty dinner,
did not say a single word, and then uttered a long
and most eloquent harangue on the Samothracian
mysteries' with profound admiration, and did not
dare to interrupt him even when he questioned
the unity of Homer and the integrity of the Homeric
poems.   In *The Monastery* he calls him the most
imaginative of our modern bards ; and in *Ivanhoe*,

after speaking of him in the text as having written but too little, he adds in a note, ' that his unfinished sketches display more talent than the laboured masterpieces of others.' For Wordsworth he felt the highest respect—a feeling compounded of admiration for his original genius, and of love for that genuineness and depth of nature, that sound moral feeling and pure enthusiasm, which he possessed in a degree only inferior to Milton.

In doing and feeling all this Scott was thoroughly disinterested. Even had he needed a *quid pro quo* and expected it, it did not come. Southey is rather stingy in his laudations of Scott ; and when he does not speak out plainly, he can hint a fault and hesitate dislike. Wordsworth never even professed any great admiration for Scott's poetry, although he loved the man warmly, and wrote a plaintive sonnet on his leaving his native land, which we shall quote in the sequel.

Coleridge eloquently eulogized many of Scott's novels ; but in this as in other matters his judgments were to a great extent neutralized by his caprice, uncertainty, and thousand-and-one wayward moods. Toryism no doubt formed an element of union between the Lakers and Scott. But we are persuaded that even had these men been Radicals, and bitter detractors of Scott withal,

N

he would have spoken of their genius just as he did,—such was the largeness of his heart, and the sweet-blooded tone of his mental and moral constitution.

With Moore, too, he was on kindly terms. And for George Crabbe he had a special affection, and did not know whether more to admire his simplicity as a man or his strong sinewy genius as a poet. And we shall find that Crabbe's poetry was read to him (as it had been a generation before to Charles James Fox) in his dying days.

Constable knew to his cost how indulgent Scott was to the inferior writers, for whom the author of *Waverley* persuaded him to publish. He said he always 'liked Scott's ain bairns, but not those of his fostering.' On the other hand, a vast number of young writers of verse and of prose from every county in England, Scotland, and Ireland, and from every civilised country in the world, sent in books or MSS. to the affable Archangel of Abbotsford ; and hundreds of instances are on record of the real kindness which he showed them,—a kindness all the more valuable that he was strictly honest in his judgments and faithful in his strictures, although mild and measured in his expressions. Merciful to all, he never praised any in whom he did not perceive real merit. Ingratitude his placid nature

prepared for, and would have forgiven ; but ingratitude, unless from Hogg in one of his wild,
senseless moods, which he lived himself to regret,
he never met. He had the art of sheathing the
sting of his censure in such honeyed phrases that
it was scarcely felt, or, as the Irishman has it,—

    ' He kicked them down-stairs with such a good grace,
      That they thought he was handing them up.'

It were well if all who in a lesser but still a large
measure are pestered with sucking writers, and feel
the penalty rather greater than the honour, could
take a leaf out of the master's book, and be enabled
to imitate his inward honesty and his outward *bon-
homie*. Not till one tries can he feel how difficult
it is to do so.

Around Scott there rose a giant brood of novelists,
in Scotland and elsewhere, inferior to him, but of
decided power and genius,—strong spurs upon his
mountain chain. Such were Professor Wilson,
Lockhart, Galt, Miss Ferrier the authoress of *The Inheritance* and *Marriage*, and, some time afterwards,
Lord Bulwer Lytton. In all of these Scott took a
warm interest, and felt for them a true admiration.
He lived long enough to read and see the promise
in Bulwer's earlier novels. And all these authors
have reciprocated his feelings,—Bulwer dedicating

his *Eugene Aram* to Scott in language glowing with gratitude and enthusiasm. Unless Bulwer, none of these writers approached their model in popularity, nor did any other, till Dickens arose,—Dickens, of whose sudden and premature death we have this day heard (the 10th of June), in whom, in common with the whole literary world, and far beyond that world's limits, we mourn a great cheerful light quenched ere it was evening, and in whom we have always traced many of Scott's qualities, specially his warmth and width of sympathies, his genial and kindly nature, and the desire, which was ever uppermost with him, to find the soul of goodness in things that are evil, and the essence of beauty in objects thought by vulgar eyes common and unclean. We called him in his youth ' Bonnie Prince Charlie,' and must now lament that in the fulness of his powers, and in the height of his benignant dominion, he has been called away !

CHAPTER XVI.

'CARLE, NOW THE KING'S COME.'

ROM London Scott came down to Abbotsford,—plans for the completion of which he had brought along with him. Lockhart and his young wife had established themselves in the little cottage of Chiefswood, and there Scott was often with them, adding fresh brightness to what was then a bright and happy spot. Often in the mornings, after his daily task was over, 'the clatter of Sybil Grey's hoofs, the yelping of Mustard and Spice, and his own joyous shout of reveillée under our windows, were the signal that he had burst his toils, and meant for that day to "take his ease in his inn." ' He was then busy with *The Pirate*, and sometimes wrote chapters of it in a dressing-room in Chiefswood, which he would hand to his friend William Erskine, who, as sheriff of Orkney and Shetland, knew the localities well, and was proud of being consulted in the progress of the book. Altogether this was a busy and joyous autumn with Scott. Besides *The Pirate*, he was writing some miscellaneous things. Among others, he had begun a series of *Private Letters* in the antique style, descriptive of manners in the time of James First of England. On reflection, he threw them aside, and employed their materials in the *Fortunes of Nigel*, the first chapters of which he wrote ere *The Pirate* was completed. His pleasure, indeed, might have been somewhat abated had he known that the sale of his novels was falling off considerably, and that their reputation was slowly waning. This, however, was carefully, but we think injudiciously, concealed from him by his publishers; and his confidence in his powers was such, that he had, ere *Nigel* appeared, exchanged instruments and received bills for four works of fiction, all unwritten, and their names unknown.

In December 1821 *The Pirate* appeared, and was, on the whole, well received. The story, indeed, was extremely improbable, and in many parts not pleasing. Norna was a fantastic character,—Meg Merrilees reproduced, and made ridiculous by her own father. But there was a strong smell of the sea throughout ; and the wild scenery of Shetland was described with picturesque and vivid power. The ancient manners of Ultima Thule were preserved in amber. The characters, as a whole, were admirable,—the Pirates, rough, fresh, and strong, with Cleveland towering above them into a man, if not into a finished hero,—Claud Halcro, capital with his catchword of 'glorious John,' and his fine, spirited songs,—Magnus Troil, genuine heart of Norway fir, true, genial, frank, and noble,—Bryce Snailsfoot, the most hypocritical of professors, and Triptolemus Yellowley, the most ludicrously unfortunate of agricultural improvers. And what a magical effect is produced by the picturesque contrast between the amiable sisters, Minna and Brenda,—one dark, starry, and beautiful as an oriental night, and the other serene and mildly lustrous as a Zetland summer day!

Nothing very remarkable occurred in his history till, in the course of two rainy mornings, he produced *Halidon Hill.* This was at first intended as a contribution to a volume of Poetical Miscellanies Joanna Baillie was projecting in behalf of a friend who had got into deep commercial waters, but, as it expanded beyond his intentions, he published it in a separate volume, and wrote for Miss Baillie instead *MacDuff's Cross.* This small mediocrity of *Halidon Hill* Constable purchased from him at

the price for which, fourteen years before, *Marmion*
had been sold—a thousand pounds!

Byron, meanwhile, had dedicated *Cain* to Scott,
—a poem which the spice of profanity it contains
rendered very unpopular at the time, but which
Scott regarded as one of the grandest of the noble
poet's productions ; certainly it is one of the most
original, and in parts the purest and most plaintive.
In May 1822 *The Fortunes of Nigel* appeared, and
was received in London with much enthusiasm ;
in other places with a kind of sober delight suitable to its general character.   As a picture of an
age, and as a portraiture of James the First, it is
almost perfect.   Alsatia is a unique sketch, as good
as could have come from one of the Elizabethan
dramatists, and with some touches of exquisite
depth and humour, as, where describing the captain and the hedge parson fighting and swearing
at each other, he says, 'A strife in which the
parson's superior acquaintance with theology enabled him greatly to surpass the Captain,' a stroke
worthy of Fielding.   Margaret Ramsay and the
Lady Hermione are both finely drawn and finely
contrasted, and so are Jin Vin and Frank Tunstall.
The three villains, Dalgarno, Captain Culpepper, and
Andrew Skurliewhitter, are all damned to divers
degrees of everlasting infamy with a discrimination

equal to the severity of the sentence. George
Heriot has full and heaped justice done to his
shrewd and benevolent character. The Prince and
Buckingham, too, are vigorously sketched. Nor
must Ritchie Moniplies be forgotten, with his
solemn countenance and coiled-up self-conceit,
dismissed in company,—surely the punishment is
too penal,—with Martha Trapbois, with her long
purse, horrible squint, and vinegar visage. *Nigel*,
in its usually quiet and subdued tone, resembles
one of the tragedies of Lillo ; and its power is as
homely in its elements as commanding in its
results. *Peveril of the Peak* was begun ere *Nigel*
was fully launched ; but whether from rapidity of
production, or some other cause, it ranked far down
in the scale of his Novels,—the first part being intolerably tedious, and the second improbable and
overdone—a long convulsive spasm. Fenella alone
(partly derived from Goethe's Mignon), like a
strange shooting meteor, crosses and relieves the
dulness ; and even she is more distinguished by
oddity than by strength. Yet this romance of
Peveril served to give a new cognomen to Scott.
Patrick Robertson, the famous wit, was busy cracking jests to the younger lawyers, when he saw
Sir Walter approaching. 'Silence, boys, here
comes old Peveril. I see the *Peak*.' Scott's reply

was ready, 'Better Peveril of the Peak any day than Peter with the *painch.*'

Besides various other matters, Scott had found time amidst all this for writing *The Lives of the Novelists* in the big, clumsy series of the Ballantynes, and had written them with consummate skill, taste, and good feeling.

In August 1822 George the Fourth visited Edinburgh; and while Byron was writing with prodigious spirit, and the very sublime of scorn, his *Irish Avatar,* where he satirizes in the bitterest terms the visit the year before of *Fum the Fourth* to Ireland, that land

> ' Which he loved like his bride,'

Scott was moving heaven and earth to secure him a triumphant reception in the northern metropolis. Among a hundred other appliances and means which he was compelled to use, not only to raise, but to direct and control the steam of enthusiasm, he consulted the Muse, and she produced a clever ballad, entitled 'Carle, now the King's come,' in which he flattered with great tact all the parties, particularly the Highland chieftains, who had conflicting claims to precedence in connection with the royal arrival. He employed means more substantial than poetry. He gave sumptuous entertainments, and these had their own conciliating influence. At length, on the 14th of August, we see 'Peveril' and his snowy Peak rowing, through thick rain, to the Royal George, which is riding at anchor in Leith roads. The King is standing on the deck of the yacht, and when told that Scott is alongside, he exclaims, 'What! Sir Walter Scott! the man in Scotland I most wish to see! Let him come up.' Scott then ascended the ship, and, with an appropriate speech, presented His Majesty, in the name of the ladies of Edinburgh, with a St. Andrew's Cross in silver, which the King of course received graciously, and promised to wear in public in gratitude to the fair donors. The 15th, the day of the landing, saw Sir Walter a proud and a busy man. He formed, of course, a prominent object in the procession from Leith to Holyrood, which must have been a magnificent spectacle, although mixed with a good deal of trumpery, with the military element preponderating too much, and certainly not so interesting as when Queen Victoria, on the 3d September 1842, with Albert by her side, rode up from Holyrood to the Castle through multitudes, every heart in which felt the loyalty which the lips were loudly proclaiming; nor so sublime as the Volunteer Review on the 7th August 1860, when the eye of royalty and the loveliest

light of autumn blended in looking down on the
collected might, manhood, and valour of the Scottish nation, and when many an enthusiast felt
Scott's words burning on his tongue,

> ' Where is the coward that would not dare
> To fight for such a land ?'

Two of the remarkable men who witnessed the
procession of 1822 we must single out from the
rest : George Crabbe, who has come from the
Vale of Belvoir to visit Sir Walter, and who stands
amidst the crowd thinking much, saying nothing,
adding not a solitary cheer to the sea of sound
which is roaring on all sides ; and Dr. Chalmers,
who has lifted off his hat from his grand head not
yet grown grey, and is waving it in the air, exclaiming the while, ' God bless him ; he is a fine
fellow.'

We need not dwell on the further particulars of
an event at which Scotland now blushes, and at
nothing more than at the share her greatest son
had in this act of public degradation. At the
time, Sir Walter received a share of attention and
applause only second to the sovereign. Sir Robert
Peel says, ' On the day on which His Majesty
was to pass from Holyrood, Scott proposed to me
to accompany him up the High Street to see

whether the arrangements were completed. I said to him, " You are trying a dangerous experiment ; you will never get through in privacy." He said, " They are entirely absorbed in loyalty." But I was the better prophet. He was recognised from the one extremity of the street to the other ; and never did I see such an instance of national devotion expressed.'

Yet some ludicrous misadventures, along with one serious calamity and one signal mortification, befell Scott during these gala days. When the King received him in his yacht, he ordered a bottle of Highland whisky to be produced, took a glass himself, and made Scott drink another. Scott requested that the King would present him with the glass out of which he had just drunk his health, and proceeded to deposit it in the safest portion of his dress. When he returned to Castle Street, he found Crabbe newly arrived. He saluted him with warmth, and, forgetting all about the King's present, sat down beside him ; the glass perished, and he screamed aloud under the advent of a considerable wound. This was only a scratch. But a day or two after this, his friend Lord Kinneder (William Erskine) died, stung to death by a base calumny, and Scott, on one of the busiest days of the royal visit, attended his funeral, and returning in a most melancholy plight, had to plunge into gaieties, or, 'as Crabbe has it,' said he,

'To hide in rant the heartache of the night.'

There were other circumstances which annoyed him. There was a general rumour that His Majesty did not fully appreciate Scott's services in the visit matters, and that he spoke of him and his everlasting clans and tartans as a bore. Lockhart, indeed, denies this, but some believe it notwithstanding. Mrs. Johnstone, the well-known author of *Clan Albin* and editor of *Tait*, then on the spot, asserted it often in print, and specially insisted on the fact that cards were issued for a royal entertainment at Castle Street, but withdrawn in disgust. If so, the King's conduct was very ungrateful to one who had done so much to gild his stained reputation, and to uphold his tottering throne both by his private and public efforts.

Another dark event blackened still more this August. Lord Castlereagh died by his own hands, it being understood that one cause at least of the sad event was his counsel, like that of Achitophel, having been rejected. He had opposed the royal visit, but opposed it in vain. It seemed the Man's Hand writing prophetic characters of lamen-

tation, mourning, and woe on the wall of a Bel-
shazzar banqueting-room, and

' Made men tremble who never wept.'

In fine, Scott's exertions on this occasion nearly
cost him his life, and, but for the safety-valve of a
prickly eruption on the skin, he would have fallen
a victim to the effects of his sincere but short-
sighted loyalty.   When recovered, he instantly resumed his gigantic labours.

CHAPTER XVII.

SCOTT IN IRELAND.

ON the close of 1822 Scott commenced *Quentin Durward*, but was considerably retarded by his environment with the various clubs,—Bannatyne, Roxburgh, Blair Adam, etc.,—of which he was a member, as well as by his connection with some of those joint-stock companies, such as the Edinburgh Oil Company, which were beginning to spring up like mushrooms around him. The subject was probably suggested to him by the return of his friend Mr. Skene from France, bringing along with him drawings and landscapes of that beautiful land, besides an accurately kept and well-written journal. It was, however, a drawback to the novelist that he had never visited the country himself, and he got at times perplexed and bewildered amidst the localities he was compelled to describe.

In June 1823 the novel appeared, fitly coming
out amidst the blaze and splendour of summer, for
it is one of the gayest and most buoyant of all his
tales. At home it was, strange to tell, not well
received at first, but was welcomed on the Continent with a burst of applause so loud and unanimous, that its spent echo returned on this country
was fame. The power was seen to lie, first of all,
in the youthful freshness breathing out of Quentin
himself, one of the most life-like of all Scott's
heroes ; again, in the unmitigated interest of the
story, and the elastic, easy force of the style ; but
especially in the contrast, drawn out with a line so
long and bold, between the bull-headed Burgundy
and the crafty, cunning, unscrupulous, cruel, and
superstitious Louis XI. Shakspeare in many of
his plays adds a fool to his *dramatis personæ*
as a foil, a wild ornament, and a running commentary. Scott often uses, for a similar purpose,
a villain with a dash of romance in him, and never
with more effect than in Hayraddin Maugrabin the
Bohemian, who is no commonplace town black-
guard, but a poetical ragamuffin, his eye flashing with
a mystic fire, with strange Oriental blasphemies
mingling with unmeasured leasings as they flow
out of his supple yet burning lips, and his swarthy
countenance, seeming to shine, not in the light of

O

sun or moon, but in the weird lustre of the star
Aldeboran, the Cynosure for ages of his wandering
race.   Scott puts into his mouth a 'dying speech,'
but there is no 'confession,' unless it be of his
hardened, hopeless, and glorying atheism.   How
he dashes his daring hand into the waters of an-
nihilation before plunging amidst them !   Danton
alone has equalled the following burst : 'Soul!
Name not that word to me again.   There is, there
can be, there shall be no such thing : it is a dream
of priestcraft.   My hope, trust, and expectation is
that the mysterious frame of humanity shall melt
into the general mass of nature, to be recom-
pounded in the other forms with which she daily
supplies those which daily disappear, and return
under different forms, — the watery particles to
streams and showers, the earthy parts to enrich
their mother earth, the airy portions to wanton in
the breeze, and those of fire to supply the blaze of
Aldeboran and his brethren.   In this faith have I
lived, and in this faith shall I die !'

In August 1823 Abbotsford was brightened still
more by the presence of Miss Edgeworth ; and a
most delightful reunion took place between two
spirits who, notwithstanding great disparity of
genius, resembled each other in nature, simplicity,
healthiness, humour, good sense, and the power of

painting the manners of primitive races. The
harvest moon of that beautiful season saw no
happier hearts,

'In all that slept beneath her soft voluptuous ray,'

than hers who produced *Castle Rackrent* and
Ennui, and his who had equalled if not surpassed
them both in *Waverley* and *Guy Mannering*. It
was a fortnight of unmingled felicity to them, and
the whole party circling round them.

About the middle of December Scott published
St. Ronan's Well, where, again, the old layer of
weak and commonplace matter made its appearance, and that so prominently, that not the most
forcible writing in parts was able to counteract its
influence. As in the story, the hostelry of Meg
Dodds was injured by the tawdry modern hotel
with its gimcrack inhabitants. The villain of the
tale was *too bad*, and as mean as he was detestable;
and the termination was painfully tragic. There
was no tedium, however, in the slip-slop matter,
and the power of the master came out ever and
anon in all its plenitude. Indeed, the characters of
this novel are wonderfully fresh and numerous.
There is Meg Dodds herself, the queen of alehouse-
keepers, the lady of *Luckies*, the modern and more
than Mrs. Quickly; Clara Mowbray, the very

crack, in whose mirror-like mind follows always
the waving line of beauty, and whose death is so
overpoweringly pathetic ; Touchwood, that noble
old Nabob ; Captain MacTurk, with his short red
nose, snuffing Glenlivet or gunpowder in every
wind, and fearing the broom of Meg Dodds more
than a whole battery of cannon ; the melancholy
Tyrrell ; Joseph Cargill, the sad, gifted, amiable,
dreaming recluse ; Solmes, the double-faced sombre
scoundrel ; Mucklewham, the well-named *doer*, or
man of Scottish business in the past age ; the
odd urchin who crosses Tekyll on his way to the
well ; Bindloose, the wary banker ; the old hump-
backed postilion, who (a thing Thomas Aird
specially notices), when Tyrrell, who had been
thought dead, reappears, flees into the stable, and
—a touch of quite Shakspearean verisimilitude—
begins in the extremity of his terror to *saddle a
horse;* and last, not least, the inimitable Widow
Blower, changing Dr. Quackleben's name at every
second sentence, and at last changing her own, and
becoming *Mrs.* Quackleben, and who is led to the
nuptial altar like a fat hog to sacrifice, rejoicing
in her fillet ‘ braws.’ ¦Such variety and richness
of character found in one of Scott's second-class
novels is something quite wonderful. The village
of Inverleithen, although not at all like St. Ronan's

in the main features of its scenery, eagerly claimed the name ; and the St. Ronan's Games were formed, and continued long to be celebrated there, being usually followed by a dinner, at which such men as Hogg, Lockhart, and Professor Wilson were the presiding spirits.

1824 produced but one novel, *Redgauntlet,*—a novel where, unlike the former, all the separate parts in point of writing are excellent, but do not blend happily into a whole. The book is an awkward compound of narrative and correspondence. Of Charles Stuart brought again into the play we cry,—

' Superfluous lags the veteran on the stage,'

and are tempted to hiss him off as a solemn, pompous noodle. Others of the characters are failures. Dairsie Latimer is, begging his pardon, a donkey ; Allan Fairford a prig ; Redgauntlet himself a spasmodic abortion ; Lilias a doll ; Pate in Peril an incident rather than a character ; Fairford's father too stiff and formal ; Crystal Nixon a villain pure and simple, almost the only villain in all Scott's Novels without a single redeeming trait ; old Tom Trumbull a hideous, incredible hypocrite ; and Joshua Geddes the driest of all dry Quakers. But Peter Peebles, with thy tow wig, thy everlasting lawsuit, and thine insatiable thirst, and Nanty Ewart, with thy sunburnt face, eyes shot with bile and blood, wasted constitution, and broken heart, ye must live for ever. And so, too, shall the boy Benjie and Wandering Willy, and that ancestor of his, riding 'bauld wi' brandy and desperate with distress' through the black wood of Pitmurkie, and forgathering there with the terrible stranger, who takes him to the mouth of hell and a step farther. Indeed, the whole of 'Wandering Willy's Tale' is Shakspearean in power of imagination and graphic ease of description.

Redgauntlet was rather a disappointment at the time, and, whether for this reason or not, no other novel appeared this year. Scott, however, found for himself full employment in furnishing his library and museum, painting his house, corresponding with his many friends, speaking at the opening of the New Edinburgh Academy,—an academy which has since produced so many fine scholars, and been presided over by such able teachers: need we name among the former the Archbishop of Canterbury and Robertson of Brighton, and among the latter Archdeacon Williams, Carmichael, and MacDougall,—writing an epitaph on his favourite dog Maida, and watching with a poet's eye the red billows of that terrible fire which, in November, reduced so many of the old buildings of Edinburgh to ashes. This year died Byron; and Sir Walter wrote, in the *Edinburgh Weekly Journal*, a generous and glowing tribute to his memory, which ranks in eloquence, if not in exquisite delicacy, with those testimonials paid by Jeffrey to Playfair and to James Watt immediately after their deaths, and which contains one very noble image. Alluding to Byron's faults, and to his early and sudden death, Scott says, 'It is as if the great orb of day were to disappear for ever from our view while *we were busy looking through our telescopes at the spots which bedimmed its lustre.'* This would have been as true as it is sublime a few years before; but at the time referred to men were rather gazing at the sun throwing off an eclipse which had been strangling his beams, and now, with the last speck of the darkness, the luminary himself had vanished. This tribute of Scott only expressed the universal feeling at the time. No death, unless that of the Princess Charlotte or Prince Albert, ever produced such a wide sensation as that of Lord Byron. It seemed to stun the very heart of the world. Enthusiasts in Greece, who were flocking to his standard, when they heard that the Pilgrim of Eternity had departed, turned back and went homewards.

Poets and literary men in all countries of the
earth, from the patriarch Goethe to the youngest
rhymster, vied with each other in pouring out
tributes to his memory, which had one unquestionable merit—they were all sincere. Old men in
London, Edinburgh, and Glasgow wept; and boys
on the verge of the Perthshire Highlands stood
dumb and awestruck at the tidings, as if an earthquake were shaking their native vale. Many
blamed destiny for his death; many the Grecian
war; none, at this time, the unhappy victim himself. Death seemed to have expiated all his
offences; and that 'late remorse of love' which he
had predicted was seen shedding tears and sowing
laurels over his early grave. Thus, in the main,
for five or six years, it continued till the year 1830,
when Moore's *Life* awoke a fresh gush of interest in
his memory, and Lady Byron, no doubt under considerable provocation, stepped forward and uttered—
what? a hint, an insinuation, a whisper; but a hint
of the most damning character,—an insinuation of
the most deadly and damaging kind,—a whisper,
methinks, resembling that of which Coleridge in
his *Mariner* speaks,—

> 'A wicked whisper came, and made
> Their hearts as dry as dust.'

And we need hardly mention how Mrs. Stowe

came out lately with her *True Story*, opening up
all the old sluices of slander, and giving to the hint-
whispers airy-nothing—foul gas of Lady Byron's
document a 'local habitation and a name,'—a rash
and rank embodiment. On this subject we shall
say no more than this, that Scott, from his letters,
seems to have known the very worst about Byron;
and yet, though he says of some things he heard
about him, 'Premat alta nox,' he continued to
love, admire, and defend him, while lamenting that
he was a *Genie mal logé*,—words we may translate
into, 'Byron was an Apollo saddled with a lame
foot, a bad temper, a bilious temperament, a
foolish mother, and the passions of a demoniac;
but, notwithstanding all his infirmities, vices, and
misfortunes, the scion of a celestial race,—an
erring man, or fallen angel if you will, but not a
monster.'

1825 began gaily with Scott; and in February
his son Walter married Miss Jobson, the heiress
of Lochore, in Fife,—the young couple repairing,
after the marriage, to the bridegroom's regimental
quarters in Ireland, where Sir Walter promised
to visit them in the summer. The *Tales of the
Crusaders* appeared in June. *The Betrothed* was
good in the commencement, and powerful near
the close. The hawking scene at the Red Pool

is in Scott's best style, but much of it was tedious
and drawling; and the novel, as a whole, had too
much of that old wives' fable shape, in which,
alas, like the *formosa mulier* of Horace, ending in
atrum piscem, his unequalled story-telling power
was doomed to degenerate. But *The Talisman*
was received nearly as *Ivanhoe* had been. Enchantment and elaborate finish were never more
thoroughly united than in this tale, which Wilson
has pronounced Scott's *only* artistic whole, and
which drew from Mrs. Hemans, after spending
some delightful hours reading it in her garden,
one of her sweetest minor strains. About this
time Archibald Constable projected his famous
Miscellany; and it was agreed that one-half of
a cheap issue of *Waverley* should begin the
series, and be followed by a *Life of Napoleon*, in
four parts, by the author of *Waverley*. To this
Scott jocularly alludes in the introduction to
The Crusaders. And no sooner was the scheme
started than he commenced, with characteristic
promptitude, the preliminary sketch of the French
Revolution.

On the 8th of July he set out, along with Lockhart, for Ireland. He went there to see his son,
to visit Miss Edgeworth, and to gratify the warm-
hearted people of that country. They sailed down

the Firth of Clyde, where Scott got very gracious with a Glasgow bailie,—a veritable Nicol Jarvie; and as they were drinking their rum punch, told him an amusing story about Thom of Govan, a witty divine of the last century, who once preached before the Town Council of Glasgow from the words, 'Ephraim's drink is sour, and he hath committed whoredom continually;' on which the bailie groaned, and said that he doubted 'Tham o' Govan was at heart a ne'er-do-weel.' They crossed to Belfast, paying *a guinea* each for the passage across. On their way to Dublin they halted at Drogheda, where Scott visited the field of the battle of the Boyne, and recited to an astonished veteran who accompanied him the famous ballad, *The Crossing of the Water.* Arrived, they went to Walter's house; and Scott looked round with joy and pride as he first sat at his son's table. Most people will remember with what a peculiar feeling they first sat at their own; but this was a purer emotion, and is well likened by Lockhart to a passage in *Pindar,* where, in order to paint the highest rapture of happiness, he represents an old man, with a foaming wine-cup in his hand, at his child's wedding-feast. So soon as his arrival in Dublin was known, he received every possible attention, both in public and private. When recognised in the street, and when visiting the theatre, he was received with loud huzzas; indeed, the enthusiasm was so great, that it scandalized the worthy Glasgow bailie, who said it was 'owre like worshipping the creature.' This is only a specimen of the droll stories with which this Irish excursion characteristically abounded. A college librarian said to Scott, 'I have been so busy that I have not read *your Redgauntlet.*' 'I have not happened to fall in with such a work,' was Scott's quiet reply. A female guide had shown him and his party some of the usual show-scenes; when he was gone, a gentleman told her he was a poet. 'Poet,' said she, 'divil a bit of him, but an honourable gentleman; he gave me half-a-crown.' On one occasion he gave a fellow a shilling when sixpence was the fee. 'Remember you owe me sixpence, Pat.' 'May your honour live till I pay you.' All Pat's clothes would have been dearly bought at the sum.

After visiting Wicklow and its romantic and famous spots, he went to Edgeworthstown, where he renewed his friendship with the gifted Maria; and she, with tears in her eyes, agreed with him when he said that all things were moonshine when compared to the education of the heart. He rebuked there one of his daughters, who was despising something as vulgar. 'What is vulgar? it is only common; and nothing that is common, except wickedness, can deserve to be spoken of with contempt.'

A mad poet amused him much, named O'Kelly, who, calling on Scott, inflicted on him the lines:

> ' Three poets, of three different nations born,
> The United Kingdom in this age adorn :
> Byron of England, Scott of Scotland's blood,
> And Erin's pride, O'Kelly great and good.'

Scott needed all these little ludicrous interludes to support his spirits under the sight of the ruined country he found Ireland to be. He visited Killarney, Cork, the Groves of Blarney, Fermoy, Lismore, Kilkenny, etc., and returned to Dublin, his whole journey being a procession of triumph; deputations meeting him at the entrance of every town, and crowds attending him all through the streets; saluted everywhere as the monarch man of the time. Yet he seems to have left the Green Isle without regret.

He returned home by the Cumberland Lakes. There took place one of the most brilliant reunions and regattas which even that classical region ever witnessed. Seldom have so many eminent men met in such favourable circumstances, as in August 1825, under Mr Bolton's roof-tree, and on the banks of Windermere. There was Canning, pale in cheek, and with the winding-sheet already well up his breast, but with his genius as lively, his eye as bright, and his brow as commanding as ever. There was Wordsworth, stooping, not yet under the load of years, but of that brooding thought and inverted reverence with which, all his life, he had admired the 'ground out of which he was taken,' and

'Worshipped Nature with a thought profound.'

There, in the prime of his majestic manhood, was Christopher North, probably by gifts, if not by culture or achievements, a greater man than any of them all; in *appearance* unquestionably the first,— the facsimile of Scott's own Cœur de Lion, but more anxious to obtain fame as the Admiral of the Lake than as a world-poet, critic, or humorist. There was Lockhart, certainly one of the cleverest and sharpest of men, if not quite on the level of his companions. And there the Mighty Minstrel, flushed with his Irish reception, with the success of the *Talisman,* and with the projected *Life of Napoleon,* spent his last thoroughly triumphant days. Ah! little thought he they were the last. Yet there was no undue or ominous elation; and when he returned to Abbotsford, he sat quietly down to his labours connected with the Life of the Emperor, and to his usual routine of country business and country pleasures.

CHAPTER XVIII.

DECAY AND DECADENCE BEGUN.

SCOTT was now fifty-four, an age when many men are at their very best, with the strength of their bodies unimpaired, and the faculties of their minds in full vigour. But ever since the attack of cramp his constitution was not so strong as it seemed; and he had, besides, complained of what he calls a 'thickening of the blood, or whoreson apoplexy,' the disease of which he ultimately died, and to which he attributed the dulness of *Peveril*. And Lockhart hints that attacks of this sort occurred now and then before his terrible seizure in 1830. But the angel of disease at present suspended his blow, and left other ministers of ruin to do their work instead.

His labour in the preparation of *Napoleon* was of a very different kind from that of his Novels. These required no previous study,—*that* had been the work of the first half of his life ; but for the other he had to consult authorities and pore over note-books, so that we may venture to say that he had to read as much for a single page in the *Napoleon* as for a whole volume in the *Waverley* series. When we looked through the library in Abbotsford some years ago, and saw the shelves crowded with folio *Moniteurs*, we said, ' These are the great French guns which laid the flower of Scotchmen low.' When he came to the work of original composition, he came well crammed, no doubt, but jaded, with an aching brow and a dim eye ; and his writing, though generally spirited, was often hasty and careless.

During the latter months of 1825 Scott entertained some distinguished visitors,—among others, Lord Gifford and his lady, Harry of Exeter, and, above all, Tom Moore, who had expressed his regret that he was not present when Scott and Killarney were introduced to each other,—a regal interview verily worth not only seeing, but, as Dr. Johnson used to distinguish, ' going to see.' The conjunction of Moore and Scott itself must have been an interesting sight—the delicious butterfly-bard of Erin, carrying, however, what butterflies do not, a bag of highly concentrated venom and a sharp and polished sting ; the slight, dapper little

P

person, looking insignificant till you noticed 'The Twopenny Post Bag' and other such dangerous explosives slung around him,—the dainty and fastidious darling of society,—the Hafiz Anacreon Catullus of his day,—the pungent morsel of a man, like Mustard Seed in the *Midsummer Night's Dream*, meeting with the brawny poet and novelist of Scotland, with his white hair, sagacious face, tall figure, and Matterhorn-like forehead; Moore in his walks armed with a smart Malacca cane—Scott with a sturdy oak plant, which Friar Tuck might have flourished; Moore at table sipping his French wines, and Scott imbibing his mountain dew; Moore warbling his *Irish Melodies* with the 'treble of a fay'—Scott adding his rough and tuneless but hearty chorus, with voice like a Westphalian boar; and yet both delighted with each other, and connected, like Goldsmith's Dwarf and Giant, in close offensive and defensive league. They had much common ground, were both intimate friends of Byron, both patriotic poets, both men who combined great enthusiasm with great common sense and a thorough knowledge of the ways of society, including the upper and the lower orders alike, and were both kindly and generous men. Moore kept a diary while there, and sent it to Lockhart, with the additional words, 'I parted from Scott with the feeling that all the world might admire him in his works, but that those only could learn to love him as he deserved who had seen him at Abbotsford.' Of course you never can *thoroughly* understand any man, or love him with sufficient warmth, till you have known him in private ; but it is the peculiarity of Scott's works that they compel you, not only to admire the author, but to love the man, and make all his readers feel as if they, like Mr. Moore, *had been* at Abbotsford.   Moore adds : ' I give you *carte blanche* to say what you please of my sense of his cordial kindness and gentleness ; perhaps a not very dignified phrase would express my feeling better than any fine one,—it was that he was a *thorough* good fellow.' This we may know and say without having lived a while with the Great Unknown. Every page of his works proves it ; and especially every character in his Novels into whom he has thrown his whole soul, such as the Baron of Bradwardine, Paulus Pleydell, Esq., Dandie Dinmont, Jonathan Oldbuck, Bailie Nicol Jarvie, John Duke of Argyle, Robin Hood, Rob Roy ; and Richard Cœur de Lion is, like his creator, a *thorough good* fellow.

Scott astonished Moore by revealing to him, without reserve, that he was the author of the Waverley Novels. The mask had been long worn ; he was beginning to tire of it; he wore it now carelessly, and, alas! did not know that his dropping it, like the dropping of the glass mask to his own Alascor, was to be the signal of doom. It was not in expectation of the ruin which was at hand, rendering concealment impossible, but in mere gaiety and triumph, that he mentioned the Novels to Moore as his own, and spoke of them as a source of great wealth; yet he added that he was not making them so good as he used to do. The two thorough *good fellows* parted, as Scott said to the other, 'friends for life.'

After Moore came Mrs. Coutts, the famous banker's widow, afterwards Duchess of St Alban's, whom Scott treated with high respect, partly because his high-born guests were disposed to *cut* her for her vulgarity, and Scott did not, as he said, recognise that word as English; and partly because, with a feeling seemingly opposite to this, he had a profound reverence for the distinction of wealth, as well as for other of the world's distinctions. This certainly was a weakness, but it were useless to hide it,—more useless still to seek to apologize for it, any more than for the wart on the brow of a noble-looking man, or the cast in the eye of a beautiful woman. Scott could afford a hundred weak points, and he had not ten.

At this time mutterings of the great commercial storm of 1825–26, so soon to break upon the country with unprecedented violence, began to startle even the echoes of Abbotsford. Pope says,—

'Now a bubble bursts, and now a world.'

But the bubble about to burst *was* a world. It had attained the most gigantic proportions, and shone with the most glittering hues. Speculation had, in joint-stock schemes, companies, mining adventures, wind bills, wild and visionary projects of every sort, come to its height, and, as it could neither climb farther nor stop where it was, it must come down, and with a vengeance. Lockhart, then in London, heard that the crash was at hand,—that the trade, and even Constable, was in danger. He hurried down to Chiefswood and told Scott his fears. Scott derided them at first, but, on reflection, ordered his carriage and rode over to Polton, where Constable dwelt, and was reassured for the time by the publisher's statement. The tempest, however, was only delayed for a season.

Napoleon, meanwhile, was in progress ; but sometimes Scott felt fagged with the researches necessary for it, and, in order to fill up the intervals of time when his historic 'line laboured and his words moved slow,' he began a journal in imitation of Byron's Ravenna Diary, with a transcript of which Murray had presented Lockhart, and Lockhart showed to Scott. Each is very characteristic of each poet. Byron's is reckless, rapid, careless in style, but extremely vivid in many of its touches, and has an air of thorough honesty throughout, although you think of a great mind going to pieces like a ship in a storm-drift. We are afraid that the keeping of a diary is, in most instances, a morbid symptom, and imagine that Scott, in the prime of his powers, would have disdained the collecting of such a dish of orts and leavings. Still his Journal is intensely interesting, and reveals, better than any biographical statement could do, the hidden man, or rather woman, of his heart,—the amiable weaknesses, the old sores and unforgotten sorrows, the palpitations of spirit, and incipient frailty of brain which the brave man concealed from the world under a firm and almost stern outward deportment.

Even this did not afford his active mind a sufficient employment. At the suggestion of Constable, who knew that Scott used sometimes to carry on two romances abreast, and who was anxious that every minute of such valuable time should be occupied, he commenced another novel, to be taken up whenever *Napoleon* was standing

still and the Journal found inadequate. Hence
Woodstock was begun.

Scott's fortunes were now nearing the edge of a
precipice. He knew it not. We of course do,
and are disposed to linger before describing in the
next chapter the terrible downfall ; and therefore
we may spend the rest of this in culling, upon the
verge, a few flowers, and thistles too, from his
Journal, which is full throughout of matter, although it is a matter which gets drearier and
darker every page.

He finds one reason of his rapid intimacy with
Moore in the fact, 'We are both good-humoured
fellows, who rather seek to enjoy what is going
forward than to maintain our dignity as lions ; and
we have both seen the world too widely and too
well not to contemn in our souls the imaginary
consequence of literary people who walk with their
noses in' the air, and remind me always of the
fellow whom Johnson met in an alehouse, and
who called himself the " Great Twalmly, inventor
of the floodgate iron for smoothing linen !"'

Here is a hint of his weakening constitution :
'My pleasure is in the simplest diet. Wine I seldom taste when alone, and use instead a little
spirits and water. I have of late diminished the
quantity, for fear of a weakness inductive to a dia-

betes,—a disease which broke up my father's
health, though one of the most temperate men
that ever lived.'

Here is his estimate, not too severe, of the late
Ugo Foscolo : ' Ugly as a baboon, and intolerably
conceited, he spluttered, blustered, and disputed
without even knowing the principles on which men
of sense render a reason, and screamed all the
while like a pig with a knife at his throat.' The
same Ugo seems, like Shelley's Sensitive Plant, to
have ' desired what he had not—the beautiful ;' for
we find one of his biographers describing him
as surrounded in his lodgings by three lovely
young women, hovering between servants and mis-
tresses,—a Satyr attended by three Graces ! Yet
he was a scholar and a poet.

Here we find Scott in an ominous fix. ' I had
a bad fall last night coming home. There were
unfinished houses at the east end of Athole Crescent, and, as I was on foot, I crossed the street to
avoid the materials which lay about, but, deceived
by the moonlight, I slipped ankle-deep into a sea of
mud (honest earth and water, thank God !), and
fell on my hands. Never was there such a representative of "Wall" in *Pyramus and Thisbe.* I
was absolutely rough-cast.' To T. S. Gillies he
thus described what was probably the same acci-

dent : 'One moonlight night I found Sir Walter standing in a newly-built street, apparently in a deep reverie. "I was considering," he said, "what it is best to do. I have been at one party, and was engaged to another; but look at these habiliments! It happened by a most ludicrous chance, and to my own very great surprise, that I found myself a few minutes ago lying at the bottom of a wet gravel-pit, from which I have just emerged; and I believe it is indispensable to steer homewards and *refit*, otherwise the whole discourse at Lady ———'s *rout* will consist of explanations why the unfortunate *lion* appears in such bad condition." And at this he laughed heartily.' His lameness began to get worse; but that, too, he bore with the same equanimity that he did such penalties of popularity as he specifies in the following: 'People make me the oddest requests. It is not unusual for an Oxonian or Cantab, who has outrun his allowance, and of whom I know nothing, to apply to me for the loan of £20, £50, or £100. A captain of the Danish naval service writes to me that, being in distress for a sum of money by which he might transport himself to Columbia to offer his services in assisting to free that province, he had dreamed I had generously made him a present of it. I can tell him his dream by contraries. I begin to find, like Joseph Surface, that a good character is inconvenient.'

The next is a kindly notice of poor William Knox, a nearly forgotten poet: 'A young poet of considerable talent died here a week or two ago. His father was a respectable yeoman; and he himself, succeeding to good farms, became too soon his master, and plunged into dissipation and ruin. His talent then showed itself in a fine strain of pensive poetry, called, I think, *The Lonely Hearth*, far superior to that of Michael Bruce, whose *consumption*, by the way, has been the *life* of his poems. I had Knox at Abbotsford, but found him unfit for that sort of society. He scrambled on writing for booksellers, and living like the Otways and Savages of former days. His last works were spiritual hymns, which he wrote very well.' Scott was very friendly to Knox, and sometimes sent him £10 at a time. We are familiar with some of his Biblical verses, which are sweet and sad, and resemble, at times, in his own words,

> 'The harp-strings' holiest measures,
> When dreams the soul of lands of rest
> And everlasting pleasures.'

Here is a characteristic touch: ' A stormy and rainy day. Walk it from the Court through the

rain. I like this ; for no man that ever stepped
on heather has less dread than I of the catch-cold,
and I seem to regain, in buffeting with the wind,
some of the high spirits with which in younger
days I used to enjoy a Tam o' Shanter ride
through darkness, wind, and rain, the boughs
groaning and cracking over my head, the good
horse free to the road, and impatient for home.'
Premature senility, nevertheless, comes out in the
following optical delusion : 'When I have laid
aside my spectacles to step into a room dimly
lighted out of the strong light which I use for
writing, I have seen, or seemed to see, through
the rims of the same spectacles I have left behind
me,—nay, at first put up my hands to my eyes,
believing that I had the actual spectacles on.'

Mingled with the following fine passage, the
last we shall quote here, we fancy a certain dim
foreboding or prevision of calamity : 'There is
nothing more awful than to attempt to cast a
glance among the clouds and mists which hide
the broken extremity of the celebrated Bridge
of Mirza. Yet when every day brings us nigher
that termination, we would almost think our
views should become clearer. Alas! it is not so.
There is a curtain to be withdrawn, a veil to be
rent, before we shall see things as they really

are. With the belief of a Deity, the immortality of the soul and of the state of rewards and punishments is indissolubly linked. More we are not to know; but neither are we prohibited from all attempts, however vain, to pierce the solemn, sacred gloom. The expressions used in Scripture are doubtless metaphorical; for penal fires and heavenly melody are only applicable to beings endowed with corporeal senses. Harmony is obviously chosen as the least corporeal of all gratifications of the senses, and as the type of love, unity, and a state of peace and perfect happiness. But they have a poor idea of the Deity, and the rewards destined for the just made perfect, who can only adopt the literal sense of an eternal concert, a never-ending birthday ode. I rather suppose this should be understood as some commission from the Highest, some duty to discharge, with the applause of a satisfied conscience.'

Lockhart says that Wilson might have been the best preacher of the age. We think that, in that department, had both *tried* it, as well as in poetry and novels, North would have had a dangerous rival in Scott.

CHAPTER XIX.

UNIVERSAL SMASH.

UT now, as Lockhart has it, 'the muffled drum was in prospect.' The fabric of prosperity which Scott had reared with such prodigious labour, and which seemed to him and others solid as Ben Nevis, was about to sink like a castle in the clouds, and to leave to the architect only the reality of ruin. We have neither inclination nor sufficient knowledge of the ways of business to dilate at large on the particular causes and circumstances of the well-known catastrophe. A few remarks, founded on a perusal of the documents on both sides of the controversy excited by Lockhart's *Life*, may, however, be adventured. Scott, as we saw before, had established a business as a printer and bookseller in connection with the Ballantynes. Owing to various causes, the bookselling firm was utterly unsuccessful. When wound

up, a vast amount of useless stock had been
accumulated ; but this, by successive forced sales
to Constable and others, Scott ultimately cleared
off, and so paid the debts of the concern in full.

After John Ballantyne's death, James Ballantyne
and Scott entered into a new partnership, James,
besides, acting as Scott's agent in procuring and
paying money, which was accomplished, as is
well known, by means of bills drawn for literary
work done, or even *to be done*, by Scott for the
booksellers, but very frequently also by recourse
to mere accommodation bills.   The enormous
expense of this system, the extravagance of Sir
Walter's building schemes and style of living,
the diminished sale and over-multiplied editions
of the novels, and the complications of the whole
business with Constable's firm, on whom most of
these bills were drawn, paved the way for the
tremendous smash, which was precipitated by a
great commercial panic,—a panic in which the
Bank of England itself shook like an oak in a
tempest,—so that, on the failure of Hurst & Co.
and Constable, which became certain on the 16th
of January 1826, Scott found himself a debtor to
the extent of about £120,000, besides a personal
debt of £10,000.

In addition to this very general outline of the

facts, there are two or three points to be noticed. In the first place, when Scott entered into partnership with the two Ballantynes, there was unquestionably a certain inequality between the parties, Scott bringing not only (after a short while) more capital into the firm, but immense literary influence, which procured a copious supply of work for the Ballantyne press. Still, secondly, the minor parties were by no means so inferior to Scott as Lockhart pretends. James Ballantyne brought some capital, and great talent both as a printer and *litterateur*, to the business. John had pleasant manners, accomplishments, vivacity, and enthusiasm; and both had unbounded attachment to Scott. Thirdly, Scott undoubtedly, as he had the chief share in raising, had also the chief share in ruining the original firm, effecting this by a number of unsaleable publications, partly his own, but chiefly by other hands, such as an ill-edited edition of *Beaumont and Fletcher*, a cumbrously got-up series of *British Novelists*, which Scott's interesting lives were not able to float, an able but heavy *History of the Culdees*, and the like. Fourthly, to stem the torrent of disaster he had himself in a great measure let loose, Scott manfully and nobly strove; and to the failure of John Ballantyne and Co. we owe some of the finest of his poems. Fifthly,

Lockhart has in vain pretended that Scott was in-
attentive to business, a 'magician wrapt in mists,'
and so forth. The facts that he demanded in one
instance *fifteen per cent.* for a sum of money he lent
to the firm ; that he forced off, as we have seen,
John Ballantyne and Co.'s bad stock upon Constable and other booksellers with whom he had
transactions ; and that, notwithstanding his intricate
and enormous money connections with James Ballantyne, he (although with no dishonourable purpose), *without* his knowledge, alienated his estate,
mansion, etc., and settled them in 1825 upon his
eldest son ;—these facts, and the whole tenor of his
correspondence, prove, to say the least, a most minute
and lynx-eyed, if not a self-seeking attention to his
own personal interests,—more, certainly, than you
might have expected in a poet. While, sixthly, not
freeing the Ballantynes from blame in point of im-
prudence and extravagance, they were in these
respects left far behind by their illustrious partner,
whose love for family aggrandisement, and whose
passion for accumulating land, and for baronial
hospitality, amounted to a degree of derangement.
And, finally, whatever may be thought of the
relative shares of fault contracted by the different
parties in these complicated transactions, there can,
we fear, be but one opinion as to the conduct of

Scott's biographer. None but a Lockhart, the un-
genial son-in-law of a most genial sire, could or
durst defend a Lockhart's conduct in seeking to
blast with scorn two men whom Scott had honoured
with his confidence and affection ; who had shared
in his success ; one, and, in a measure, both of whom
had been ruined through their connection with him,
and who idolized as well as materially served him.
He that allows the biographer to be swallowed up
in the satirist, who pollutes the stream of the record
of a great man's life by foul and gratuitous personalities, may be compared to the Oriental despot
who offers up all the kindred of a deceased king as
a propitiation to his Manes. Now Lockhart has
done all this. In his reply to the first pamphlet
published by the trustees of James Ballantyne, his
usual talent deserts him, while it abounds in more
than his usual hauteur ; the reasoning is as feeble as
the language is coarse ; and his whole spirit reminds
you of that of a pampered menial, who uses liberties
of insolent language which his master would dis-
dain. From the whole subject we may draw the
conclusion, that the less a man of genius, however
acute, entangles himself in the complications of
this world's affairs, the better for his peace and
prosperity.

It is painful to watch the shadow of disaster

Q

slowly gaining upon the great orb, and to see every
inch of the observation registered in his Journal.
In vain did Constable make every effort to keep
off the ruin, 'searching impossible places,' like Ford
in the *Merry Wives*, proposing impossible measures,
rushing to London, and there fretting, fuming,
and plunging about in downright desperation.
Scott must, on the 16th of January 1826, write
thus : 'Came through cold roads to as cold news.
Hurst & Robinson have suffered a bill to come
back upon Constable, which I suppose infers the
ruin of both houses.' He went that evening to
dine with Mr. Skene, and appeared in his usual
spirits. On going away, he whispered to his host
to call on him next morning, as he had something
to say to him. Skene called accordingly, and
found Sir Walter writing in his study. He rose
and said, 'My friend, give me a grasp of your
hand ; mine is that of a beggar.' He was working
at *Woodstock* ere he made this declaration ; and
when Skene went away, he resumed it. And during
that dark week, in which every post brought him
tidings of some new calamity, he wrote several
chapters of the novel.

His mind was speedily made up. Instead of
declaring himself bankrupt, as he might have
done, he determined by his own exertions alone to

liquidate all the bills accepted by Constable & Co., and bearing his indorsation. He said, 'My own right hand shall pay my debts.' He surrendered everything to his creditors. He reduced his establishment, left dear old Castle Street, and took a lodging in St. David Street. With a quietness and depth of resolution almost unparalleled, he sat down under the darkened sky of his fortunes, and proceeded, with a constitution prematurely old, a heart wounded, and a brain partially enfeebled, to execute his vast literary projects. He had, besides, insured his life in favour of his creditors for £25,000, and signed a trust-deed over his own effects at Abbotsford, including an obligation to pay in cash a certain sum annually until the debts were liquidated.

In all this he met with great and all but universal sympathy. A few, indeed, of his creditors grumbled, and were disposed to recalcitrate, and some cantankerous persons out of that circle joined with them in this ; but the majority were kind and generous. Some people of wealth made him munificent offers of help, which he respectfully but most decidedly declined ; and the feeling of the general public on the subject was healthy, and in a high measure kind. 'The author of *Waverley* ruined!' cried the Earl of Dudley. 'Good

God ! let every man to whom he has given months of delight give him a sixpence, and he will rise to-morrow morning richer than Rothschild.'

During the crisis his Journal is full of melancholy entries. It, in fact, formed the safety-valve to those wretched feelings which he was able to conceal from the world under a look of stern and silent magnanimity. He says: 'I have walked my last on the domains I planted, sat the last time in the halls I have built. My poor people, whom I loved so well! There is just another die to turn up against me in this run of ill-luck. If I should break my magic wand in the fall from the elephant, and lose my popularity with my fortune, then *Woodstock* and *Boney* (Napoleon) may both go to the paper-maker, and I may take to smoking cigars and drinking grog, or turn devotee, and intoxicate my brain another way. In prospect of absolute ruin, I wonder if they would let me leave the Court of Session. I would like, methinks, to go abroad,

> " And lay my bones far from the Tweed."

But I find my eyes moistening, and that will not do.'

Again : ' I have a funeral letter to the burial of Chevalier Yelin, a foreigner of learning and talent, who has died at the Royal Hotel. He wished to be introduced to me, and was to have read a paper at the Royal Society, where this introduction was to have taken place. I was not at the Society that evening, and the poor gentleman was taken ill at the meeting and unable to proceed. He went to his bed, and never rose again ; and now his funeral will be the first public place I shall appear at. He dead, and I ruined : this is what you call a meeting.'

He thus describes his first visit to the Court after his downfall : ' I went to the Court for the first time to-day, and, like the man with the large nose, thought everybody was thinking of me and my mishaps. Many were undoubtedly, and all rather regrettingly, some obviously affected. Some smiled as they wished me good-day, as if to say, " Think nothing about it, my lad ; it is quite out of *our* thoughts." Others greeted me with the affected gravity which one sees and despises at a funeral. The best bred just shook hands and passed on.'

In reference to the meeting of his creditors he speaks in the following terms of his ancient and successful rival in love : ' Sir William Forbes took the chair, and behaved as he has ever done, with the generosity of ancient faith and early friendship.

That house is more deeply concerned than most.
In what scenes have Sir William and I not borne
share together!—desperate and almost bloody
affrays, rivalries, deep drinking matches; and,
finally, with the kindliest feelings on both sides,
somewhat separated by his retiring much within
the bosom of his family, and I moving little beyond
mine. It is fated our planets should cross, though,
and that at the periods most interesting to me.
Down, down—a hundred thoughts.' The following will be understood and felt by many: 'Have
set to work to clear away papers and pack them
up for my journey. What a strange medley of
thoughts such a task produces! There lie letters,
which made the heart throb when received, now
lifeless and uninteresting, as are, perhaps, their
writers; riddles which have been read; schemes
which time has destroyed or brought to maturity;
memorials of friendships and enmities which are
now alike faded. Thus does the ring of Saturn
consume itself. To-day annihilates yesterday.'

Calamities, like crows, fly in crowds. And this
poor Sir Walter Scott now felt in his experience.
His favourite grandson, John Hugh Lockhart,
became unwell of the illness from which he never
recovered. And, to put the copestone on all, his
poor wife, who had long suffered under nervous

irritation, died at Abbotsford on the 15th of May. He was in Edinburgh at the time, but had visited her a few days before, and on the tidings of her death returned instantly. He describes his feelings as sometimes firm as the Bass Rock, and sometimes weak as the water that breaks on it. 'It is not,' he says, ' my Charlotte, it is not the bride of my youth, the mother of my children, that will be laid among the ruins of Dryburgh Abbey, which we have so often visited in gaiety and pastime. No! no!' She was buried on the 22d of May; and next day he says: ' The whole scene floats as a sort of dream before me : the beautiful day, the grey ruins covered and hidden among clouds of foliage and flourish, where the grave, even in the lap of beauty, lay lurking and gaped for its prey.' Surely his heart was entombed along with her ; and his body, too, has long been at her side. A week later we find him returned to Edinburgh, and resuming his ordinary labours, although now *alone*, and to be alone till the close.

CHAPTER XX.

'THE UNVEILED PROPHET.'

A WRITER in a forgotten magazine, dated 1826, says something to the following effect :—' There has the author of *Waverley* been the other day putting out *Woodstock*. The man has been often called a magician, but never so much deserved the name as now. How but by sorcery has he in these dreadful times, when money, credit, and confidence are all alike gone, been able to get £10,000 for a novel, by no means the best, either, of his productions?' The sum here is overstated,—it was only £8228; but the wonder, though lessened by several hundreds, remains great. The price undoubtedly was enhanced by the competition among the booksellers, anxious, now that the Constable monopoly was broken down, to secure an interest in the most popular works of their time. The shock of sympathy, too, produced by the news of Scott's misfortunes had its own share in increasing, for a time, the value of his productions. The novel consequently sold well, and its success came upon the author like a gleam of sunshine in a cloudy eve.

About *Woodstock* the anonymous writer is correct. It by no means comes up to the first, no, nor yet to the second, nor yet to the third file of his fictions. It is in many parts exceedingly tedious. It ought to have embraced the period closing with the battle of Worcester, and had the Royal Oak for FINIS, instead of which 'the mere lees' of that impressive story are 'left the vault to brag off.' The apparitions at Woodstock are managed with very little skill, not certainly as even Mrs. Radcliffe would have managed them. Scott admits himself that when he wrote the novel he had not the spirits to caricature the Puritans as he had done the Covenanters ; so, instead of making them ridiculous, he has made them simply loathsome. Witness Trusty Tomkins. And, above all, his picture of Cromwell, the greatest historical character he ever grappled with, is a failure. He halts between two opinions in his estimate of him ; and this irresolution is fatal to the power and fidelity of the likeness. Charles II., too, is a wretched daub. But there are many scenes

and passages of striking interest. The characters
and connection of Sir Harry Lee and his daughter
are exquisitely tender,—the more so if we suppose
that Scott was here shadowing out his own family
history. Bevis, the noble hound, is his own Maida ;
and altogether, when we remember that the tale,
like the fatal bark in *Lycidas*, was 'built in the
eclipse,' we are astonished to find it built so well.
It resembles the work of a blind architect, where
faults are forgiven and merits exaggerated, on
account of the circumstances surmounted and the
difficulties overcome. He no sooner finished and
launched *Woodstock* than he began *The Chronicles
of the .Canongate.* Frequently since his failure he
had contemplated the possibility of taking refuge
from his creditors in the ancient sanctuary of
Holyrood, and this gave a strange charm to the
Canongate, that fine old street opening upon it,
and led to the conception of Chrystal Croftangry.
We wish he had given us what we believe he
at one time intended, a series of Tales of the
Abbey. No one certainly could have thrown such
vivid light as Scott upon the numerous paths of
misfortune, carelessness, extravagance, and crime,
leading so many victims to this Scottish city of
refuge, defended almost superfluously, and consecrated, too, by a royal palace, the giant-snouted

crags of Salisbury, and the couchant lion of
Arthur's Seat!

Napoleon, however, was still his *magnum opus*,
and he devoted to it his more earnest and intense
moments. He now carried on his labours, not
merely in the morning before breakfast, which had
long been his chief time for composition, but in the
evening, as well as in the forenoon, to the great
detriment of his health. Mr. Gillies says, ' I have
always thought that to the domestic affliction, the
painful impressions and incessant labours of the
year 1826, was imputable the break of his constitution, although the injury was not then apparent.
In St. David Street he kept earlier hours than
ever ; and sometimes in one morning, before the
meeting of the Court at ten o'clock, he had finished
an entire sheet of twenty-four pages for the printer.
His handwriting was now so small and cramped,
that one of his ordinary quarto pages made at least
double that amount in print ; "and, after all," he
observed, "it was really no great exploit to finish
twelve pages in a morning." But, on his return
from the Parliament House, however wearied he
might be, the task was again resumed. Seldom
receiving any company, he scarcely sat a quarter
of an hour at dinner, but turned directly to his
writing-desk. Yet there never seemed the slightest

flurry or irritation in his demeanour. He never seemed vexed or in a hurry, but took up the pen with a smile on his countenance, and as if he had been writing merely for his own amusement.'

In this way, besides his ordinary tasks, he had found time for writing some very spirited letters on the monetary questions of that agitated period, under the *nom de plume* of ' Sir Malachi Malagrowther,'—letters which made a sensation, although not quite equal to the Drapier or to Junius. Almost his only relaxation all this dreadfully hot summer of 1826 was joining the Blair Adam Club for two or three days about the longest day, where, however, the heat compelled them to creep about and lounge under the shadow of great trees, and prevented any extended excursion.

In October he interrupted, or rather varied his labours, by a journey, undertaken along with his unmarried daughter Anne, to London and Paris, in search of materials for *Napoleon*. At London he saw some of his old friends, and made a few new acquaintances. In Paris the honours of his Irish reception were renewed with interest. He describes the French as absolutely ' outrageous in their civilities,' and seemed as glad to get safe out of Paris as if it had been a forest of officious baboons. He bore it all, however, with great apparent equa-

nimity. Cooper, the American novelist, was there
at the same time. Hazlitt (who was also then in
Paris, we think) describes the different behaviour
of the two with his usual sarcastic vigour,—Cooper
going about with his chin in the air, and assuming
vast consequence as the '*American* Scott,' while
the real Scott was entirely untouched and unmoved
amidst the palaver, seeing the usual sights, meeting
with some famous people, and pursuing quietly the
main purpose for which he had crossed the Channel,
—the getting fresh materials for his book. Attending the Odeon one evening, he found the play to
be *Ivanhoe*. The story was sadly mangled, and
the words nonsense, 'yet it was strange to hear
anything like the words which I (then in agony of
pain with spasms in my stomach) dictated to
William Laidlaw at Abbotsford now recited in a
foreign tongue, and for the amusement of a strange
people. I little thought to have survived the completing of this novel.'

In London, on his way back, he met Allan Cunningham, Theodore Hook, Croker, Peel, the Duke
of Wellington, and many others. He dined once
especially with Wellington, Peel, Huskisson, Melville, and Canning, and on returning said, 'I have
seen some of these great men at the same table
for the *last time*,'—words which seem in a twofold

sense prophetic, since he never, we think, dined with any of them afterwards; and since, owing to their divisions and separations, they seldom afterwards ever dined amicably among themselves. He sat at this time again to Lawrence, and was pleased with the portrait, as conveying the idea of 'the stout blunt carle who cares for few things and who fears nothing.' He valued this journey as having caused 'his thoughts to flow in another and pleasanter channel' than for some time previously. On his return to Scotland in the end of November, he took a house in Walker Street, Edinburgh, and spent there the winter months, tormented with rheumatisms, which he had caught in France from damp sheets, and often sunk in deep depressions; but, ill or well, serene or melancholy, always tugging on at the oar.

We quote one or two painfully interesting passages from his Journal of this year. On the last day of 1826 he held a little party: 'The Fergussons came, and we had the usual appliances of mirth and good cheer; yet our party, like the chariot-wheels of Pharaoh in the Red Sea, dragged heavily. It must be allowed that the regular recurrence of annual festivals among the same individuals has, as life advances, something in it that is melancholy. We meet like the survivors of some

perilous expedition, wounded and weakened in ourselves, and looking through diminished ranks to
think of those that are no more ; or they are like
the feasts of the Caribs, in which they held that
the pale and speechless phantoms of the deceased
appeared and mingled among the living.' Thus
he describes a walk and what followed : ' Wandered
from place to place in the woods, chewing the cud
of sweet and bitter fancies which alternated in
my mind, idly stirred by the succession of a thousand vague thoughts and fears,—the gay strangely
mingled with those of dismal melancholy ; tears
which seemed ready to flow unbidden ; smiles
which approached to those of insanity,—all that
wild variety of mood which solitude engenders.
Came in and assorted papers. I never could help
admiring the concatenation between Achitophel's
setting his house in order and hanging himself.
The one seems to follow the other as a matter of
course. But what frightens and disgusts me is
those fearful letters from those who have been long
dead to those who linger on their wayfare through
the valley of tears. What is this world ? a dream
within a dream. As we grow older, each step is an
awakening. The youth awakes, as he thinks, from
childhood ; the full-grown man despises the pursuits of youth as visionary ; the old man looks on

manhood as a feverish dream. The grave the last sleep! No; it is the last and final awakening.'

The following is gloomier still : ' Heard the true history of ——[1] (a suicide). Imagination renders us liable to be the victims of occasional low spirits. All belonging to this gifted but unhappy class must have felt that, but for the dictates of religion, or the natural recoil of the mind from the idea of dissolution, there have been times when they have been willing to throw away life as a child does a broken toy. I am sure I know one who has often felt so. O God! what are we? Lords of nature! Why, a tile drops from a house-top, which an elephant would no more feel than the fall of a piece of pasteboard, and there lies his lordship! or something of inconceivably minute origin,—the pressure of a bone, or the inflammation of a particle of the brain takes place,—and the emblem of Deity destroys himself or somebody else! We hold our health and our reason on terms slighter than one would desire, were it in their choice, to hold an Irish cabin.'

These extracts are rather in the mood of John Foster than of Walter Scott ; more like the gloomy misanthrope and ascetic than the broad, benignant Scottish Shakspeare, and seem to point to begun disease. And yet we could quote from his earlier

[1] This was, we think, Irving, Scott's early companion.

writings passages sprinkled here and there of a
similar purport, as where, in *Waverley*, he says,
'If this compound of fools and knaves called the
world be still in existence.' And it is singular how
so many of his most powerful characters are soured,
disappointed, and disrespectable beings,—gipsies,
villains, smugglers, and caterans,—and might augur
that he had, like Shakspeare, a dark sore deep
sunk in his nature, which he relieved by creat-
ing such queer, ambiguous, and somewhat savage
people. Every castle of old had its dungeon, and,
we suspect, every lofty mind has its deep misan-
thropic pit, with plenty of sullen, waveless water,
and many reptiles, living or dead, swimming or
rotting within ; yet Scott mingled even his dark
portraits with kindly elements, and his very devils
are brown, not black. To show the good that is
in evil characters is a more amiable task than to
show the evil that is in good, or to make the good
incredibly perfect.

One splendid and gratifying incident occurred
this otherwise disastrous season. This was the
dinner of the Theatrical Fund, which took place
on the 23d of February 1827, and at which he presided. Lord Meadowbank, as it was the first time
Scott had appeared at a public entertainment since
his misfortunes, determined, after consulting him

R

in private, to give his health as 'the Author of
Waverley.' He did so, accordingly, in glowing
terms. A storm of applause is said to have followed. A Glasgow litterateur present on the
occasion says, on the contrary, that the applause
was rather cold, and would have been much more
enthusiastic had the toast been given in the capital
of the West. Be this as it may, Scott's reply was
in admirable taste ; and the last sentence *must*
have brought down the house : 'I beg leave to pro-
pose the health of my friend Bailie Nicol Jarvie
(Mackay the Actor) ; and I am sure that, when the
author of *Waverley* and *Rob Roy* drinks to the
health of Nicol Jarvie, the applause shall be *prodigious.'* To which Mr. Mackay replied, 'My
conscience ! my worthy father the deacon could
never have believed that his son would have such
a compliment paid him by the Great Unknown.'
Lockhart adds a ludicrous thing. 'After resuming
the chair, Scott sent a slip of paper to Patrick
Robertson, begging him to confess something too ;
why not the murder of Begbie ? but this, if done
by the facetious Peter, must have been at a late
hour of the evening.' We can imagine the solemn
gravity with which Peter of the Painch would rise,
like a penitent Sir John Falstaff, as if some awful
birth of guilt were riving his continental bosom ;

what profoundly ludicrous sorrow would sit upon
his heavy features and half-shut eyne; and how,
after some beatings of breast and *painch*, sepulchral
sighs, and genuine Burgundy begot tears, he would
proceed, in tones as dolorous and guttural as those
of his famous Gaelic sermons, to deliver himself of
his dread secret; and how, when from the Man
Mountain in labour there sprang to light the old
story of the robbery and murder at noonday of
the bank porter, thunders of applause, dying away
in convulsive laughter, would welcome the off-
spring, and almost drown its parent as he sank
exhausted in the chair! We can fancy all this,.
and fancy, too, with what delight Scott would have
witnessed it had he waited, and prided himself on
being the grandfather of the joke of the evening!

The *Waverley* secret had ceased to be one from
the date of the failure. It had been well kept,
considering that twenty persons had been apprised
of it. Scott says in his diary: 'Funny thing at
the theatre last night. Among the discourse on
High Life below Stairs, one of the ladies' ladies
asks, "Who wrote *Shakspeare?*" One says, "Ben
Johnson;" another, "Finis." "No," said an actor,
"Sir Walter Scott; he confessed it at a public
meeting t'other day."' And thus the Prophet
was at last unveiled.

CHAPTER XXI.

'NAPOLEON TO THE RESCUE.'

GREAT things had been expected of his *Napoleon*, at least by the general and distant public. They imagined that it would at once re-establish his fading fame and redeem his ruined fortunes. 'Napoleon to the rescue!' became the cry along the line of his wavering battle. The initiated, however, knew better. They were aware that the sum he might get for this work, however large, was a mere drop in the great bucket of his engagements, and they were aware of the difficulties with which disease, sorrow, bereavement, and his careless habits of composition, had environed his task. Some of them must have known that, although two years had elapsed since he began the work, the actual time consumed in the writing was hardly more than a year. And what a year of 'pain, sorrow, and ruin!' None less than a Michael Scott, or some similar supernatural personage, could have been expected in such a time to write a work worthy of such an author and such a subject. Wreathing ropes of the ribbed sea-sand, or splitting the Eildon Hills in three, were child's play to the task of recording worthily, in the course of a few hundred sittings, the career of the most marvellous man of modern times,—himself, too, the centre of the most multiform and marvellous events in the grandest of eras,—the 'man without a model and without a shadow,' whose flag for twenty years had been Victory, and his will Fate.

In June 1827 Scott's *Life of Napoleon* appeared in nine volumes, and met, if not with a rapturous reception, with an enormous sale. It realized, first and second editions included, a profit of £18,000,— a fabulous sum in itself, but which, placed against his debts, was a wart to Ossa. Scripture critics speak of 'notes of time' in portions of the ancient volume. Scott's *Napoleon* bore but too distinctly its note of time. Haste was visible in every page; and this not the haste of his novels, in which he had been emptying his oldest and richest repositories, spreading out like the wise men of old his far-brought treasures, gold, frankincense, and myrrh, but the haste of one who loads his waggon with goods in one street to catch the market in another. Many of the descriptions, indeed, especially of battles, are worthy of the author of *Marmion* and *Old Mortality;* and the spirit of the whole, particularly in reference to Napoleon himself, is wonderfully impartial. But altogether it ranks rather with compilations than with works of genuine history, and classes its author's name with the Smolletts rather than with the Humes and Robertsons of his country. In profound political and philosophical sagacity it is deficient. Of its sketches of individuals we remember none, unless where he speaks of Danton as a character worthy of the treatment of Shakspeare or Schiller, and as the 'Mahomet of the Revolution.' The style is in some parts exceedingly bald and careless, and in others too florid for narrative ; and the flowers have not the natural beauty and bloom of those in his earlier works. Burke was an older man than Scott when he wrote his *Regicide Peace,* and the figures in its style are as numerous, but they never seem to disguise weakness, always to augment as well as adorn strength. Indeed, Scott's book is not nearly so good, so clear, so compact, and so strong as Lockhart's own two little volumes of *Napoleon's Life* published in John Murray's Family Library.

William Hazlitt wrote shortly after Scott's work,

and in almost avowed rivalship, his *Life of Napo-leon.* Hazlitt is a poor describer of battles, unless of *racket* and pugilistic contests, where he shines ; while Scott has the old cavalier blood in him, and evermore rises when he smells the battle afar off. Scott has always great ease, and sometimes a grand sweep of style, but has not that constant watchful, lynx-eyed intellect, like a whole com-mittee of vigilance in permanent session, which distinguished Hazlitt. There are no descriptions in all Scott's nine volumes to be compared to Hazlitt's pictures of the Reign of Terror, of the poetical power and charm of the Catholic religion, and of the Fire at Moscow. This last is specially fine. There is something, indeed, very grand in the thought of the two great elements, Fire and Snow, making common cause against this new Kehama or Man Almighty, and checking his pro-gress.. Snow as an enemy in Russia he might have expected ; but Fire too—there was something he could not have calculated on, and which seems for the first time to have awed Napoleon's spirit. And how little he and his army look, first in the glare of the Kremlin, and then in the white boundless waste of the snow !

Apart from the splendid passages of Hazlitt's *Life,* it is a book which raises materially our estimate of his sense. There is less paradox and personal feeling than in his other writings, and a vast deal of strong, sagacious, weighty reflection. Having been himself a flighty thinker at times, he is excellent at exposing flightiness in others ; and *Napoleon* had a good deal of it blended with his great general soundness of judgment.

The effect of Scott's book on the public was to produce a mixture of wonder, sympathy, considerable admiration, and much disappointment. Everybody read, few criticised it. Goethe, as we saw, stated the truth in saying that its chief value lay in its satisfying the interest felt as to the general impression which a career like Napoleon's had produced on such a mind as Scott's ; although a captious critic now, comparing Scott's fierce and vulgar abuse of Bonaparte in those letters, written during his brilliant career, with the estimate in the *Life*, might allege that the impression varied so much at different times as to be of less consequence. There would, however, be more captiousness than sense in this criticism. Compare the abuse poured out by the Northern journalists on Stonewall Jackson and General Lee, while both were in arms, with the language of universal admiration, softening in the one case into a deeper feeling because the object is dead, which is employed to both *now!* Scott only passed through a process which is as common in, as we think it is honourable to, human nature.

After all that Scott, Lockhart, Hazlitt, Thiers, and a hundred others have done, the life of Napoleon is not yet adequately written, nor his portrait fully taken. We see only as yet a few scratches on the canvas, and dim outlines of the future photograph. It may never be done ; it cannot be done, we suspect, for long ages. The only man now alive who could have painted Napoleon with a force and fire, a sweep and mastery at all worthy of the subject, has devoted himself to other and surely not worthier heroes, such as Frederick the Great,—the life of whom, by the most powerful pen extant, must be pronounced a clumsy compilation, a colossal blunder, and might, were we using his own metaphorical language, be called a 'Sphinx Swine,' the size enormous, the shape disgusting. Curious employment, certainly, that of Thomas Carlyle, with his almost last (authorial) breath inflating an unprincipled scoundrel, with the talents of a clever corporal or drill-sergeant and the habits of a satyr, into a hero, and the 'last of the kings !' Napoleon, whom Carlyle now abuses, had probably as many faults as Frederick, although of a less offensive kind ; but his genius was of a far loftier order, and his achievements transcendently greater. And when did Frederick ever blend such feeling, poetry, and common sense, as Napoleon in the following instance? Talking in the park at Malmaison to one of his counsellors, he said, ' I was here last Sunday, walking out in this solitude in the silence of nature. The sound of the bells of the church at Ruel suddenly struck my ear. I was affected, so great is the power of early habit and education. I said to myself, What an impression must it not make on simple and credulous minds! Let your philosophers, your metaphysicians reply to that : a religion is necessary for the people !'

Scott now stood relieved, as Atlas when Hercules took his place under the weight of the heavens, from a tremendous load. New tasks he instantly undertook, but they all seemed easy to him after *Napoleon.* Lockhart and his family having come to spend part of the summer at Portobello, Sir Walter was often there in the long days of June, strolling along the beautiful beach, and inhaling the sea breeze. When the Court rose, he returned to Abbotsford, where Lockhart's household, too, were gone ; and there the Wizard might be seen riding through the woods with little John Hugh Lockhart, his grandson, and telling to him one of those stories from Scottish history which in the

evening or next day he was to write down for the
whole world in his book already begun, *Tales of a
Grandfather.* He was working, too, at his *Chronicles
of the Canongate.* This summer the Blair Adam
Club met in Charleston, Fife, and enjoyed some
pleasant little excursions. Scott once more visited
St. Andrews; and while his friends climbed St.
Rule's Tower, which his lameness and rheumatisms
prevented him doing, he thus meditated: 'I sat
down on a gravestone and recollected the first visit
I made to St. Andrews, now thirty-four years ago.
What changes in my feelings and fortunes have
since then taken place,—some for the better, many
for the worse! I remembered the *name* I then
carved in Runic characters on the turf beside
the Castle gate, and I asked why it should still
agitate my heart? "Still harping on my daughter."'
His friends, however, came down from the tower,
and the sad, delicious reverie fled away.

While he was, soon after, at Minto, he heard the
news of the death of Archibald Constable, who
died utterly broken down by his misfortunes, and
sketched him'in his diary with generous fidelity.
One curious thing he mentions about him: 'He knew
the rare volumes of his library, not only by the eye,
but by touch when blindfolded. Thomas Thomson
saw him make this experiment, and, that it might

be complete, placed in his hand an ordinary volume instead of one of these *libri rariores.* He said he had overestimated his memory,—he could not recollect that volume.' Scott grants to him to have been the 'prince of booksellers; his views sharp, liberal, and powerful ; too sanguine and speculative, but who knew more of the business of a bookseller, in planning and executing popular works, than any man of his time. He was generous, and far from bad-hearted ; in person good-looking ('The Crafty,' he said on another occasion, 'is a grand-looking chield, but not equal to Jupiter Carlyle'), but very corpulent latterly ; a large feeder and deep drinker, till his health became weak. I have no great reason to regret him, yet I do. If he deceived others, he deceived also himself.' Constable was only fifty-four, but looked ten years older. He died the occupant of an obscure closet called by courtesy a shop, in poverty and wretchedness ; and most of his great schemes had perished before him. Yet he must be remembered as long as the *Edinburgh Review* and the Waverley Novels.

In August died a greater man, who had also been closely connected with Scott, George Canning. We remember no eminent person of this century whose reputation is now so much a tradition as Canning's. Byron said of him : 'Canning

is a genius,—almost a universal one,—a wit, a
statesman, and a poet.' But his speeches are
forgotten,—all save a few bold strokes, such as, 'I
called a new world into existence' (by acknowledging the South American States); his wit lingers in
such scraps of sarcasm, of questionable taste and
unquestionable bad feeling, as 'the revered and
ruptured Ogden' (a worthy patriot, who had contracted a rupture while confined for a political
offence); his poetry never deserved the name,
and is now nowhere, unless in obsolete books of
extracts, where you may find still his *Knife-
grinder*, and his ballad of *The German Student*,
who exclaims,—

> ' Here doomed to starve on water gru-
> El, never shall I see the U-
> Niversity of Gottingen !'

Yet he was a most brilliant and a most useful
man. His power over the Commons and country
was immense ; his oratory at once refined and
brilliant. As Scott says of him: 'No man possessed
a gayer and more playful wit in society ; no one,
since Pitt's time, had more commanding sarcasm
in debate in the House of Commons. He was
the terror of that species of orators called the
"Yelpers." His lash fetched away both skin and
bone, and would have penetrated the hide of a

rhinoceros.' As a statesman, he was given somewhat to intrigue, but had large views and progres-
sive tendencies, although the Tories accused him,
as they have since accused Gladstone and D'Israeli,
of breaking down their ranks; and certainly, as
Falstaff has it, 'he led his rogues where they were
well peppered.' As a man, although irritable,
haughty, and not willing to work amicably with
inferior statesmen, he was frank, if not always
open, and often yielded, as in his defence of
Queen Caroline, to generous impulses. When
appointed Premier, he said the office was his
by inheritance, and as he could not from constitution hold it more than two years, it would
descend to Peel. But he did not enjoy it for
even that brief space. He was hunted to death
by the organs of the extreme party he had left,
which openly shouted out, ' *We are killing him ;*'
and was mourned by Scott the more tenderly
that he strongly disapproved of his latter policy.
It is singular to find in Scott's Journal, immediately after a feeling notice of Canning's death,
the following sentence: 'My nerves have for
these two or three last days been susceptible of
acute excitement from the slightest causes. The
beauty of the evening, the sighing of the summer
breeze, bring the tears into my eyes, not un-

pleasantly.' This was nature's untimely signal that he must at no distant day follow his great statesman friend.

Before the close of the year he had two dangerous rencontres,—the one with a vapouring Frenchman, General Gourgaud, who had taken offence at some statements in *Napoleon's Life*, and wished personal satisfaction, and another with Abud the Jew, who threatened him, on account of a debt, with incarceration; but, as Bunyan would say, 'the Lord being merciful to him, he escaped both their hands.'

CHAPTER XXII.

STRUGGLES OF THE PROSTRATE.

THE vigorous rally made by *Napoleon* had on the whole failed. Even had the work been as good in the historical style as *Waverley* was in fiction, we doubt if, at that stage of the business, it could have redeemed him. Its success would have probably led to a second effort, and, had *that* triumphed, the victory would have been bought by the author's life. More probably it would have been a failure, and Scott might have had to return to novel-writing over the ruins of his historical reputation. As it was, he was compelled to do this to some extent; and most of his after efforts in novel-writing appear like the convulsive struggles of his own Dirk Hatteraick after he was mastered and bound, strong but ineffectual.

Early in the winter appeared the first series of the *Chronicles of the Canongate*, heralded by one of Christopher North's splendid jubilates of applause in *Blackwood.* They were, however, rather coldly received by the public. At this *we* wonder, who look at them simply on their own merits, and do not remember that the generation of 1827 were compelled to compare them with their more brilliant predecessors. *We* land in France, and find a day warm, which the natives, contrasting it with the previous part of the week, vote to be somewhat dull and chilly. Scott himself liked *The Highland Widow* while writing it, and thought it written in his 'bettermost manner.' It is certainly a powerful Ossianic pro-duction, quite a prose poem ; and the style is grave and solemn as the 'stalk of the bold wolf in the harvest moon.' The Woman of the Tree has some slender resemblance to his Nornas and Elspeth Mucklebackits, but is on the whole as original, as powerful. And who can forget her exclamation over her lost son, 'My beautiful, my brave !' The others are spirited and varied tales. *The Two Drovers* is little more than a newspaper incident, but it is admirably told. In *The Surgeon's Daughter* Middlemas is an unredeemable and unnatural scoundrel; and the part of the story

S

described as passing in Scotland is commonplace enough. But the scenes in Hindostan, such as the story of the Indian whose bride is devoured by a tiger, and who keeps a life-long watch over her tomb, and the unveiling of Hyder Ali, are most excellent, and create the desire that Scott had given us a full-length portrait of that extraordinary man, and opened up a little more of the 'gloomy recesses' of a mind so 'capacious,' as Burke has it, of wild justice and wide retribution, as well as of that severe and measured mercy which often mingled with it in his actions, and the descent of which resembled less the gentle rain from heaven than the first slow, large drops of a thunder shower.

If *The Chronicles*, however, did not create any sensation, *The Tales of a Grandfather*, which came forth immediately after, did. They were welcomed, according to Lockhart, with greater rapture than any of Scott's productions since *Ivanhoe.* They extended his fame into a place where it had not got full footing before,—into the nursery,—and tended to confirm it in all other directions. Sir Walter now, for the first time, ranked with such enviable writers as the authors, many in number, of *The Arabian Nights*, and as Bunyan, Defoe, and Goldsmith, whose works are equally relished by boys and bearded men, and whose praise is perfected out of the mouths of babes and sucklings as well as in the encomiums of critics, and in the thanks of all. At first, indeed, the language of *The Tales* is rather babyish even for babes; but after a little practice the author finds out the true golden mean of style which, while children crow and clap their hands over it, glues elder people (as we are told of Sir Joshua Reynolds when reading *The Life of Savage* in a country inn) to the mantelpiece till their arms are stiff and cold. Often, when it appeared in its three small volumes, was it read at one sitting. It is often read at a single sitting still, and may be called the history of Scotland illuminated by a fairy's lantern,—so tiny and so true, so childlike and so real, the radiance it casts upon a story, romantic enough of itself, and which, even in its barest version, is stranger far than fiction.

In the course of two years Scott had cleared off about £40,000 of his debt. Still the remainder loomed large before him. But now Cadell, who had been Constable's partner, and had recently purchased the copyrights of the Novels, projected,—it was a project worthy of Constable, and, indeed, was in its original germ his,—the *Magnum Opus*, *i.e.* a new, cheap, and uniform edition of the Waverley Novels, illustrated by eminent artists, and accompanied with notes from the pen of the author. This became ultimately a mine of wealth.

The first announcement of Scott's literary labours in 1828 was that he had a volume of sermons in the press,—an announcement which sounded then as strange as though a few years ago Dickens had advertised a reply to Colenso. In spring, accordingly, there appeared a thin octavo volume entitled *Religious Discourses*, which we remember seeing when a boy in a parish manse that summer, and hearing highly commended by a respectable Established minister as good, sensible discourses, 'better than he expected from Sir Walter,' but did not read then, and have never met with since. They were written out of a kindly motive for a young man named Gordon, who had acted as Scott's amanuensis ; had studied for the Church, although labouring under an infirmity of deafness ; who got a presentation to a parish, but had been seized with a nervous dread of appearing before the presbytery to deliver the necessary discourses,— something like Cowper's terror at facing the House of Lords,—and came to Scott with tears in his eyes, telling him that his pen was powerless. 'Never mind,' said the kindly Scott, 'I'll write two sermons for you which will pass muster ;' and next morning

presented him with them. They were not ultimately required, but Gordon retained them in his
possession, and being pressed with pecuniary difficulties, sold them (after getting Scott's consent)
for £250, the largest price which had ever hitherto
been paid for two sermons. They were published
by Colburn, then the great vender of fashionable
novels, and we suppose had a run alongside of
Pelham, *The Disowned*, *The Kuzzilbash*, and the
O'Hara Tales, with which that year his press was
teeming.

In March appeared *The Fair Maid of Perth*, the
reception of which was, in Scotland at least, enthusiastic. We remember in Glasgow, where we
were then attending college, that the estimate of
the press,—a press very ably conducted at that time
by Sheridan Knowles, Malcolm, Kerr, Northhouse,
and others,—was exceedingly high. It has undoubtedly here and there an appearance of forcing and
uneasy elaboration, but is on the whole a most
successful production, with the genius great, but
the art greater; indeed, we may call it Scott's last
real novel. It is full of spirit-stirring incident, of
graphic painting, and of admirably portrayed
character. In reference to its pictures of scenery,
we often regret that the season selected is early
spring, or rather winter, so that we have the

beauties of the Fair City and Loch Tay rather cast in statuary than revealed in the rich colours of painting. What he would have made of Killin in summer, and of Kenmore and Kinfauns in autumn! The Highland funeral and the battle of the Inch are splendid descriptions,—the latter perhaps too frightfully accurate, although there gleams on us a raw and bloody glory from that field of desperate and all-devouring death, over which are echoing the cries, 'Another for Hector! Death for Hector!' like accompaniments of thunder! Harry Wynd is a portrait drawn with a mixture of care and boldness worthy of Scott's very best days. Catherine Glover has character, though it is hardly the character of the time; is a fair maid, but not the Fair Maid of Perth in that age. Louise is more true to her, perhaps to any, period. All the Court scenes ranging round Rothesay are powerfully pictured; and his frightful death is artistically relieved by Catherine's tenderness and his own patience. Conachar is a coward whom we pity more than we despise; nay, properly speaking, he is not a coward at all. Morally he is brave, constitutionally he is timid; he unites a nerve of aspen with an heart of oak. It is himself, not death, that he fears; and his suicide seals not his disgrace, but his restoration to our respect.

But Henbane Dwining is in our judgment the flower of the flock. He is the most original character of them all. Strange how he always suggests to our mind the image of Thomas De Quincey, and seems to resemble him in his small stature, extremely complaisant, almost cringing manners, unsearchable eye, and transcendent powers, although De Quincey was an amiable man and a believer. Dwining, on the contrary, represents the last result of Materialism ; and to his eye frequent dissection of the human frame has reduced man to the level of a worm hacked to pieces by a schoolboy's knife. Yet he assumes a certain sublimity of aspect from his powerful intellect and his worship of intellect, the contempt with which he regards the brutal desperadoes with whom he is nevertheless mixed up, and whom he uses as his tools, and from his undoubting conviction of his miserable creed. The Bohemian in *Quentin Durward* avows himself an atheist, but he does so in a fierce defiant spirit, which may after all disguise a fear lest his creed be false ; but Dwining is cool, collected, absolutely certain of his, and dies with the sneer of its avowal sculptured upon his lips. How you tremble at the lean little incarnation of malignity, skill, cunning, sarcasm, infidelity, and intellectual pride, and at the 'he, he, he !' the

fatal chuckle which proclaims his diabolic presence; and still more when he says to Catherine
on the battlements of Falkland, pointing to Ra-
morny's soldiers, who are turning traitors to him,
' These things thought themselves the superiors of
a man like me! And you, foolish wench, think so
meanly of your Deity as to suppose that wretches
like them are the work of Omnipotence!' Byron
has been called the searcher of dark bosoms; but
Scott could search them too, although with a very
different spirit and purpose from the other.

After Scott had completed this tale, he set out
for London, in or near which were his eldest son,
his second son, Lockhart and his family, and
where he spent six weeks, on the whole pleasantly,
although little Johnnie Lockhart was still very
unwell; and this and other family distresses prevented him going much into general society. He
saw, however, on this, as on former occasions, a
good many distinguished people, such as Sir
Robert Inglis, Sotheby, and Coleridge; sat to
poor Haydon, and also to Northcote, who reminded him of an 'animated mummy;' dined
and remained all night at Holland House; visited
the Duchess of Kent, and was presented to the
little ' Princess Victoria,' who, being then nine,
must still have some faint recollection of the tall,

lame, white-haired baronet, probably introduced
to her as the cleverest man in the British empire.
He says of her : ' This little lady is educating with
much care, and watched so closely that no busy
maid has a moment to whisper, " You are heir of
England." I suspect that, if we could dissect the
little head, we should find that some pigeon or
other bird of the air had carried the matter.'
And ere he went north he spent a pleasant day
at Hampton Court, where his son Walter then
resided, in the company of Samuel Rogers, Tom
Moore, Wordsworth, and his wife and daughter,—
Rogers presenting the Scottish poet with a pair
of gold-mounted spectacles, and Scott valuing the
gift and giver highly.

This was the last visit paid by the unmutilated
Scott to London. With some little infirmities,
and although his eye had waxed dim, his natural
strength was not yet abated. One slight symptom,
however, of begun loss of memory he gave during
this journey. Hearing Mrs. Arkwright singing,
with great power and beauty, the lines,—

> ' Farewell, farewell ! the voice you hear
>   Has left its last soft tones with you ;
> The next must join the seaward cheer,
>   And shout among the shouting crew,'—

he said to his neighbour in the room, ' Capital

words,—whose are they? Byron's, I suppose; but I don't remember them.' He was astonished when I told him they were his own in *The Pirate*. He seemed pleased at the moment, but said next minute, ' You have distressed me. . If memory goes, it is all up with me, for that was always my strong point.' Ere he visited London again, he was the mere wreck of what he had been in memory, mind, and body. When he returned to Scotland he recommenced his literary labours, and during the remainder of this year completed his second series of *Tales of a Grandfather*, wrote some interesting papers for *The Quarterly*, worked at the *Magnum Opus*, and commenced *Anne of Geierstein*. This novel was published in May 1829. Lockhart speaks of its being as well received as *The Fair Maid of Perth*. This is a misstatement. We remember its publication distinctly, and that a general feeling of disappointment prevailed. One of the cleverest students we knew in Glasgow College could with difficulty, we remember, read it through; and we were prevented by his experience from even making the attempt. The opening scene in the Alps we found afterwards, and find still, at every renewed perusal, magnificent, and shall not soon forget the picture contained in it of Pilate washing his hands in the ' Infernal

Lake' for ever in vain. But with this exception, and one or two other passages scattered through the book, it is a mere piece of senile garrulity,—like a long, endless story told by an old man half asleep in his easy-chair ; and the first chapter or two, contrasted with the rest, reminds us of one of the passes from the low country to the Highlands, very grand, but leading up often to dreary monotonies of desolation. Ten years before, *Anne of Geierstein* would have come out from his hands a

> ' Child of strength and state ; '

and Switzerland would have hailed Scott as her novelist as indisputably as he had long been that of his native land. '

CHAPTER XXIII.

THE STRONG MAN BOWED DOWN.

BY the close of 1829 Scott had done a great deal more work. He had written the first volume of a *History of Scotland* for Dr. Lardner's *Cyclopædia;* he had ready for publication by December the last of the Scottish series of *The Tales of a Grandfather;* and had been working diligently at the prefaces and notes to the *Opus Magnum.* The sale of this last was most cheering. Ere 1829 was over, eight volumes had been issued, and the monthly sale amounted to 35,000 copies. This gave the prospect that, with the continuance of health and his usual capacity of work, his debts in a few years would be entirely liquidated.

But, alas! although his industry could always be calculated on, his health now could not. Besides rheumatisms, symptoms of *diabetes,*—a here-

ditary trouble from which his father had suffered,—
and other minor ailments, he complained for some
weeks of headaches and great nervous irritation, till
hæmorrhage gave him a doubtful and ominous
relief. Cupping became necessary, and he manfully submitted to it, although he describes it as a
'giant twisting about your flesh between his finger
and thumb.' He felt for the time better than he
had been for years before ; but his friends were
alarmed, for they knew that the first preliminary
blow of the axe of apoplexy had been struck. In
his Diary, among its last entries this season, he
records an interview, the first and last, with Edward Irving. His description will interest more
now than when it was first published: 'I met
to-day the celebrated divine and *soi disant* prophet
Irving. He is a fine-looking man (bating a dia-
bolical squint), with talent on his brow, and madness in his eye. I could hardly keep my eyes off
him while we were at table. He put me in mind
of the devil disguised as an angel of light, so ill
did that horrible obliquity of vision harmonize
with the dark, tranquil features of his face, resembling that of our Saviour in Italian pictures, with
the hair carefully arranged in the same manner.
There was much real or affected simplicity in the
manner in which he spoke. He spoke with that

kind of unction which is nearly allied to cajolery.
He boasted much of the tens of thousands that
attended his ministry at the town of Annan, his
native place, till he well-nigh provoked me to say
he was a distinguished exception to the rule that
"a prophet was not esteemed in his own country."'
There is a spice of prejudice in this picture, though
we presume it is in the main true. We imagine
Irving would not be quite at ease, or altogether
himself, when meeting at a dinner party with
Edinburgh lawyers, litterateurs, and fashionables.
Had he met Scott alone, they would have taken
to each other at once; for Irving was the most
genial of men, and as thorough a Scotchman as
Sir Walter. Perhaps Scott, too, was under the
influence of Lockhart, who speaks here of Irving
'as deposed on account of his wild heresies,' and
who, in a letter inserted in Mrs. Gordon's *Life of
Professor Wilson*, talks of him as a mere quack,
whose popularity was entirely owing to his atti-
tudes and the tones of his voice. How differently
the world rates Lockhart and Irving now! And
how all must regret that two such noble beings
as Irving and Scott had not got into *rapport* with
each other,—the one the great Border Preacher,
and the other the great Border Poet,—both men
of the warmest heart and the most exalted genius!

Tom Purdie died this autumn in a moment. Scott mourned his loss greatly. We gave before an extempore epitaph he proposed for him; his more deliberate one, written by the heart as well as hand of his master, may be found over his grave near the Abbey of Melrose.

Early in 1830 Scott published *The Ayrshire Tragedy*, a piece of some interest as a story, but not much poetical merit. On the 15th of February a tragic event occurred to himself. At two o'clock afternoon he returned home from the Parliament House, and while conversing with an old lady, a Miss Young of Hawick, who had called to show him some MS. memoirs of her father, a Dissenting clergyman of eminence in his day, sunk down, with a slight convulsion agitating his features. He ultimately fell at all his length on the floor, speechless and senseless. He was instantly bled, and then cupped, submitted to a severe regimen, and after some weeks he partially recovered. He resumed, of course, his pen, and became as busy as he had been in 1829, with *Letters on Demonology and Witchcraft* for Murray's Family Library, the second volume of his *History of Scotland* for Lardner, and the fourth series of *Tales of a Grandfather on French History*. All of them bore unmistakeable indications of the shock he had sustained,—unmistakeable *now*, although his contemporaries out of the circle of his own friends seem, while aware of the weakness of these productions, to have been ignorant of its cause. Thus we find even Wilson, in one of his *Noctes*, tearing the *Letters on Demonology* to pieces in a style which, savage as it seems at any rate, would have been cruel in the extreme had he known that they sprung from a diseased brain. The *Phrenological Journal*, on the other hand, discovered from the same production that Sir Walter Scott had no philosophical faculty, but added that neither had Shakspeare. Certainly neither Scott nor Shakspeare had in the same sense as George Combe. But we would have credited these philosophers with more acuteness had they discovered from these *Letters* that Scott's brain was not in a normal state. Toward August he had very much rallied, and wrote a pleasant review of Southey's *Life* and edition of *John Bunyan.*

In June died George IV., who, whatever were his relations to the country, had certainly been Scott's warm friend. Before his death, hearing that Sir Walter was to retire from the clerkship, he suggested that he might come to London to spend the winter, and overlook the MS. collections of the exiled house of Stewart, which had come into the King's hands by the death of the Cardinal of York. Scott heard of this gladly; but when offered the rank of privy councillor, he, as Dickens too has since done, at once and decidedly refused.

When the term ended in July, Scott ceased to be a Clerk of Session, but was told that, in lieu of his salary, £1300, he should have a retiring allowance of £800. He received also an intimation from the Home Secretary that the Ministry were prepared to give him a pension covering the difference. He laid the matter before his creditors, who advised him to consult his own feelings in the matter. In fine, he declined respectfully, acknowledging the intended favour, but declaring that he would accept of no more than had been allowed to his former colleagues, over whom he did not feel himself entitled to preference.

He received this eventful summer—was it leap-year?—an offer of marriage from a lady of rank, which he somewhat roughly declined to her brother, who had been the medium of the communication. Yet probably, worn out, diseased, and only recovering from ruin, lame, half-blind, and deaf, his constitution twenty years older than his years, he may have felt flattered by the proposal, the lady being young and wealthy. But although he felt, he never

T

acted on flattery; and his mind was made up, he
tells us, to regard woman as no more to him than
her picture.   Instead of yielding to the siren
strains of the present, he was ever recurring to
the past.   We find him, for instance, writing thus
in his Journal: 'I went to make a visit, and fairly
softened myself, like an old fool, with recalling
old stories, till I was fit for nothing but shedding
tears and repeating verses for the whole night.
This is sad work.   The very grave gives up the
dead, and time rolls back thirty years to add to
my perplexities.   What a romance to tell! and
told, I fear, it will one day be.   And then my three
years of dreaming, and my two years of wakening,
will be chronicled doubtless.   But the dead will
feel no pain.'   Again, three days afterwards: 'At
twelve' I went again to poor Lady ———— to talk
over old stories.   I am not clear that it is a right
or healthful indulgence to be ripping up old sores;
but it seems to give her deep-rooted sorrow words,
and that is a mental blood-letting.   To me these
things are now matter of calm and solemn recollection, never to be forgotten, and yet scarce to
be remembered with pain.'   Somehow the pain the
reader feels connected with these entries points to
the grave of poor forgotten Charlotte Carpenter,
the wife of his youth, and the mother of his

children. But Scott was of imagination all compact; his brain, too, was affected; and, as a poet
in decay, he must be forgiven and deeply pitied
too.

When the Court rose, he went to Abbotsford,
which again seemed to have resumed its ancient
glory and happiness. Lockhart and his wife and
family were once more in Chiefswood; William
Laidlaw had returned to Kaeside. There was
now, indeed, no Tom Purdie to lean upon in his
walk through the woods; but he had his pony
Douce Davie to ride on, and his grandchildren to
surround him on donkeys as he rode. And the
woods were green this moist summer, and he
thought them again as soon to be his own.
Report had magnified the success of the *Magnum;* his debts were generally believed to be
paid; and once more, where the carcase was,
the eagles were gathered together. The table
of Abbotsford was surrounded as deeply as ever
by distinguished guests; and Scott, although he
now passed the ˙˙bottle himself, and sipped his
toast-and-water, had much of the old jollity of
'mine host,' and found his friends in mirth as
well as in meat and wine. Few suspected that
he was all the while sinking more and more daily
into the arms of his disease, and that, while he was

writing as much as ever, his pages were beginning to smell of decay, like the last sodden leaves of autumn.

Cadell came out one September day with his 'horn filled with good news.' By October, he told Scott, the debt was to be reduced to £60,000, about one-half of its original amount. One object of this visit was to induce Sir Walter to confine himself entirely to the notes and prefaces of the *Magnum* and let novel-writing alone. He suggested also to him that he should employ some time in drawing up a catalogue of the most rare and curious articles in his library and museum. Next morning, on this hint, he spake and began dictating to William Laidlaw a book, entitled, 'Reliquiæ Trottcosienses, or the Gabions of Jonathan Oldbuck.' But after a few days he threw it aside, and reserving it for hours of leisure, he commenced a romance. This was *Count Robert of Paris*, destined to be the last and least of his long line of fictions. As he had now with the weakness much of the obstinacy of a child, all opposition was in vain. The usual agreements for publication were made, and the story proceeded.

Lockhart expresses pity for Scott's friends at this crisis and afterwards. We share in this feeling, and particularly for William Laidlaw. How different the circumstances when he wrote at Scott's dictation in 1819-20 and now! Then Scott was in disease, now in decay. Then the sturdy oak was shaken by a tempest; now it was stooping heavy-laden under infirmities, and its proud apex touched the ground. Then, as the author warmed with his theme, spirit triumphed over matter, and, after demoniac tortures, there was an angelic birth; now the flow of the thought was free and full in general, but the result was feeble. Then Laidlaw's feeling, as he contrasted the pained Titan with the glorious product, was delighted astonishment; now pity and sorrow predominated, especially when at times the mighty Wizard seemed to have dropped his wand, lost his way, and, instead of seeing the invisible, saw nothing but clouds and thick darkness. It seemed a transfiguration inverted,—a god turning into a man,—a giant dwindling into a dwarf; and it might be said of this strong man, like Sisera of old, 'At his feet he bowed, he fell, he lay down; at his feet he bowed, he fell; where he bowed, there he fell down dead.' And Laidlaw such an idolater too! We wonder his pen was not petrified,—it surely sometimes trembled. And how Scott must have missed those interjections of praise, 'Eh, sirs! heard ye ever the like o' that!' which were wont to burst from

the lips of the enthusiastic henchman, and to cheer
him on his task. Now there was a sad silence,
broken only by the voice of the author, waxing
feebler and lower every hour, and by the racing
over the paper of the amanuensis' reluctant and
hurrying pen.

The times were not of the kind to infuse new
energy into Sir Walter, or to recall old. The
three days at Paris had uttered their voice, and
all Europe, Britain included, were returning it in
assenting or angry echoes. Charles X. had taken
refuge in Holyrood, and was even there so in-
secure that Scott had to write a letter to the
newspapers, imploring for him common courtesy
and respect. The Whig Government was big with
the Reform Bill. Scott became greatly agitated,
and threw out his agitation into a political pamphlet, which had of course plenty of zeal, but was
exceedingly feeble in composition, and which his
friends strongly condemned, and with some difficulty persuaded him to destroy.

Previous to this he had another slight touch
of apoplexy, which was followed by others; and
greater severity of regimen, and abstinence from
work, were enjoined on him by his physicians.
Cadell and James Ballantyne had been compelled
to condemn *Count Robert* as altogether unworthy

of his reputation. Frightened, however, almost out of their senses by his political pamphlet, they were driven in despair to advise him to return to his novel; and this, nothing loath, he consented to do. 1830 closed in one point well with Scott. In December his creditors, gratified by the success of the *Magnum*, presented him with his furniture, plate, linen, paintings, library, etc.,—an act which gave him great satisfaction.

His debt was now reduced to £54,000. The *Magnum*, notwithstanding the disturbed state of the country, continued to flourish, its sale being scarcely at all diminished. When told of what the creditors had so handsomely done, he thought his affairs in such a satisfactory state that he determined to execute his last will, which he did the next year.

He resumed his Journal, and on the 20th of December we find him saying: 'Ever since my fall in February I have seemed to speak with an impediment. To add to this, I have the constant increase of my lameness. I move with very great pain, and am at every minute, during an hour's walk, reminded of my mortality. My fear is lest the blow be not sufficient to destroy life, and that I should linger on "a driveller and a show."' He often repeated the lines in Johnson's

Vanity of Human Wishes, of which this is an extract,—

> 'From Marlborough's eyes the tears of dotage flow,
> And Swift expires a driveller and a show.'

CHAPTER XXIV.

VISIT TO THE CONTINENT.

SCOTT closed his Journal for 1830 gloomily. He opens it for 1831 in language more melancholy still :—'January 1st, 1831. I cannot say the world opens pleasantly for me this new year. There are many things for which I have reason to be thankful, especially that Cadell's plans seem to have succeeded, and he augurs that the next two years will nearly clear me. But I feel myself decidedly wrecked in point of health, and am now confirmed that I have had a paralytic touch. I speak and read with embarrassment, and even my handwriting seems to stammer. This general failure,

> "With mortal crisis doth portend
> My days to appropinque an end."

I am not solicitous about this. Only, if I were

worthy, I would pray God for a sudden death, and no interregnum between. I cease to exercise reason, and I cease to exist.'

On the 31st of January he went to Edinburgh to execute his last will. At Mr. Cadell's, where he lived, he saw some articles of furniture which had belonged to his house in Castle Street, and the sight of them moved him deeply. He wrote in the mornings at *Count Robert*, and sometimes saw an old friend, Clerk, Skene, or Thomson, at a quiet dinner. On the 4th of February the will was signed. A storm of snow had detained him in town; but when the thaw came he returned to Abbotsford.

The times continued portentous; and when a meeting of freeholders was called in March in Jedburgh, to discuss the Reform Bill, he, to the great alarm of his daughter, determined to attend and speak on the Tory side. His tone was low, and his utterance hesitating. At one point of the speech, the crowd who had filled the courthouse hissed and hooted. He became silent, but when the interruption ceased resumed his speech. Again they broke out into clamour. He abruptly and unheard proposed the resolution, and then, turning to the crowd, said, a glow of indignation passing over his face, 'I regard your gabble no more than

the geese on the green.' He soon, however, recovered his equanimity, and as he retired bowed to
the assembly. Two or three renewed their hissing ;
he bowed again, and added, as he took leave, in the
words of the doomed gladiator, '*Moriturus vos
saluto.*'

Still he was labouring on, *invitâ Minerva*, at his
novel. When Dr. Abercromby remonstrated, he
replied : 'As for bidding me not work, Molly
might as well put the kettle on the fire and say,
"*Now don't boil.*"' To another of his friends who
used similar language he said : 'I understand you,
and I thank you from my heart ; but I must tell
you at once how it is with me. I am not sure that
I am quite myself in all things, but I am sure that
in one point there is no change. I mean, that I
foresee distinctly that if I were to be idle I should
go mad. In comparison with this, death is no risk
to shrink from.' For months he abstained from
wine and similar stimulants. One day, however,
having given a dinner party, where Lord Meadowbank was present, he neglected the prescriptions of
his physician, and took two or three glasses of
champagne, and was seized, on retiring for the
evening, with another severe shock of paralysis,
which forced him to keep his bed for days, and
changed his appearance in the most lamentable

manner. When he got a little better, he resumed and recast his novel; and there was something sublime yet ghastly in beholding this mere wreck of a man, after several apoplectic seizures, and ill besides with cramp, rheumatism, gravel, and increasing lameness, still struggling shorewards against the breakers, and keeping his eye upon Laidlaw as his faithful pilot. On the 18th of May he says: 'Went to Jedburgh greatly against the wish of my daughter. The mob were exceedingly vociferous and brutal. Henry Scott was elected for the last time, I suppose. *Troja fuit.* I left the borough in the midst of abuse, and the gentle hint of "Burke Sir Walter." Much obliged to the brave lads of Jeddart!'

He now, after the elections with their turmoil were over, got a little better; but no sooner felt himself in a measure restored than he commenced a new romance, *Castle Dangerous.* Lockhart was with him at the time, and in order to see the scenery of the novel, the twain set out on an excursion to Lanarkshire, passing on the way his dear old places, Yair, Ashestiel, Inverleithen, and Traquair. During his journey to Douglas Mill, Lesmahagow, and Castle Dangerous, he was in a state of great nervous excitement, repeating poetry from Winton, Barbour, and Blind Harry. He met with an old friend,

Borthwickbrac, also suffering under paralytic affection. They had a joyous, too joyous a meeting; and next day Scott was informed that his friend had had another severe stroke, and was despaired of. He was greatly struck, and insisted on going home immediately, saying, 'I must home to work while it is called to-day, for the night cometh when no man can work. I put this text many a year ago on my dial-stone.' (Dr. Johnson inscribed the same on his watch-seal.) He set out straightway, and never rested till he reached Abbotsford.

Returned, he finished *Castle Dangerous* and *Count Robert*. Shortly after it was suggested that he should spend the next winter in Italy. His son Charles was attached to the British legation at Naples, and to Naples his heart naturally turned. The kind and indefatigable Basil Hall, learning Scott's intentions, wrote Sir James Grahame, without Scott's knowledge, suggesting that the King's Government should place a frigate at his disposal for his voyage to the Mediterranean. Sir James at once and in the handsomest manner consented. Scott was gratified, and said he was glad to find things were still in the hands of gentlemen. He resolved to remain at Abbotsford till September, and make himself as happy as he could, revisiting the principal points of interest in the valley, calling on his old friends, and gathering as many around him as possible. Thus engaged, and freed from the drudgery of authorship, his spirits and health revived wonderfully.

On the 17th of September James Glencairn Burns, returned on furlough from India, along with MacDiarmid of Dumfries, visited Abbotsford; and once more, and for the last time, a party was held, and a most delightful day ensued. We quote some of the verses which Lockhart wrote on the occasion, which are really good :

'A day I've seen whose brightness pierced the cloud
    Of pain and sorrow ; both for great and small
A night of flowing cups and pibrochs loud,.
    Once more within the Minstrel's blazoned hall.
Upon this frozen hearth pile crackling trees,
    Let every silent clarshach find its strings ;
Unfurl once more the banner to the breeze,
    No warmer welcome for the blood of kings !
What princely stranger comes ? what exiled lord
    From the far East to Scotia's strand returns,
To stir with joy the towers of Abbotsford,
    And wake the Minstrel's soul ?—the boy of Burns.

'The children sang the ballads of their sires.
    Serene among them sat the hoary knight ;
And if dead bards have ears for earthly lyres,
    The peasant's shade was near, and drank delight.
As through the woods we took our homeward way,
    Fair shone the moon last night on Eldon hill,
Soft rippled Tweed's broad wave beneath her ray,
    And in sweet murmurs gushed the Huntly rill.

Heaven send the guardian genius of the vale
　　Health yet, and strength, and length of honoured days,
To cheer the world with many a gallant tale,
　　And hear his children's children chant his lays.
Through seas unruffled may the vessel glide
　　That bears her poet far from Melrose glen ;
And may his pulse be stedfast as our pride,
　　When happy breezes waft him back again.'

Wordsworth came and took farewell of him, and wrote then the beautiful sonnet :

'A trouble not of clouds, nor weeping rain,
　　Nor of the setting sun's pathetic light
　　Engendered, hangs o'er Eildon's triple height ;
Spirits of power assembled there complain,
　　For kindred power departing from their sight,
While Tweed, best pleased in chanting a blithe strain,
Saddens his voice again, and yet again.
　　Lift up your hearts, ye mourners, for the might
Of the whole world's good wishes with him go ;
　　Blessings and prayers, in nobler retinue
Than sceptred king or laurelled conqueror knows,
　　Follow this wondrous potentate.　Be true,
Ye winds of ocean and the midland sea,
　　Wafting your charge to soft Parthenope.'

On the 23d September, Scott, accompanied by his daughter Anne and Lockhart, set out for London. They spent one day at Rokeby, and Scott took a solemn farewell of his ancient friend Morritt. They reached London on the 25th of the month, and found it in a state of terrific excitement connected with the rejection of the Reform

Bill,—the Duke of Wellington's house having suffered along with some others from a popular eruption.

During the month he was in London, Scott went very little into society, although he saw a few old friends. He was very far indeed from being well, yet Sir Henry Halford and Dr. Holland, while recognising incipient disease of the brain, thought that with great care and complete abstinence from literary labour he might recover.

Moore, Milman, Sir David Wilkie, and Washington Irving saw him sometimes in the evenings. Croker rose from his seat at dinner to make one of his brilliant speeches against the Scottish Reform Bill, and said that Scott's company had inspired him. But his most frequent visitor was one he had known but slightly before, Sir James Mackintosh. He as well as Scott was in delicate health,—both, indeed, were prematurely arrived at second childhood,—and whenever they met, the dear old men! their conversation, wherever it might begin, was sure to fasten ere long upon Lochaber. When in Edinburgh he had given orders to erect a monument to Helen Walker, the prototype of Jeanie Deans, in the churchyard of Irongray, her native parish. He now, before starting on his journey, wrote that fine epitaph on her,

which may be read, as we read it once on a lovely
autumn day, on the monument standing in the
centre of its wood, the Cluden murmuring near,
and which for exquisite simplicity has few rivals in
the literature of the churchyard.

We can conceive no event more interesting and
suggestive than a visit from Scott to the Mediterranean in the prime of his health and powers.
Although Scandinavia and the North might, in
some respects, have been more congenial to his
Scald-like genius, yet Italy too, and Malta, had
very great attractions to him as a lover of chivalry
and a worshipper of nature. How, had he gone
abroad ten years previously, would he have enjoyed

> 'The Alps and Apennine,
> The Pyrenean, and the river Po ;'

the blue sweep of the Mediterranean, with the
mountains of Africa seen in the distance ; the Bay
of Naples, with Vesuvius as a pillar of fire and
cloud towering above it ; the Cities of the Dead ;
Rome, the capital of the Catholic world and the
grave of the ancient ; the Rhine singing its old
psalm in the ears of Europe with changeless
and unwearied melody ; Frankfort, where Goethe
was born ;—what living power would Scott have
brought to and derived from these time-hallowed

U

scenes! what materials for superb fiction would he have accumulated! How his expectations would have been exceeded, and his imaginative dreams been verified! But now, alas! in his enfeebled state, while going to see the ruins of empires, he seemed carrying dust to dust, and ashes to ashes.

On the 29th of October, in company with his son and two daughters, he sailed from Portsmouth in the Barham. He was sick, like everybody else, in the Bay of Biscay; but when it was passed, he got on deck and greatly enjoyed the feeling of the air, the sea scenery, and the arrangements of the frigate, which were admirable. The vessel seemed his yacht. It 'wandered at his own sweet will,' often altering its course to allow him to see some famous place, and would have halted at Algiers had not a favourable breeze arisen. There had shot up, some few months before, from the depths of the sea, as if to salute the mighty Wizard as he passed, a submarine volcano. It had lingered its allotted time, got a name, 'Graham's Island,' and was beginning to crumble down into the ocean again when Scott arrived. Nothing would prevent him landing on it; and he was soon seen limping over its lava with all his old agility, finding on it two suffocated dolphins and one starved robin redbreast; looking down into its tiny crater and breathing its brimstone gales, and coming on board again with no other trophy than a nautilus shell he had found, and meant to turn into a fairy cup. On this subject a most interesting painting might be founded,—Sir Walter Scott on Graham's Island. It was a meeting of two worn-out and half-quenched volcanoes on the lone salt deep: full of cold scoriæ; fires going out in steam and smoke; creations dead; footing uneasy and full of dreary chasms; both crumbling and soon to disappear in the immeasurable abyss. Alike, Scott and Byron, were lighted on their last pilgrimage by volcanic fires,—Scott by the dull embers of this smouldering island, Byron by the fresh flames of Lipari,—both pointing to doom, to death without return, or to a return more disastrous still.

At Malta Scott found himself very much at home,—in the midst of old friends, such as Hookham Frere, who was residing there, 'the captive of the enchanting climate and the romantic monuments of the old chivalry;' Sir John Stoddart, chief judge of the island, who had known Scott in his early and happy days, when Lasswade was his real and Glenfinlas his imaginary home; and Dr. John Davy, brother of the great chymist. He spent

much of his time in visiting La Valetta with its
knightly antiquities, the church and monuments of
St. John, and the deserted palaces and libraries of
the Knights of Malta. He met a lady, too, here,
a Mrs. John Davy, daughter of a brother advocate,—a Mr. A. Fletcher, whose house had stood
close to 'poor dear 39,' as he called his own old
house in Castle Street. This lady, who watched
him with all the truth of a woman's eye and the
tenderness of a woman's heart, has left in her
diary some pleasingly pathetic glimpses of the
faded but amiable poet as she saw him at Malta,
and contrasted him with the Scott she had known
in Scotland only five or six years before : ' His
articulation was manifestly affected, though not, I
think, quite so much so as his expression of face.
He wore trousers of the Lowland small-checked
plaid, and, sitting with his hands crossed over the
top of a shepherd-like staff, he was very like the
picture painted by Leslie and engraved for one of
the annuals ; but when he spoke, the varied expression that used quite to redeem all heaviness of
features was no longer to be seen. . . . Hearing the
sound of his voice as he chatted sociably with Mr.
Greig, on whose arm he leaned while walking from
the carriage to the door of the hotel, it seemed to
me that I had hardly heard so homelike a sound

in this strange land, or one that took me so back
to Edinburgh and our own Castle Street, where I
had heard it as he passed so often. Nobody was
at hand at the moment for me to show him to but
an English maid, who, not having my Scotch interest in the matter, only said, when I tried to
enlighten her on the subject of his arrival, " Poor
old gentleman, how ill he looks !" It showed how
sadly a little time must have changed him ; for
when I had seen him last in Edinburgh, perhaps
five or six years before, no one would have thought
of calling him an old gentleman. At dinner parties
he retired soon, being resolutely prudent as to
keeping early hours, though he was unfortunately
careless as to what he ate or drank, especially of
the latter.'

She met him afterwards at a party where he was
all himself, with the same rich felicitous quotation
from favourite authors, the same happy introduction of old traditionary stories—Scotch especially
—in a manner so easy and so unprepared. To Dr.
Davy, then preparing a life of his great brother,
Scott made a feeling and characteristic remark : ' I
hope, Dr. Davy, your mother lived to see your
brother's eminence. There must have been such
great pleasure in that to her.' Neglecting medical
advice, he had one or two additional shocks while

at Malta.   On Tuesday the 14th December he and
his party went again on board the Barham, and
reached Naples on the 17th of the same month,
where his son Charles was waiting to receive
him.

CHAPTER XXV.

RETURN HOME AND DEATH.

AT Naples a similar reception with that of Malta awaited Scott. The British minister — Mr. Hill, afterwards Lord Berwick — took the lead in showing him every attention, and the English nobility and gentry vied with him in the task. Some remarkable men were then in Naples, such as Mr. Auldjo, who gained fame in his day by an ascent of Mont Blanc, and published an account of it which will be found noticed in the *Edinburgh Review* for 1829–30. There, too, was old Matthias, whose *Pursuits of Literature*, seldom read now, had great vogue about the beginning of the century. Few are aware that it was a lengthy poem, with much lengthier notes, and that alike text and notes were steeped in the bitterest personalities and Tory prejudices, blended with vast learning and classical taste. The author had outlived his power, though not his powers; had had the mortification to see the authors he had underrated, such as Parr and Godwin, universally acknowledged, and the party he had vilified—the Whigs—in place; and was now in Naples resting under the shadow of withered laurels. Scott in his ruins he must have surveyed with something of a Sir Mungo Malagrowther satisfaction. Metal more attractive was found in Sir William Gell, the famous topographer, a gentleman who at fifty-six was nearly as complete a wreck as Sir Walter, and this fellow-feeling secured their intimacy. They leaned on each other like two half-fallen pillars in the same crumbling temple.

Sir Walter appeared each morning at the Neapolitan court in the dress of a Scottish archer, of light green and gold embroidery, following in this the same fine instinctive taste which led O'Connell, when he stood on the Calton Hill in 1835, to stand

'In Erin's verdant vesture clad,'

with a gold band around his cap, while all else was green as emerald! Scott would thus cut a gallant figure; and only those near could see in the loose hanging lips and the vacant eye, marks of deep-seated decay. In the evenings the old *cacoethes*

scribendi came upon him. He at first busied himself in collecting Neapolitan and Sicilian ballads
and broadsides, and was aided in this by Matthias ;
but by and by, to the horror of his friends, began
two tales, one a novel entitled *The Siege of Malta*,
and the other a story entitled *Bizarro*, both tend-
ing to excite the deepest pity for the proud genius
that had now, even before his body, become dust.
On the 16th of January he heard of poor Johnny
Lockhart's death, which he simply notices thus :
' This boy is gone whom we made so much of. I
could not have borne it better than I now do, and
I might have borne it much worse.'

Sir William Gell and Scott employed much of
their time in visiting interesting spots near Naples.
One was the Lago d'Agnano, where he was delighted with the tranquil beauty of the spot, and
to find that he had overtaken the autumn, and
found the leaves yet lingering on the trees, while
the meadows around were green as in summer.
It reminded him of a lake in Scotland, to which
country his thoughts were already beginning to
revert with an incipient home - sickness. They
visited Pompeii ; and Scott, being soon fatigued,
allowed himself to be carried through the disen-
tombed city in a chair, and as he went along he
murmured repeatedly, ' The City of the dead ! the

City of the dead!' Probably Dryburgh was as much in his thoughts as Pompeii. He now sometimes imagined that his debts were all paid, and thought that as this was the case he should again take to poetry for his amusement; and Gell encouraged him to think of Rhodes as a subject. He spent a day among the hills at La Cava and Paestum, and visited the grand Benedictine monastery of La Trinita de la Cava, situated in a noble forest of chestnuts, which spreads over very striking hills. Something in the view again reminded him of Scotland, and he repeated Jock of Hazeldean with great emphasis and in a clear voice. In the convent, mass was sung upon the organ. He examined some of the curious MSS. in the archives, and was shown a book containing pictures of the Lombard kings. The whole day was spent delightfully; the fine weather, too, aided in raising his spirits, and in the forest the voice of the Minstrel might be heard, while the evening shadows were descending, repeating once more,

> ' Aye she loot the tears doon fa'
> For Jock o' Hazeldean,'

and some stanzas from his favourite ballad, *Hardyknute*. He was interested when told that his *Old Mortality* was translated into Italian under the title of *The Scottish Puritans.*

Gell took him, in fine, to Pozzuoli and to Cumac. On the way Monte Nuovo was pointed out, and Scott's eye kindled as he heard of its springing up in one night,

'Like fiery arrow shot aloft from some unmeasured bow,'

destroying the village of Tre Pergole and part of the Lucrine Lake. At an elevated spot on the road Gell showed Scott an extensive prospect of the Lake Avernus, the temple of Apollo, the Lucrine Lake, Monte Nuovo, Baiae, Misenum, and the sea; and being more a topographer than a poet, tried to enforce on him the names and knowledge of the localities. Scott listened with respect, but it soon became manifest that, while his ear seemed attentive, his soul was far; for scarcely had they resumed their journey than he repeated in a grave tone, and with great emphasis,

'Up the craggy mountain, and down the mossy glen,
We canna gang a-milking for Charlie and his men.'

Grantully, the lochs of the Stormont, — those seven sisters of beauty,—the braes of Angus, the distant Dunkeld and Rannoch hills,—in short, the scene of the first half of *Waverley* was now in the view of the poet, from which Avernus, Baiae, and even the blue Italian sea had vanished.

He had wished to return by the Tyrol and Germany, partly to see the monuments at Inspruck and the feudal ruins on the Rhine, chiefly to visit a grander ruin still—what had once been Goethe—at Weimar. On the 2d of March Goethe died, and the melancholy luxury was denied the world of beholding the momentary conjunction of the two waning stars—the two grand old leaning towers. Scott heard of his death with surprise and a fearful sorrow. Like that of Borthwickbrae, it was a warning cry,—'Be ye also ready.' 'Alas for Goethe!' he exclaimed; 'but he at least died at home. Let us to Abbotsford.'

On the 16th of April his son Charles (who had obtained leave of absence, Walter having been compelled to return to his regiment) set out with his father on their homeward way, travelling in a barouche, which could be easily turned into a bed. The journey revived him, and still more the reception he met at Rome. In the ancient city of the Cæsars, with its massive ruins and gigantic death-smiles of art, he took little interest now,—perhaps never would have taken so much as many vastly inferior men. Into the treasures of the Vatican his strength forbade him to penetrate. He was not, as he had been, 'a gigantic genius grappling with whole libraries,' but a feeble valetudinarian, creeping and stumbling through them. For Rome as the Catholic metropolis he now cared little or nothing ; but there was still another aspect of the Eternal City which proved attractive to the mighty novelist. He valued it as the centre of intrigues, plots, dark assignations, darker assassinations, and all those abnormal incidents and strange characters which make up the wild romance of history, and form the elements of sensational fiction. To this kind of style there had always been a lurking tendency in Scott's mind, but his good sense had suppressed and modified it, till now, in his second childhood, it came out in full force, and would have produced a great deal in the most extravagant vein had it not been that a dead hand was holding the pen. Hence we find him listening with extraordinary delight to the Duke of Corchiano, when he told him he was possessed of a vast collection of papers, giving true accounts of all the murders, poisonings, intrigues, and curious adventures of all the great Roman families during many centuries, all of which were at his service to copy and publish in his own way as historical romances, only disguising the names, so as not to compromise the living descendants. Scott was so captivated that he at one time thought of remaining for some time in Rome, and at another of returning there the next winter. 'Too late,' of course, was inscribed on this and many other schemes. At an earlier date he would undoubtedly have made much of these Italian stories. Yet we need hardly regret his lack of service, when we remember, first, that the selection of such themes might have given a morbid hue to his writings, and left on them a sort of Monk Lewis savour, instead of the fresh smell of the *gowans* which was natural to them ; and, secondly, since such masters as Schiller, Shelley, Croly, and Washington Irving have treated them so well,— Schiller in his *Ghost Seer ;* Shelley in his *Cenci ;* Irving in some of his better *Tales of a Traveller ;* Croly in his magnificent *Colonna the Painter ;* not to speak of Aird's beautiful *Buy a Broom,* which is essentially of an Italian type ; and not inferior to any of all we have named, that very powerful and thrilling anonymous story which appeared in *Blackwood* during 1828, and is entitled 'Di Vasari, a Tale of the Plague at Florence.'

Whatever might be the cause, and feeble and diseased as Sir Walter was now, the records of his conversation at Rome are as rich as are to be found in any part of his biography. One reason doubtless was, that he was watched as a setting sun is watched; every parting gleam registered, and its zodiacal light fancied if not seen above. Sparks of intellect and wit shone forth occasionally. Speaking of a ruined castle which he loved to visit, and where he used to stand uncovered : 'If it had remained uncovered for a century, surely he might uncover for an hour.' He quoted with great humour Mrs. Siddons' solemn hexameter, when asked by the Provost of Edinburgh if the beef were not too salt :

> 'Beef cannot be too salt for me, my lord ;'

and seemed to agree with another of the party, who said he should eat salt to a limb of Lot's wife. His criticism on Lord Holland was, that his 'language illustrates and adorns his thoughts as light streaming through coloured glass heightens the brilliancy of the objects it falls upon.' Even when wit was thick and intellect wandering, the good humour and the heart remained. When asked once why he had done for another party something very disagreeable for him to do, he replied, 'Why, as I am now good for nothing else, I think it is as well to be good-natured.' How many, on the other hand, religiously retain their ill conditions when all else is gone, as if there were some commandment somewhere for a man who may have lived a fool to die a devil! Scott always and most emphatically near his close acknowledged that he had much reason to be grateful to the public for their indulgence, yet who, after all, in the present age has been so kind to *them?* Perhaps his most affecting saying was to Mr. Cheney. They had been speaking of Goethe, and Scott was deploring the tendency of some of his famous works. 'I answered that he must derive great consolation in the reflection that his own popularity was owing to no such cause. He remained silent for a moment, with his eyes fixed on the ground; when he raised them, as he shook me by the hand, I perceived the light blue eye sparkled with unusual moisture. He added: "I am drawing near the close of my career; I am fast shuffling off the stage. I have been perhaps the most voluminous author of the day; and it is a comfort to me to think that I have tried to unsettle no man's faith, to corrupt no man's principle, and that I have written nothing which on my deathbed I should wish blotted."'

On the next day, Friday the 11th of May, Scott had determined to leave Rome. Mr. Cheney tried in vain to get him to stop, because he should not begin his journey on a Friday. He laughed, and replied, 'Superstition is very picturesque, and I make it at times stand me in great stead, but I never allow it to interfere with interest or convenience.' Yet he had hurried to Scotland, we saw, to prevent his daughter being married in May. On Friday, therefore, the 11th of May, Scott left Rome, with indifference, if not with delight. What although every street was filled with his admirers, every book-shop and book-stall with his works, and every playhouse echoing with operas founded upon them? What although every door was thrown open to receive him, and every curiosity, from the *Codex Vaticanus*, that sacred book kept with sacerdotal jealousy, downwards, would have been free to his inspection? Homewards was now his watchword; 'Scotland's hills for me' the burden of his song, although he knew right well that he would only see them and die. Every hour in his carriage lessened his distance from home, but increased his impatience to arrive there. As he went along, Terni thundered with a louder voice, as if to attract his ear; but he could scarcely be persuaded to turn aside to see this great sight,

'Charming the eye with dread, a matchless cataract.'

He looked at it, and also at the grand church of

X

'Santa Croce in Florence, but derived no inspiration from the lion roar of the one or the 'frozen music' of the other.   On the 17th of the month he crossed the Apennines, and dined on the top of the mountains.   Here he felt at home.   Here was snow, and here were pines, and these suggested Scotland, his own Scotland,

'O'er the hills and far away,'

and he expressed himself delighted.   He hurried through Bologna and Ferrara, but would not even look at any of their interesting objects.   On the 19th he arrived at Venice, and remained there four days, but would see none of its wonders, unless that he leaned a little pensively over the Bridge of Sighs, and scrambled down with difficulty and danger into the dungeons which are beneath it. Entering the Tyrol, that magnificent country had no charms, and on a page of the Book of Guests an after traveller found Scott's name registered by himself thus, 'Sir Walter Scott, *for Scotland.*' The chapel even of Inspruck started no enthusiasm, and through Munich, Ulm, and Heidelberg he moved on as if in his coffin to Frankfort. There, on the 5th of June, he entered a bookseller's shop, and the people, seeing an English party, produced some lithographs, among others one of

Abbotsford. He said, 'I have that already, sir,' and hastened, as if a serpent had stung him, back to the inn, unrecognised.

On the 8th of June they embarked at Frankfort on the Rhine steamboat, and during the first two days, as they descended that 'abounding and rejoicing river,' he seemed placidly happy. At Nimeguen, however, on the 9th, some hours of great depression were succeeded by a serious attack of apoplexy, combined with paralysis. His faithful attendant Nicholson bled him, which produced partial reanimation; but he immediately insisted on renewing his journey, and on the 11th was lifted at Rotterdam into an English steamboat. He reached London on the 13th of June, and was carried to the St. James' Hotel, Jermyn Street. Here many of his friends in London, some from Edinburgh, and all his family, rallied round him. He recognised and blessed, but could not converse with his children. The first medical men were in daily attendance, but could do nothing for him. He lay in a stupor which seemed changeless as death.

Allan Cunningham was in London then. He had been in Dumfries while Burns was dying, and says : 'During his illness Dumfries was like a besieged place, and the whole conversation on the streets was about him and him alone.' He found

it, strange to tell, much the same in reference to
Scott in London. Walking home late one night,
he found several working men standing at the
corner of Jermyn Street ; and one of them asked
him, as if there had been only one deathbed in
London, 'Do you know, sir, if this is the street
where *he* is lying ?' Yes, a king lying in state !

Messages without number were incessantly sent
to his hotel, including daily inquiries from all the
members of the royal family. Reports being
circulated that his funds were exhausted, the
Government most munificently offered him whatever sum from the public treasury might be necessary, but the offer was respectfully declined.

Whenever the cloud partially broke, Abbotsford
still shone out on the eyes of the sufferer, and
seemed by its summer beauty to beckon him northwards. It was as if, like his own Meg Merrilees
with Derncleugh, his spirit would not leave the body
but in his favourite spot. Toward it, therefore, he
proceeded on the 7th July in the James Watt
steamer, accompanied by Lockhart, Cadell, Dr.
Thomas Watson (a medical man), and his two
daughters. The party arrived at Newhaven on the
9th, and being still, as he had been all the voyage,
unconscious, he was conveyed to Douglas' Hotel,
St. Andrew Square. Here he lay for two days,

Edinburgh on the whole unaware that he had returned ; at least, no demonstration whatever was
made.   We forget if even the newspapers recorded
the arrival.   And hence, too, to preserve *incognito* as
much as possible, it was at a very early hour of the
morning of the 11th that Sir Walter Scott, lifted
into his carriage, left, and knew not that he was leaving his own romantic town for ever.   He remained
torpid, till, descending the valley of the Gala, he
raised his head, and began, like a man waking from
a dream, to gaze about him.   Suddenly he murmured, ' Gala Water surely, Buckholm, Torwood-
lee.'   When he saw the Eildons, he became greatly
excited; and when, turning on his couch, he caught
a glimpse of Abbotsford, he uttered a cry of delight,
and could hardly be kept in the carriage.   His excitement continued ungovernable till he reached
the threshold of the door.   Laidlaw was in waiting,
and assisted in carrying him to the dining-room.
Here he sat bewildered for a few minutes, when,
resting his eye on his old kind friend, he said, ' Ha !
Willie Laidlaw ; how often, man, have I thought
of you !'   By this time his dogs assembled around
his chair.   They fawned on him, and licked his
hands.   He now sobbed and now smiled, till exhausted nature laid him asleep in his own Abbotsford.

Next day he awoke perfectly conscious where he was, and was wheeled round the garden, the grandchildren pushing the chair before them, and the venerable patriarch smiling serenely on them, on the dogs, on the house, and on the July roses in full bloom. He even talked a little, said he was better of being at home, and might cheat the doctors yet. ' Nothing like my ain house in all my travels. Just one turn more.' And then he slept like an infant.

Next day he was again wheeled round the garden, and then into the library, and placed by the central window, that he might look out on the Tweed. He expressed a wish that Lockhart should read to him, and when he asked from what book, he replied, ' Need you ask? there is but one.' Very impressive, certainly ! This man had read the most of the books in the literature of his own country and of other lands ; he had written himself hundreds of volumes ; he was surrounded at the moment by a vast library of books in all languages ; and yet, now in his dying hours, there was but one book he thought worth listening to. Lockhart read him the 14th chapter of John. What pencil shall give us the aged and worn-out Wizard, with velvet cap, faded features, but brilliant eye, listening in the library of Abbotsford to the blended sounds of the Tweed gently murmuring o'er its pebbles, and the accents of the divinest love and compassion flowing from the lips of the Man of Sorrows? 'Let not your heart be troubled, neither let it be afraid : ye believe in God, believe also in me. In my Father's house there are many mansions. I go to prepare a place for you.' Scott, when the chapter was read, said to his son-in-law, 'Well, this is a great comfort. I have followed you distinctly, and I feel as if I were yet to be myself again.' He again was put to bed, and sunk into a deep, sweet slumber.

Next day was much the same, only he asked Lockhart to read him something amusing,—something of Crabbe. Lockhart complied ; and Scott, imagining it was a new production, cried out, 'Capital ! Crabbe has lost nothing.' It was the attack in *The Borough* on players. 'How will poor Terry endure these cuts ?' At last he could not stand it. 'Shut the book ; it will touch Terry to the quick.'

Next day, he again mistook *Phœbe Dawson* (a story which had been read to C. J. Fox on his deathbed) for some part of a new volume published by Crabbe while he was in Italy. 'That evening he heard the Church Service, and when I was about to close the book, said, "Why do you omit the

Visitation for the Sick?"' which Lockhart accordingly added.

On Tuesday the 17th he tried once more to write, but the right hand had lost its cunning, and the pen dropped from it helplessly. It was like Napoleon resigning his empire. The sceptre had departed from Judah: Scott was to *write no more.* Little wonder that he sunk back on his pillow with the large tears flowing down his cheek; or that, when after a brief sleep, Laidlaw having said, 'Sir Walter has had a little repose,' he exclaimed, 'No, Willie; no repose for Sir Walter but in the grave!' and again he wept bitterly.

Deliriums and delusions without number followed. Now he thought himself administering justice as the Selkirkshire sheriff; anon he was giving Tom Purdie orders anent trees; now, it is said, he dreamed he was in hell,—a dream not uncommon with imaginative persons *in extremis.* Sometimes, according to Lockhart, his fancy was in Jedburgh, and the words 'Burke Sir Walter' escaped him in a dolorous tone; and anon his mind seemed for the last time time to

'Yoke itself with whirlwinds and the northern blast;'

and, as it 'swept the long tract of day,' words issued from it worthy of the Great Minstrel, snatches from Isaiah or the Book of Job, some grand ragged verse torn off from the Scottish Psalms, or an excerpt sublimer still from the Romish Litany, such as,

> ' Dies iræ, dies illa,
> Solvet sæclum in favilla ;'

or, in a more pensive mood, when the whirlwind was moaning its last,

> ' Stabat mater dolorosa,
> Juxta crucem lachrymosa,
> Dum pendebat Filius.'

Perhaps his family, who remembered how, to the harp of Allan Bane, Roderick Dhu's

> ' Freed spirit burst away,
> As though it soared from battle fray,'

wished that the soul of the 'old Makkar' would spring up on one of those words of winged fire to return no more ; but it was otherwise ordered. The end was near, but it was not yet, and it was not thus.

On the 17th September Sir Walter awoke from those whirling dreams, conscious and composed. He told Nicholson to bring Lockhart instantly to his side ; and when he came, he said to him, 'Lockhart, I may have but a minute to speak to you. My dear, be a good man; be virtuous, be religious; be a good man. Nothing else will give you any comfort when you come to lie here.' He paused; and Lockhart said, 'Shall I send for Sophia and Anne?' 'No,' he replied, 'don't disturb them. Poor souls! I know they were up all night. God bless you all.' He fell into a deep sleep, and seemed scarcely again conscious, except on the arrival of his sons, who were now both summoned in haste to see the close. This came about half-past one P.M. on the 2d September, when, in the presence of all his children, the sun of autumn shining softly in at the open window, and the Tweed uttering its silver monody as it crept along, the spirit of Scott was released from its body of death. His eldest son kissed and closed his eyes.

A *post mortem* examination discovered that the cause of his death was a slight softening of the brain.

He was buried on the 26th September in Dryburgh churchyard,—a very large company, some of them from distant parts of Scotland, following his remains, which were carried by the hands of his old domestics and foresters, the pall being borne by his sons, his sons-in-law, his little grandson, and his cousins. Prayers were offered up in the house by Dr. Baird, and Dr. Dickson of St. Cuthbert's, Edinburgh. The train of carriages extended over a mile, and the Yeomanry followed on horseback in great numbers. Some accident made the hearse pause for a few minutes on the top of the hill at Bemerside, a point where Scott used often in admiration to rein up his steed,[1] and the view from which the late Angell James pronounced the grandest he had ever seen.

The trees of Dryburgh were waving with a stormy wind, and the sky was lowering as the coffin was, about half-past five P.M., deposited in the dust. A sob burst from a thousand hearts, but was stilled by the voice of Archdeacon Williams reading over him the beautiful service of the Church of England, and laying him down in the sure and certain hope of a blessed resurrection.

All the newspapers in Scotland, and many in England, clothed their columns in black for his death ; and on the day of his funeral the bells of most of our cities rung a muffled peal,—those of Glasgow, as heard on that dark September morning, are still sounding in our ears.

Sir Walter died free of debt. The sale of his

---

[1] The horse of the hearse is said to have been the one Scott used to ride.

works, the insurance of his life, and a sum advanced by Cadell on the security of his copyrights, completely cleared his engagements. The subsequent fates of his family and estate are too well known to be rehearsed here. We happened to be present at the meeting held in Edinburgh to pave the way for a monument to his memory, and listened with delight to the speeches of Lord Jeffrey, who spoke of all classes coming into the Assembly Rooms as if 'into the temple of the Deity,' to do honour to the great departed ; and of Professor Wilson, who closed by quoting, in tones of trembling pathos, the lines of the poet,—

> ' Ne'er to those dwellings, where the mighty rest,
> Since their foundations came a nobler guest.'

The Duke of Buccleugh, too, spoke in a good spirit, as became a chief over a bard. The result of this meeting is now that superb column which, towering above the city of palaces, almost challenges equality with the mountains which do around it, as with ancient Jerusalem, 'stand alway.'

CHAPTER XXVI.

SCOTT, THE MAN AND POET.

EW literary characters have been so blameless as Sir Walter Scott. Genial, gentlemanly, frank, open, homely, kindhearted, considerate, utterly free from vanity, jealousy, envy, malice, or guile, he was also distinguished by high principle and the most honourable feelings. He had plenty, withal, of prudence, with the slightest spice of what the Scotch call pawkiness, but duplicity and craft were unknown to, perhaps inconceivable by him. We forget if in all his characters there be one that is *sly*, or, properly speaking, cunning. His very hypocrites wear glass masks and dissolving cloaks, and are all too transparent. He had strong sensuous appetites and passions, as most healthy men have, but he kept them under strict control. He ate an enormous breakfast, but it was his main meal. He picked away at dinner, and seldom supped at all. While the richest and most sparkling wines were circulating at his board; he preferred a little spirits and water, and diminished his quantity latterly to almost zero. He slept, after working double tides, on a tankard of porter and a single cigar; and a great deal of his talk about 'flowing quaichs' and sturdy 'morning draughts' was rather antiquarian than real. One amusing little story we heard in Cumberland about him. Wordsworth and he were to climb Helvellyn, and on the way passed a small public-house, the proprietor of which, standing at the door, saluted Wordsworth as a neighbour but no customer; Scott, whose name he did not know, more warmly as a stranger but a customer. It turned out that Wordsworth, being in his house as well as habits a very strict teetotaller, Scott had walked out on various occasions alone, and enjoyed his 'morning' at the little hostelry. A hearty laugh followed the eclaircissement, and the immortal pair proceeded (*morningless*) up the mountain! But to excessive or habitual drinking he was in his latter years a determined foe,—led to this by warnings connected with more than one of his relatives; and he said to Lockhart once, 'Depend on it, of all vices intemperance is the most adverse to greatness.' Like most men of such

unbounded popularity as he,—and especially in the
past age,—he might have encountered temptations,
to intrigues, but such follies he seems invariably
to have waved away from him ; and his life on this
point stood in edifying contrast to many of the
most celebrated men of his period. We have heard
him called an indifferent husband ; but this, we
believe, does not convey the full truth on the subject,—hardly a fond husband, he was a kind and a
faithful one. As a father he was tender and con-
fiding to a degree. In friendship he was steady
as steel ; and as a landlord was eminently kind-
hearted, considerate, and dutiful. This his foresters
and small tenants felt as they hoisted aloft the
coffin of their father and friend ! In all private
and business and family and literary matters he
was the most methodical of men. He despised the
litter and gown-and-slipper tricks of literary men.
His study was not a Chaos but a Kosmos; and he
the Demiurge who had reduced it all to comely
order, and sat in the midst clothed as well as in
his right mind. He liked order in others too.
When a correspondent sent him a letter sealed
with a wafer, he replied, ' I am not a particular
man, but I detest wafers.' To his brethren on
the Bench, and his contemporaries or juniors at
the Bar, he was ever courteous without fudge,

accessible, and on easy terms. He never needed and never tried on the airs of the great man. There is often as much pride in the mode and angle of stooping as in going on tiptoe. Scott did neither the one nor the other; he simply stood erect and walked straight forward. To young and rising authors he was indulgent rather than severe, as a rule; and his purse as well as criticism was ever open to those of them who required and deserved aid,—nay, sometimes whether they deserved it or not. According to Hogg, he almost literally supported some unfortunate authors.

In political zeal, as well as in family pride, he was at one time excessive, but experience tended much to modify his feelings. He mourned more, ultimately, over his own hard treatment of his brother Daniel than over that brother's pusillanimous and unworthy conduct. The 'greatest of these is charity' rose gradually into the centre of his moral code. In his sheriffdom he was the father of the fatherless, the shield of the oppressed, and known and welcomed as a sudden sunbeam in the dwelling of the poor and the dependent, acting in the very spirit of the grand words of Burke when he speaks of Howard 'remembering the forgotten.' From his flaming Pittism of 1806 he was subsiding into a very moderate Conservative, when the

panic of the Reform Bill came over the land, and
he proceeded to adjust his Tory mantle round him
ere he fell,—fell, as he thought, with his country
and his race! Had he lived a few years longer, he
might have gone on with Peel in his slow but
certain movement toward Liberalism. He was by
far too wide-minded and warm-hearted to have
stood sullenly still, or come in last in such a
generous and inevitable advancement.

Scott's great fault, as is now universally con-
ceded, was his desire of territorial acquisition and
family aggrandizement. To be a *laird*, to found
a family, to reach a patriarchal or feudal ideal,
was his ambition,—an ambition partly springing
from his idiosyncrasy as a lover of Scotland, as
an echo of past ages, and which we could not
sternly blame, had it not led to reckless speculations, and to an extravagance of expenditure in-
volving a certain degree of moral turpitude. As
it is, the turreted mansion of Abbotsford looks
like a Castle Folly, and worse, because it rose
over the head of one of the most sensible as well
as gifted men that ever lived, reminding you of a
cap and bells on the brow of some hoary senior,
who has attained more than the age, and deems
that he has all the wisdom of Solomon. There
is almost an immoral incongruity in the spectacle.

Y

Hundreds of anecdotes are floating through the south of Scotland anent Scott's kindly private ways. One of the Ettrick Shepherd's children was born with a weak foot. Scott never met the father without inquiring, 'How's the footie?' At Altrive a curious little incident occurred. Scott was dining with Hogg there. Before dinner he was looking at Hogg's library. He drew out a volume, one of several, labelled 'Scott's Novels.' It was *Waverley.* Putting back the volume, he said, 'Your binder has put a "t" too many in the word Scots.' 'Not at all,' said Hogg; 'I wrote out the copy.' Scott smiled. The secret had not yet been divulged.

He used to call those he knew well by their Christian names,—Willie Laidlaw, Jamy Ballantyne, Johnnie Ditto. The late Mr. William Banks, engraver, Edinburgh, was assistant to Mr. Lizars. Whenever Scott entered the office, he would sit down beside the assistant, with the kind words, 'How are ye, Willie?' Lockhart does not relate that Sir Walter was elected Rector of St. Andrews University in March 1825. The election was contrary to the then existing laws of the University. When a deputation of the students waited on him, he kindly thanked them, and begged them to 'mind the laws and their studies.'

His appearance need not be described, and cannot be well described by one that never saw him. It had great variety of aspect and expression. Edward Irving insisted on it to De Quincey that the permanent expression on Scott's face was that of the Border horse-jockey,—shrewd, gruff, and rather selfish. Ordinary people, who saw him in his ordinary moods in the Parliament House, have described his look to us as that of dense stolidity, like the face of a heavy country bumpkin. But he had higher and more characteristic expressions. Those who waited on his countenance till it 'waukened,'—till the angel disturbed the placid pool,—were well rewarded for their patience, when the blended fires of the poet and the warrior looked out at his eyes, and his tall brow lightened up like a mountain in the morning sun ; and even on that cold bench, and surrounded by those dry, keen lawyers, he was suddenly

> 'Attired
> In sudden brightness like a man inspired.'

Latterly, when his hair had become snow-white, such moments of glory 'made him seem like Mont Blanc with the dawn shining on his summit.' Wilson and Lockhart both describe him well ; and in Carlyle we find his familiar features shown us in a new and strange light, as if in the gleam of an apothecary's evening window, ghastlily, luridly like him, liker his corpse. Scott the man and Scott the poet may seem at first to furnish rather elements of contrast than of harmony. As a man, he was plain, practical, worldly even to some extent; as a poet, chivalrous, impulsive, full of minstrel enthusiasm, selecting by choice all his subjects and all his characters in the wildest and most out-of-the-way corners. Hence some others besides Carlyle have been led to believe that, unless we can conceive him formed on the principle of the composite figures in Ezekiel, half ox and half eagle, half business man and half Border minstrel, we must doubt the thoroughness of his poetic vein, and deem his mantle put on for the nonce. We grant, however, at once his bifold nature, and Carlyle himself admits his sincerity. He says, indeed, that he was not a *Vates*, that he was possessed by no great idea, that he wrote most of his poetry and prose to *order*, and that there was ' not fire enough in his belly to consume all the sins of the world.' Much of this might be alleged with equal truth against Shakspeare. Shakspeare was not consciously a *Vates*. Shakspeare would have been puzzled to reply to Carlyle or to Ulrici, had they been alive to ask what

his main idea was. Shakspeare 'was great, nor
knew how great he was.' Shakspeare taught, and
guided, and cheered the world very much as the
sun does, in grand, unconscious might, ' God being
in him, and he knew it not.' Shakspeare wrote,
we believe, most of his plays to secure that moderate competence on which he retired at the
early age of fifty. Shakspeare had even less out-
standing personality than Scott. A munificent
and modest benefactor, he knocked at the door
of the human family by night, threw in inestimable
wealth, fled, and the sound of his footsteps dying.
away in the distance was all the tidings he has
given of himself. Carlyle, indeed, sees the resemblance of Shakspeare to Scott, but he grossly per-
verts it, calling Shakspeare's utterance ' living fire,'
and Scott's 'futile phosphorescence,'—an asser-
tion we must denounce as absurdly false and in-
consistent with his other statements. Nothing but
futile phosphorescence from a most 'genuine man !'
Impossible ! As to fire-eating and fire-bellied
consumption of evil, we venture to say that Scott,
with little definite purpose in him, with a contempt
for most of the so-called *moral* and *religious* novels
which were then pouring from the press, and with a
greater scorn still for such *im*moral and *ir*religious
tales as *The Elective Affinities*, which Goethe was

sweating out with the animus of a Priapus, and polishing after production with the skill and pains of an Ovid, has, by the healthy tone of his morals, and his usually reverent spirit, done a vast deal to purify the literary atmosphere; and if he did not forcefully blast, yet he silently sapped many of the vices of the times, meeting them on what is their strong point, namely, the pleasure they give, and substituting for that a rarer and purer enjoyment.

Carlyle accuses Scott of 'want of finish,'—a charge which had been more worthy of a Voltaire blaming Shakspeare for putting a seaport in Bohemia, or for violating the unities, than of a critic who glories in being an admirer of a chartered libertine like Jean Paul, and whose own writings in general set finish, order, logic, grammar, and a hundred other conventionalisms at defiance. But the truth is, that when Carlyle wrote his estimate of Scott, noble and true as it is in many points, he was himself steeped to the lips in disappointment and disgust; his own wheel had reached its lowest and most wintry point; and the cry, 'Ho! we go up to summer now,' had not yet been raised. He would probably write differently at present. Yet his closing words are very beautiful: 'When he departed, he took a man's life

along with him. No sounder piece of British manhood was put together in that eighteenth century of
time. Alas! his fine Scotch face, with its shaggy
honesty, sagacity, and goodness, when we saw it
latterly on the Edinburgh streets, was all worn
with care; the joy all fled from it; ploughed deep
with labour and sorrow. We shall never forget it;
we shall never see it again. Adieu, Sir Walter,
pride of all Scotchmen, take our proud and sad
farewell!'

Whether a *Vates* or not, and whether his poetry
was written, like Peter Pindar's razors, simply to
sell, there can be no doubt that the article he
produced was a very pleasant one. Scott's poetry,
considerably over-rated in its day, has since received rather sparing justice, and this mainly
because it has been compared to that of others,
with which it has scarcely one element of simi-
larity. You may say it is not deep like that of
Wordsworth, nor exquisitely artless like that of
Burns, nor soaringly spiritual like Shelley's, nor
passionately powerful like Byron's,—but what is all
this to the point? It does not seek nor pretend
to be aught of all this,—no, nor to be everlastingly
witty like Butler's, nor polished to the pitch of
pin-points or fire-irons like Pope's, nor artistically
and elaborately perfect like Tennyson's, nor para-

doxical like Browning's, nor splendidly smutty like Swinburne's. It pretends to be Scott's poetry —coming after Homer's and the *Ballads of the Border;* and it has, besides their martial energy, a picturesque force, a chivalric spirit and fire, a free and graceful movement, and at times an aerial charm and sweetness, all its own. Call *Marmion, The Lay of the Last Minstrel,* and the rest, as Coleridge does call them, rhymed romances, and not poems, if you please; they are so delightful, that, in spite of the critic, the delight will overflow into all ages, as it has already into all lands.

Ere we can do justice to Scott's poetry, we must remember what it succeeded and supplanted. Previous to his rise, Darwin, with the cold ingenuities of his *Botanical Garden;* Hayley, with the turgid tameness of his *Triumphs of Temper;* and Monk Lewis, with the clever monstrosities of his *Tales of Terror,* were among our most popular authors. Coleridge, Southey, and Wordsworth were all singing indeed, but singing to an audience rather few than fit. Campbell alone, of the true poets of the time, had gained the popular ear, and he was fallen sound asleep—a boy Apollo —under the early laurels which the *Pleasures of Hope* had given him. In such a state of things, even had the merit of Scott's poetry been much

less than it was, it would have done good service.
For it was, if not great, eminently true; if not
thoroughly original, the models it imitated were
the best; and if not charged with profound
thought, it was fresh, natural, unconventional in
spirit, and eminently free, flowing, and unhack-
neyed in style. And then it had characters of
much interest, and contained many passages of
transcendent power. The Last Minstrel himself,
Brian the Hermit, Roderick Dhu, Allan Bane,
Margaret of Branksome, and Ellen Douglas,
belonged to the former. Melrose Abbey by
Moonlight, Love of Country, the Battle of Flodden, the Battle in *The Lady of the Lake* by the
side of Loch Katrine, the Death of Roderick
Dhu, and the Picture of Skye, belonged to
the latter class, and were worthy of any poet,
living or dead. Altogether, at that period, and
before Byron had written his strong poetry, and
Wordsworth and Coleridge had been appreciated,
and Campbell had been again aroused to indite
his later and better strains, and the wild genius
of Shelley had flashed and died in the horizon
like a monster meteor, we cannot blame Scott
for captivating the public with his song, or the
public for being captivated with Scott. It was
the best thing of the kind going. The author

was a true poet, and it was scarcely his misfortune, and certainly not his fault, that his poetry was even more popular than it was good.

Carlyle himself, although he had spoken of Scott as producing little but futile phosphorescence in comparison with Shakspeare, is compelled to admit some real merit in his poetry. 'We in this age have fallen into spiritual languor, destitute of belief, yet terrified at scepticism ; reduced to live a stinted half-life, under strange, new circumstances. Now vigorous whole-life, this was what of all things these delineations afford. The reader was carried back to rough, strong times, wherein these maladies of ours had not yet arisen. Brawny fighters, all cased in buff and iron, their hearts, too, sheathed in oak and triple brass, caprioled their huge horses, shook their death-doing spears, and went forth in the most determined manner, nothing doubting. The reader sighed, "Oh that I too had lived in these times, had never known these logic cobwebs, this doubt, this sickliness, and been and felt myself alive among men alive !"'

So that, after all, Scott's poetry was not mere phosphorescence, nor mere honeycomb, nor yet, as Carlyle calls it immediately afterwards, 'a beatific land of Cockaigne and Paradise of Donothings.' It had tonic and bracing qualities withal. It had something of old Homer in it ; and, like his poetry, and others of that grand age,

> ' Flashed o'er the soul a few heroic rays,
> Such as lit onward to the Golden Fleece,
> And fired their fathers in the Colchian days.'

What Scotchman, at least, has not felt his blood boil while singing or hearing sung *Blue Bonnets over the Border*, or the *Gathering of Gregarach :*

> ' There's mist on the mountain, and night on the brae,
> But the clan has a name that is nameless by day.
> Then gather, gather, gather, Gregarach.'

Or Norman's song in the *Lady of the Lake :*

> ' No fond regret must Norman know ;
> When bursts Clan Alpine on the foe,
> His heart must be like bended bow,
> His foot like arrow free, Mary.'

Or Flora's fine chant in *Waverley :*

> ' O high-minded Moray, the exiled, the dear,
> In the blush of the dawning the Standard uprear ;
> Wide, wide on the winds of the North let it fly,
> Like the sun's latest flash when the tempest was nigh.'

We venture to assert that the poetry in the Waverley Novels alone would have entitled its author to rank as one of our foremost modern bards.

CHAPTER XXVII.

THE MASTER OF THE NOVEL.

E come, while admiring Scott's poetry, to speak of his prose with greater pleasure, because, while exhibiting all the finer traits of his verse, it manifests qualities not to be found in it, and which serve to bring out better the strength, breadth, richness, and originality of his genius.

Surely those were halcyon days for Scotland; and though then a boy of ten or eleven, we remember the latter portion of them well, and watched them as closely as we would do now, when twice or thrice every year it was announced: 'A new novel by the author of *Waverley* may be expected.' What interest was excited! What an almost, yea, altogether audible smacking of lips was heard! What speculations were started about the probable era of history to be embraced, or

particular portion of country to be described!
How many were saying, 'Will he give us a novel
on Wallace by and by, supplanting the small
swipes of Miss Porter, and forming a pendant to
his picture of Bruce in the *Lord of the Isles?*' Not
a few in the country districts of Scotland were ask-
ing, 'Will he fix the scene this time in our county,
or, oh joy! in our native parish?' If an elderly
gentleman, with tall, rather clumsy form, white
hair, and a little lame withal, were seen prowling
about the environs of a Highland village, the
rumour instantly ran, 'This is the Great Unknown
studying for his next novel.' (We knew a case
where the name of Walter Scott and a grey head,
possessed by a dissenting preacher,—a very worthy
man, but one of the dullest dogs that ever barked in
a pulpit,—had nearly procured for him the freedom
of a northern county town, and did, dexterously
used by a wag, elicit a peal of bells on his entrance.)
How proud were Perthshire and Perth when
Catherine Glover stepped forth, leaning on Sir
Walter Scott's stalwart arm! We remember how
the quidnuncs and critics of an old Scottish village
were puzzled, and even somewhat alarmed, at the
possible meaning of the word 'Redgauntlet,' when
it was first announced. And when each expected
tale appeared, what crowding of booksellers' shops!

what enormous parcels, making the stage-coaches in those ante-railway days tremble and vibrate to and fro, and carriers' carts collapse! what copious extracts filled· the papers! how critics perspired and panted in uttering words vast enough to express their admiration! and how, while Edinburgh, Glasgow, London, Paris, Copenhagen, Leipsic, Vienna, and New York were rejoicing over the humours or weeping at the pathos of the new story, the shepherd was *guffawing* upon the mountain side, or wiping his tears with his maud ; the young maiden reading it on a garden-seat, or on her father's house stairs, with her long golden hair falling neglected over her shoulders ; while the enthusiast boy, after he had waited for it for long weeks, when it did at last arrive, perhaps in the dimness of the late summer evening, when it could not be read, would take it up and clasp it to his bosom! We know something from personal observation, too, of the delight with which the better writings of Dickens, such as *David Copperfield*, were welcomed in London ; but if they produced more laughter, we are certain they did not make such a deep and permanent impression, had not the same broad, natural interest, or the same ideal, poetical, and most romantic charm.

All this is long over. The man is long dead. The

works, stripped of their halo of novelty, must be
judged of as they are in themselves, and in the severe
and searching light of the new age which has risen
around us ; and that test they can stand, and that
light they have already borne. Often a century
must elapse ere a writer attain his true niche in
the temple of Fame. About half that time passed
from the appearance of Milton's *Paradise Lost* till
Addison made it popular by his criticisms in the
Spectator ; but Scott, though dead not forty years
ago, is already a classic, has had his popularity
confirmed, and his fame endorsed by the civilised
world, and is as secure of his place in the future,
although not precisely the *same* place, as Milton,
Homer, and Shakspeare. Not the slightest danger
of this verdict being reversed. A writer of great
ability, in the *Westminster Review*, predicted a few
years ago that the future popularity of the three
principal idols of our present literary hour, Carlyle,
Tennyson, and Ruskin, was precarious ; and this
he grounded on what *he* thought their imperfect
and belated political and religious opinions. But
whether this vaticination be true or false, it is
the glory of Scott, as well as of Shakspeare and
Homer, that the power of his writings is altogether
irrespective of any political principles, and of
aught except the broadest and most humane

religious sentiments. He, although a Conservative by blood and training, has never, no, not in *Old Mortality* itself, defended tyranny, never become the devil's advocate, never entangled any esoteric or exoteric creed into his writings, never indulged in senseless outbursts against commerce, or law, or logic, or metaphysics, nor in outbursts against anything. He has identified his genius with the deep, general principles of humanity, and has learned and used a language understood and felt wherever man eats and drinks, falls and rises, sins and suffers, loves and hates; and aims at being neither a politician, nor a philosopher, nor a theologian, but at being what many politicians, philosophers, and theologians are not—a man.

In the Waverley Novels the poetic element which was in him so strongly, is held quite subordinate to that of the noble humanity and the wide reflection of all that swept across his universal soul. Scott never pauses too long on a description of nature, never dallies with a fine image; seldom, if ever, indulges in the luxury of rounding sentences merely for the sake of the euphony thereby produced. He looks at dead scenery by the side of living characters, and they must move and he must move along with them; he makes, but has not time to mount his metaphor and turn it into a hippogriff, hobby-horse, or velocipede; and although he often drops the most beautiful sentences in the language,—sentences not surpassed in Burke, or Addison, or Robert Hall,—it is half consciously, and as he is pursuing, without pause or thought of pausing, the path of his story. As Scott is generally read fast, and more for his plot or his characters and the incidents of the tale than for his writing, we would refer our readers, without quoting at present, to such passages in his works, as authenticating our statement, as the night scene in one of the first chapters of *Guy Mannering;* the description of Bothwell Bridge in a summer evening in *Old Mortality;* the pictures of autumn in the *Monastery* and in *St Ronan's Well;* the description of the glorious achievements of alchymy in *Kenilworth;* and there are hundreds besides.

Carlyle recites with approbation a saying of somebody : 'No man has written so many volumes with so few sentences that can be quoted,'—that *have* been quoted were nearer the truth ; and the reason of this is obvious enough : what good or profit in quoting a writer who is in everybody's hands ? Besides, the power of many of our best writers lies in the *whole.* But we are prepared, whenever we deem it necessary, to prove that in no other novelist—not even in Cervantes, or Bulwer,

z

or Godwin—do we find a greater number of sepa-
rable and quotable beauties than in Scott. And
were all these beauties shorn away, there would
remain a residuum of worth and power, of interest
and invention, enough to secure their pre-eminence.
How copious they are in matter; how sweet-
blooded in spirit; how strong, yet simple and
limpid in style,—'simple as the water, strong as the
cataract!' How profound, without any laboured
search or ostentatious anatomy, in their knowledge
of human nature! how minutely accurate usually in
their historical costume! how their characters teem
with life, and move and walk and seem blushing
with the blood which a master spirit has shot into
their resuscitated veins! how delightfully true, yet
splendidly ideal, in their pictures of battle scenery
and historical incident! how pure, amidst all their
genialities and generosities, in their moral tone!
and how sound in the main, healthy and Christian,
broad and charitable, in their religious spirit!

In regarding him as the master of the novel, the
greatest by far that ever lived (Cervantes pos-
sibly was a greater genius, and his *Don Quixote* is
perhaps a better novel than any one of Scott's;
but we look at Scott as the creator of a whole
world of fiction), more minutely we have to speak
of the width of his sympathy, of the use he makes

of the power of contrast, of his immeasurable variety, and of the moral and religious character and influences of his Novels.

Scott's main quality is his exceeding breadth of sympathy. Shakspeare has been called the greatest of men *because* he was the widest of sympathisers. Scott on this point was not very far inferior, and this enabled him to furnish a table with viands adapted for every taste. He presented pictures of nature in her grandest and most solitary aspects; sketches of romantic character; incidents of heroic adventure and sublime superstitions; traditions for the lovers of the strange, the mysterious, and the poetical. Then for antiquarians he had

> ' A rowth o' auld nicknackets,
>   Rusty airn caps and jinglin' jackets
> Wad haud the Lothians three in tackets
>   A towmont guid ;
> And parritch pats and auld saut backets
>   Afore the flood.'

Then for the lovers of sport he could intersperse the liveliest descriptions of hunting, fishing, dogs, horses, and falcons. To the lovers of the military art his Novels were a perfect study,—valuable for their strategic details as well as for the martial fire which burns in them. In courts he is as much at home as in camps, and has been called peculiarly

the poet of princes; and yet, who has painted
the life of the lower ranks with greater force,
fidelity, and sympathy? How many gentlemen
have come glowing from his plastic hand, and yet
with what gusto he has depicted blackguards and
villains of every shape and hue! To scholars every
page teems with recondite lore; to the students of
human nature he unbares the deepest secrets of
the heart. Readers of history find his writings
nearly as true, and far more delightful, than the
works of Robertson and Hume. The books teem
with stories for the lovers of the *Ana;* and ladies
are attracted to them by the purity of their tone
and the chivalric gallantry of their spirit. Gour-
mands even, revel in their imaginary meals so
heartily described, and Scott's Novels are the best
appetizers in the world. In all countries, too, and
in most ages, he is at home,—as strong among the
lilies of France as on the sands of Syria, on the
green turf of Sherwood Forest as on the heather of
Caledonia. All this not only proclaims powers
nearly Shakspearean in width though not in depth,
but proves prodigious culture; and the mere mass
of miscellaneous knowledge in Scott's works were
enough to have founded a brilliant reputation.
Scott's breadth of sympathy is not confined to the
human race. His dogs and horses are much better

drawn than most other novelists' men and women, aye, than the most of nature's ordinary productions in the human line. Witness the terrier Wasp and the mare Dumple; the cow Brockie in *The Heart of Midlothian;* Klepper the Bohemian's palfrey, in *Quentin Durward*; Bevis in *Woodstock;* Roswal, that nobler hound of the Scottish knight, in *The Talisman;* and, best of all, Gustavus, the faithful and congenial horse, who long bears and at last clothes the immortal limbs of Sir Dugald Dalgetty of Drumthwacket, and who was the namesake of Gustavus Adolphus, the lion of the North, and the bulwark of the Protestant faith! Scott had lived much with the lower animals (not the brute but the mute creation, as Lord Erskine used to call them), and learned to understand their habits, and had entered further than most men do into their natures, and those souls of theirs so mysteriously hid in God, but which do really exist, and connect them by strangest cords and sympathies with the human family.

Connected with his breadth is his extreme *fairness* to all his characters,—except, perhaps, the wilder of his Cameronians,—and the justice he does to them even when bad or dubious; faithful thus to his poetic—let us call it rather his Christian— instinct of finding a 'soul of goodness in things

that are evil.' Few men of his time were freer
from evil than Scott, and yet, as Shelley says of
Leigh Hunt, 'none had a more exalted tolerance
for those who do and are evil.' He looks on all
his characters with the benevolent regard of a
creator, and gives them all their due, and nothing
more : if bad, makes the best of them ; if good,
faithfully registers their evil as well as good qualities. Hence his homicides, caterans, and smugglers are all human, and have virtues of their own.
Meg Merrilees, 'harlot, thief, witch, and gipsy,'
has wild fidelity and undaunted resolution. Henbane Dwining is a careful and kind leech to those
whom it is not his interest to poison. Ranald
MacEagh loves his grandchild, and robs from a
hundred Campbells to support Dalgetty his de-
liverer for nothing. Varney is devoted to Leicester.
The Bohemian loves Klepper, and the star Aldeboran and his brethren, and has a lurking liking for
Quentin Durward. Dirk Hatteraick, when charged
with the want of a single virtue, replies, 'Virtue,
Donner! I was always faithful to my owners,
always accounted for cargo to the last stiver ;' and
his last action ere he hangs himself is to write an
account of the state of the trade to Flushing, and
we have no doubt it was a very accurate account !
The murderess, Meg Murdockson, loves Madge

her mad daughter, and will not betray Staunton because she had nursed him at her own breast. Thus ever will the great artist, like the dog in Byron's Darkness, be 'faithful to a corpse, and keep the hounds and wolves away from it,' as much as to a living subject, place every picture in its best possible light, and feel himself bound to express something of that ideal which his genius and his heart see hovering over all beings that God has made. Akin to this fairness is his total want of exaggeration. How well is this shown in the trial scene of Effie Deans! After the heart-rending scene, an ordinary writer would probably have described the crowd as still agitated on leaving the court. Scott, more true to reality, says, 'The crowd rushed shouldering each other out of the court, and soon forgot whatever they had felt as impressive in the scene which they had witnessed.' We find the same moderation and 'moral sweetness' in nearly all his works; and it is in this respect, more than in subtlety of thought or power of imagination, that he approaches Shakspeare. Yet he has occasional touches which, in sudden and almost supernatural felicity and pathos, are worthy of the great English poet. Such is Meg Merrilees saying, 'I am nae good woman. I am bad eneugh; but *I can do whai*

good women canna and darena do.' Such is Rebecca's reply when ordered to remove her veil:
' I will obey you. Ye are *elders among your people ;*
and at your command I will show you the features
of an ill-fated maiden ;' and the wonderful words
she utters when about to spring from the battlements of Torquilstone. Such is the entire scene
between Jeanie and Effie Deans in prison, and the
account of Sir Hugh Robsart's illness in *Kenilworth.* The once celebrated John Scott of Aberdeen (cut off prematurely ere he had established
fully his claim to be one of the finest prose writers
of the day, but whose *Trip to Paris, Character of
Robert Hall as a Preacher,* and paper ' On the
Waverley Novels' in the first volume of *The London Magazine,* will long survive as most admirable
specimens of chaste yet vigorous composition)
thus notices one of his inimitable hits: ' The
Bailie in *Rob Roy* assures his kinsman that if
ever a *hundred pound,* or even *twa !* would put
him and his family into a settled way, he need but
just send him a line to the Saut-market ; and Rob
returns the compliment by squeezing the Bailie's
hand, grasping his basket-hilt, and protesting that,
if any one affronted his kinsman, he *wad stow the
lugs oot of his head were he the best man in Glasgow.* How exquisite is all this ! The citizen, in

a moment of enthusiasm, offering a hundred pounds, or even *twa!* It is like the spring of a cripple, who, not being able to walk a moderate pace, throws himself forward four feet at a time. His liberality bursts out with impetuosity, like a dam of water when the sluice is raised. Such touches as these are not the fruit of study. The giving of them is not probably accompanied with a preconception of their effect. When given, they escape, as it were, like natural oozings from a mind gifted with a wonderfully quick and true feeling of what is picturesque in the operation of the principles of character.'

Still more obvious and equally delightful are the uniform healthiness of Sir Walter's spirit ; the simplicity, clearness, and flexibility of his style, which, capable of the highest eloquence, elaboration, and passionate fervour, pursues in general the tenor of its way as evenly as a common letter; his constant vein of strong sound sense ; his rich but never excessive or ostentatious use of imagery ; his dramatic power; his vivid, if not always minutely accurate, descriptions of scenery; his intense nationality, beautifully blended with a true cosmopolitan width, and the sudden breaking out, amidst prosaic details and mere commonplace, of the bardic spirit, like Hecla's fire spouting out of Hecla's ice. His faults may be summed up thus : frequent carelessness of language; occasional quaintness of thought; a trick of introducing learned terms into conversation, and, as with Baron Bradwardine and Jonathan Oldbuck, pursuing the humours of an odd character to a wearisome length ; a frequent awkwardness in the disentanglement of plots, and, in the latter tales, prolixity of introductions; occasional repetition of himself; an overloading of his page with antiquarian details; an obvious walking through his part at times, and now and then, though very rarely, a profusion of dreary prose. His broad humour, too, is apt to degenerate into farce; nor is his wit always so felicitous or finished as are the efforts of his fancy and imagination.

Scott uses *contrast* with great frequency and uniformly powerful effect in his Novels. Contrast, indeed, producing unity may be called Scott's artistically great and peculiar power,—the two-handed sword of his genius. One of the main merits in *Waverley* lies in its blending of the past and the present in such a thorough union, that you are reminded of the phenomenon described in the grand old ballad of Sir Patrick Spens, 'of the auld mune in the new ane's arms;' and the eagle flying over the Pass of Ballybrough, at which Evan Dhu aims his fowling-piece in vain, seems a lofty link between the Highland hills and the Lowland braes, and a metaphor of the splendid tale itself as connecting the Sassenach and the Gael together! In *Guy Mannering*, over the quiet pastoral scenes and simple characters hovers the weird light of the supernatural like an electric arch, and one feels that there was intense beauty if not truth in that old astrology, of which it is not perhaps too much to say,—

> ' Surely no fantasy that ever crossed
> The heaven of midnight like a golden haze,
> Making the lovely lovelier, as a crown
> Of halo does the moon, so fair as thou,
> Divinest falsehood called Astrology !
> Wild dawn of science ! morning dream of Truth !'

In *Rob Roy*, the life of a counting-house in London and the abode of a cateran in Balquhidder are brought into sharp, and, on the whole, very striking contrast. In the *Heart of Midlothian*, the extremes of Edinburgh Canongate and of Court life in London, Meg Murdockson and Queen Caroline, John Duke of Argyle and Daddie Ratcliffe, are reconciled. In *Old Mortality*, we have Cameronians of the very straitest sect pitted against Claverhouse ; Mause Headrigg and Edith Bellenden brought into juxtaposition. In *Kenilworth*, the inn at Cumnor balances the castle of the

Earl of Leicester, and the dwarfish Dicky Sludge determines the fate of the beautiful Amy Robsart. In *The Bride of Lammermuir*, the extravagant humours of Caleb Balderstone relieve yet deepen the horrors of Lucy Ashton's tragedy ; and we have already seen the magical effect produced in *The Pirate* by the contrast between Minna and Brenda, as well as between both and the savage rovers of the sea. Many trace a deepening degeneracy in those novels following *Ivanhoe ;* but others, we think with more justice, find the same spirit and power working quite as freely, if not with such conscious and exuberant force, in his *Nigel* and *Quentin Durward*, and even in parts of his *Abbot, St. Ronan's Well,* and *Redgauntlet,* not to speak of his splendid and sustained *Talisman,* which, occurring very late in the series, exhibits all the original strength and glory of his genius under the subjugation of an art more exquisitely perfect than any other of his Novels, or perhaps any other fiction whatever, has displayed. *Contrast* in that superb story, too, is the great charm, the contrast especially between Saladin and Cœur de Lion,—a contrast including that of race and religion, as well as of the two persons and characters, and extending to the very exercises in which they both approve themselves matchless proficients,—the one cutting a bar of iron in sunder with his two-handed sword, and the other severing a pillow in twain with his delicate scimitar! No narrow-minded man could ever have done such justice as Scott does in this novel to the better parts and spirit of Islam; and he, be it noticed, did so fifteen years before Carlyle wrote his *Heroes and Hero-worship*, with its warm commendation of Mahomet, and forty-four ere the *Quarterly Review* startled the literary world with its recent extraordinary paper entitled 'Islam,'—a paper which, had it appeared in the days of Gifford, or even Lockhart, would have terminated the existence of that venerable organ of Conservatism. Genius like Scott's is 'before all ages;' and even philosophy must take many rests ere it can overtake it.

The variety and originality of Scott's characters is another point in which he may be likened, though still at a great distance, to Shakspeare. What galleries they form of the bold, the bad, the grotesque, the ludicrous, the beautiful, and the noble, now arranged in graceful groupes, now projected in striking contrast, and now standing out in strong relief like solitary pines upon a mountain side! Let us notice a very few out of multitudes. In *Waverley*, we have the venerable Baron Bradwardine, the gallant Vich Ian Vohr, the adventurous Charles Edward, the beautiful Flora MacIvor, and the sweet and girlish Rose, set in the front of a picture, the background of which is peopled by Bailie MacWheeble (Coleridge's special favourite), Callum Begg, the Gifted Gilfillan, Mrs. Flockhart, Balmawhapple, and David Gellatley dancing to the wild wind of his own music. In *Guy Mannering*, there is room under the tall shoulder of Meg Merrilees, the real heroine of the tale, for the stalwart Dandie Dinmont, the rugged Hatteraick, Paulus Pleydell, Esq., the most astute of advocates, Gilbert Glossin, the wiliest of lawyers, Jock Jabos, prince of postilions, and Duncan MacGuffog, most ugsome of turnkeys. In the *Antiquary*, two of the humbler characters, Edie Ochiltree and Elspeth of the Craigburnfoot, are the best; but the dropping of Oldbuck's grey shaggy eyebrows when he is angry is a trait taken from Scott himself, as James Hogg in his *Memoirs* often testifies; and he bears, besides, a striking resemblance in his early love disappointment to his creator. Old Caxon, though he does not rise much higher than Morland's asses, is depicted with equal power; his daughter Jenny is sweetness and modesty itself; and alike Lieutenant Taffril, Hector MacIntyre, and the Phoca who robs him of his cane, are fine animals. In *Rob Roy*, the Bailie and Rob form a pair altogether inimitable, united by downright dissimilitude, cemented by the elements of explosion; and besides them, and Andrew Fairservice and Diana, there are the precentor, Mr. Hammorgaw; Mattie, the lassie quean, afterwards Mrs. Jarvie; Clerk Jobson, the pettifogger; Clerk Touthope; Garschattachin, with his drunken courage; Iverach, with his singed plaid; and last, not least, the hack, Souple Sam, with his 'curious and complete lameness, making use of three legs for the sake of progression, while the fourth appeared as if meant to be flourished in the air by way of accompaniment.' And even in some of his later novels we have seen already how this wealth of character continues startling, although the quality is not always equal. We have often regretted that Sir Walter did not commence writing novels ten years sooner than he did, in which case we would have had other twenty novels as fresh and overflowing with life, and character, and poetry, and fun, as those we are privileged at present to possess.

We pass now to some closing remarks on the moral and religious influences of Sir Walter Scott's Novels. And let us observe here, once for all, that if we look in Scott for any narrow, contracted, or merely conventional morality, we shall look in vain. The morality that crushes natural instincts, that confounds the positive with the moral, that refuses to grant innocent recreations or gives them with a grudge which taints them with bitterness, that identifies duty and life with austerity, gloom, and useless self-denial, and founds its rules and regulations very much on the old Manichean hypothesis that matter is evil and the body the creation of the Wicked one,—that nature is fallen as well as man; this is entirely opposite to Scott's spirit, as it is, indeed, if we err not, to that of the Great Teacher Himself. Scott felt that morality on these terms may be possible, but can never be attractive and scarcely permanent; for, while casting out some evils, it often introduces others worse and wickeder than those superseded, leading to pride, formality, cold-heartedness, and the want of that broad charity which thinketh no evil (having enough to do with the evil which requires no thinking to see, and no search to find), and that beareth and believeth all things. Scott's moral code is founded on a deep knowledge of human nature in all its strength and weakness, and sympathy with its sore struggles and thick temptations; on a firm conviction that comparatively few men are in themselves much better or worse than their neighbours; that morality is far more a matter of the inward heart and soul than of the outward deportment, depends more on the soundness of the kernel than on the completeness of the shell; and that in loving our neighbour as ourselves lies the marrow of the Law, just as in loving God with all our mind and strength lies the essence of the Gospel. In showing us the faults of the generous and the good, he uniformly acts on the principle of first getting us warmly to appreciate their merits, to feel for them as personal friends, and to be as anxious as are personal friends to wean those they love from their errors. He delights, too, rather in lashing the sins of the soul than those of the temperament and passions; and so did the Master of Christian morals before him.

On the other hand, he is not afraid, whenever occasion serves, to show vice its own feature with all the fidelity of Solomon and all the force of Hogarth. What vice has Scott not exposed, what villany has he spared! Is it hypocrisy? Think of mine Host of the Candlestick in *Waverley*, Tom Trumbull in *Redgauntlet*, and Ned Christian in *Peveril*. Is it legal chicanery, leading by sure gradation to darker crime? Think of Glossin in *Guy Mannering*. Is it sottishness? Think of Michael Lambourne and Nanty Ewart. Is it seduction? Remember George Staunton. Is it quackery?

2 A

Down, Dousterswivel, on thy knees and confess
what an impostor and charlatan thou art! Is it
accomplished, far-stretching, but self-destroying
fraud? Think of Rashleigh Osbaldistone and his
hideous dying moments. Is it idleness and the
self-indulgent frivolity of youth? Think of his
cousin Francis. Is it selfish family pride? Think
of Lady Ashton. Is it that somewhat loftier but
equally ruinous ambition, which, mounting the
ladder of power, is ready to trample on the ten-
derest ties, and to moisten its rounds by the
dearest blood? Remember the Earl of Leicester.
Is it a thorough want of principle and almost of
human feeling? Think of such men as Varney
and Etherington, and the Templar, Giles Amaury,
in *The Talisman*. Is it even the excess of human
affection mismanaged to madness? Think of
Elspeth MacTavish, the Highland Widow, or
Woman of the Tree. And let it be marked that
Scott is as faithful in administering the ideal
punishments as he is in branding the crimes, or
exposing the errors. His works, in one view of
them, may be called a long hymn to Retribution,
and a many-volumed proof that justice is done
certainly, if not fully, in this present preliminary
life. Yet he is aware of important exceptions to
the rule, as will be proved by a remarkable quota-

tion from one of his prefaces: 'The writer of
Ivanhoe was censured because he had not assigned
Wilfred to Rebecca rather than to the less interesting Rowena. But, not to mention that the
prejudices of that age rendered such a union impossible, the author may, in passing, observe that
he thinks a character of a highly virtuous and
lofty stamp is degraded rather than exalted by
an attempt to reward virtue with temporal prosperity. Such is not the recompense which Providence has deemed worthy of suffering merit; and
it is a dangerous and fatal doctrine to teach young
persons, the most common readers of romance,
that rectitude of conduct and of principle are either
naturally allied with, or adequately rewarded by,
the gratification of our passions or the attainment
of our wishes. If a virtuous and self-denied character is always dismissed with temporal wealth,
greatness, or rank, the reader will be apt to say,
Verily virtue has had its reward. But a glance at
the great picture of life will show that the duties of
self-denial, and the sacrifice of passion to principle,
are seldom thus remunerated, and that the internal
consciousness of their high-minded discharge of
duty produces in their own reflections a more
adequate recompense, in the form of that peace
which the world cannot give nor take away.'

After all this, it may seem poor praise to say that not only do Scott's writings never inflame the passions, or seek to shake the moral principles, but they are entirely free from that levity and coarseness of language which are often found where there is no corruption, and unite a manly code of morals with a feminine delicacy of feeling. The best proof of this will be found in the great improvement which has taken place in the moral tone of fictions since he wrote. Godwin, no doubt, Mrs. Inchbald, Miss Austen, and Miss Edgeworth were pure, and so far purified the taste ; but Scott, a mightier genius than all of them put together, set the copestone on the reformation they had begun. And, with the exception, of course, of some of the French school abroad and their imitators at home, most fictionists are now compelled to observe decency of language, and to pay outward respect, at least, to those great common laws of morality which the world has sanctioned as essential to its well-being and its healthy action.

In reference to Scott's religion, so far as that was a *personal* matter, we have nothing to say. He always professed himself an attached member of the Church of England, in love with her liturgy and worship, if not, perhaps, exactly *en rapport* with all her articles. Yet if we take his Journal as a

full, as it was a final exponent of his religious sentiments, his deviations from the orthodox creed were
exceedingly slight, and his general belief in Christianity seems never to have been shaken. We
have quoted above his significant and earnest
dying words to Lockhart. We are not prepared
to deny that he had somewhat strong prejudices
against what is called the Evangelical School, that
he disliked *very* pious females, and that no more
than Jonathan Oldbuck was he a regular attender
on church : but he paid, on the whole, a satisfactory homage to the Sabbath, always spending
a portion of that day in religious exercises and the
instruction of his children ; he believed as well as
admired the Bible, and religious reverence was
indeed an essential part of his constitution. How
his views and feelings might have been modified in
our strange, faith-shattering, or rather faith-shifting
days,—days in which, perhaps, after all, faith is gaining in breadth what it is losing in intensity ; less
drying up than changing its channel,—cannot, of
course, be either stated or surmised. But, without
contending for the evangelical character of any of
his works in the strict sense of that term, we maintain that no one who had not drunk into the very
depth of the spirit of Christianity could have
created a Jeanie Deans. He did not, indeed, create,

he only copied her from many living examples he had met with among the Christian women of his native land; but unless he had admired and understood, he would not have condensed these examples into this consummate *one,* or would have dared—and in that age it required some daring—to make Rebecca the Jewess the finest character and the truest Christian in the most brilliant of all his tales, and put into her lips that noble strain which ranks almost beside the old Psalms of David:

' When Israel, of the Lord beloved,
    Out from the land of bondage came,
Her fathers' God before her moved,
    An awful Guide in cloud and flame.

' By day along the astonished lands
    The cloudy pillar glided slow,
By night Arabia's crimsoned sands
    Returned the fiery column's glow.

' There rose the choral hymn of praise,
    And trump and timbrel answered keen,
And Zion's daughters poured their lays,
    And priests' and warriors' voice between ;'

or could have sustained throughout his numerous tales that general respect for the institutions and the ministers of religion, that reverence for the Scriptures, or that all-embracing charity, which so distinguish his every page. He that is not against us is on our part, says the Founder of Christianity Himself; and His words, we venture to say, may be applied fearlessly to the author of the Waverley Novels.

Old Mortality, all may remember, spent his life in visiting the tombs of the martyrs; and there exists at least one remarkable man of the day who might earn the name of 'New Mortality' from a similar habit. We refer to the author of the *Life of Chalmers* in the present series. The tendency, however, is rather now-a-days to repair to the tombs of the poets. It has been at least our own fortune to have stood at some of the most celebrated of the resting-places of the renowned. Years ago we visited the mausoleum which, in Dumfries,

> 'Directs pale Scotia's way
> To pour her sorrows o'er her poet's dust,'

with many conflicting emotions, as we remembered how much power and weakness lay buried there; although the feeling left last and uppermost was that expressed in the words,

> 'The glory dies not, and the grief is past.'

Some time after we visited Wordsworth's grave, as evening was dropping her dewy curtain over Grasmere Lake, and the Rotha, blue darling of her poet's eye, was softening her voice amidst the stillness, and the New Moon had suddenly shone out in the west, as if to certify the immortality of his song and himself, and to cut with her silver sickle whatever doubts as to either might have been crossing our souls. A year or two later we visited the grave of Southey, with Derwentwater spreading out her beautiful bosom on the left; Portinscale, the loveliest of English villages, laughing through roses in the foreground; and old Skiddaw standing up like the poet's everlasting monument behind. But none of these visits moved us more than when, one splendid September forenoon in 1859, we stood in Dryburgh Abbey, and leaned over the tomb of Scott, with a vast yew that might have formed a coronet for the head of Death shadowing it, and the sound of the Tweed—the sound of all others sweetest in the ear of the mighty Wizard—coming up through the woodland as a lullaby to his dust;—and thus leaning and musing there, thought of the benign creations of that man's mind; of the stores of knowledge it had accumulated; of the entire literature which had emanated from it; and of the intellectual, moral, and purely and loftily spiritual influences which that literature had produced, was producing, and would produce for evermore;—we felt as if a multitude of men, as if a nation were slumbering below, and, full of blended awe and love, turning away, we left him alone with his glory!

CONCLUSION.

THE COMING CENTENARY.

WE cannot close this brief and imperfect, but not, we trust, inaccurate or insincere life of Sir Walter Scott without a very few closing words in reference to the centenary of his birth which is at hand.

The time draws nigh when Scotland is to do herself and her most gifted son the honour of a centenary celebration; and certainly, if it exhibit the loyalty and enthusiasm, or even a portion of it, which saluted that of Robert Burns, it will add a lustre and a laurel to the year 1871 that shall render it only second to the year 1771, when the great Minstrel of the Border and the prose Shakspeare of Scotland appeared in the metropolis of his native land.

We use the words 'a *portion* of it' advisedly, for we are aware that there were circumstances connected with the Burns celebration which secured greater enthusiasm than we can expect in the case of Sir Walter Scott. Mrs. Stowe, in her *Sunny Memories*, notices that, at the public meetings held in Scotland in her honour in 1853, any allusion made to Burns brought down the house, while Scott's name was received rather coldly. We may supply some reasons for what seems to have puzzled her considerably ; and these reasons will be found to apply to the point in hand. In the first place, Mrs. Stowe's admirers—and we state it in her honour, not in her disparagement—belonged principally to the people, the very class among whom Burns is most highly admired ; the upper classes were not so fully represented at her gatherings, and they in general prefer Scott to Burns. Secondly, there is a feeling very prevalent in Scotland that Burns was a shamefully used man ; that his treatment at the hands of the nobility, and middle class too, of his time led to much of his misery and reckless conduct ; and that his country had contracted a debt to his memory which must be publicly and in the amplest measure discharged. Every rapturous cheer Mrs. Stowe heard at her meetings, when the name Burns was pronounced, was a separate instalment in the clearance of that debt ; and it seemed entirely liquidated on the memorable 25th of January 1859. Scott, on the other hand, had been for the greater part of his life a prosperous gentleman, and, so far as money was concerned, had received his reward. His misfortunes afterwards were to a great extent the result of his own extravagance and ambition. Ebenezer Elliott says of the Scotch people and Burns :

> ' They gave him more than gold,
> They *read the brave man's book.*'

But the people of Scotland, England, and the world read Scott and gave him gold besides. Thirdly, there was lingering in 1853, and there lingers still, a certain prejudice, partly political and partly religious, against Scott, founded on his Tory principles, and on his treatment of the Covenanters. That this prejudice has to a great extent subsided since, we fondly believe ; but it is not entirely gone. Burns, on the contrary, although sometimes profane enough, was a Radical in politics ; and his *Cottar's Saturday Night*, like charity, covered a multitude of sins. Hence nothing will shake him in the estimation of his countrymen. While admitting Scott's general superiority, they trace it partly to his happier circumstances and greater success, and determinedly hold to it that Burns is the representative poet of his nation.

This, we say, is the feeling of the majority. With
some, again, Scott stands on a much higher vantage-
ground ; and by all he is admired. This ought to,
and must, secure a noble centenary ; but we question if it will have the same heartiness of celebration as that of 1859, although it shall be far more
enthusiastic, in Scotland at any rate, than the tre-
centenary of Shakspeare in 1864.

About the propriety of such a centenary celebration there can, we think, be no reasonable doubt.
The Scotch are slow to recognise their great men
in their lifetime, and their recognition, even when
it comes, seldom takes any very enthusiastic or
demonstrative form. It sometimes amounts to little
else than a cessation from abuse ; and we are reminded of the one privilege which befell Wordsworth's old Cumberland beggar through his long
lingering on the road, that

> ' The dogs turned away,
> *Weary of barking at him.'*

Such is, too, the inherent, call it coldness, or
reticence, or bashfulness of the Scottish character,
that whenever we hear of any great testimonial
to living national merit suddenly paid, or any
keen enthusiasm suddenly excited, we begin to
ask, Why, what evil has the recipient been doing ?

over what flickering *fama* is this meant to be
the golden extinguisher? or, if not, Is there
not some political end to be thus served, or
party *animus* to be thus covertly gained? When
death comes, this is all changed, and then every
opportunity for the outflow of the pent-up feeling
is given and welcomed. And even after the great
man has been dead, as Scott has been, for nearly
forty years, it becomes incumbent on the people to
prove that their feeling has not been of the mere
de mortuis nil nisi bonum kind,—not a mere evan-
escent and got-up sensation,—but a deep, quiet,
sober, and growing conviction of the solid worth of
his achievements, and of the thorough identification
of his name and works with the nation's pride and
the nation's glory. Since Scott departed, some
great changes have taken place in literature, and
especially in the novel. New dynasties of power
have sprung up abroad and at home. Names to
conjure with—such as those of Victor Hugo, and
Alexandre Dumas, and Balzac, and Bulwer Lytton,
and Thackeray, and Dickens, and others scarcely
inferior—have been placed by their admirers, if
not by those who bear them, not very far from Sir
Walter's own; and it behoves Scotland to embrace
the opportunity afforded by the 15th of August
1871 to declare, in a manner worthy of herself, and

unmistakeable in the certainty of its sound, that she prefers her own child still, while most cheerfully conceding the transcendent merit of others ; and is ready to exclaim (as Scott himself said in reference to the candidate he proposed at Jedburgh at the last election before the Reform Bill),—

> ‘ We hae tried this *Border lad,*
> And we ’ll *try him* yet again.’

He is to us the Master of the novel, and the Master of the song too. There may be larger and brighter suns in other regions of space,—and let those other lands glory in and admire them,—but Scott is *our sun* here in the north, and we are content to continue to bask in his beams and to rejoice in the anniversary of his rising. Other ends may be served by the celebration of the great Scotchman’s centenary,—such as ‘the vindicating the true greatness of our national genius and of our national character ; the asserting that the language of Scotland is not the language of a province but of an independent kingdom ; and the resistance or modification of that centralizing tendency which is sucking in the Scotch manners and literature, and all that is Scotch, into our southern Maelstrom. Not very long ago we remarked to an English Dissenting clergyman of great eminence, how England had so many large towns. His reply was, 'Yes, sir ; England's one vast city turning, and Scotland is *our pleasure-ground.*' We must go, we thought, and inform our *gardeners* of this. When Queen Caroline threatened to turn Scotland into a hunting-field on account of its complicity with the Porteous mob, the Duke of Argyle replied, with a low bow, 'Then, Madam, I must go north and get my *hounds* ready.'

With regard to the manner of a celebration, for which there exist such strong and various reasons, we need only say, to be worthy of Scott, it must be carefully pondered, and not spoiled by undue hurry or enthusiasm. The details, as well as the general programme, must be thoroughly digested ere they are presented to the public. While national, it should be of a most catholic character ; and the memory of the Minstrel should on that occasion be severed, even in idea, from all petty associations and political or religious prejudices. It should be imposing and splendid in its circumstances, but without an atom of sensationalism. It should be connected, as we believe it is to be connected, with some permanent institution,—some bursary or fund which may, peradventure, encourage and educate future Scotts, if there be virtue in the coming ages to produce such prodigies; it should be, in short, a celebration which shall not only attract but enrich the eyes of the whole world, express worthily cosmopolitan gratitude and admiration, and be such as the benignant but solemn shade of the departed himself may regard with pride and complacency.

MURRAY AND GIBB, EDINBURGH,
PRINTERS TO HER MAJESTY'S STATIONERY OFFICE.

Handsome crown 8vo volume, price 7s. 6d.,

Homiletics and Pastoral Theology. By William G.
T. SHEDD, D.D., Baldwin Professor in Union Theological Seminary, New York City.

'The work will be found to be an admirable guide and stimulus in whatever pertains to this department of theology. The student finds himself in the hands of a master able to quicken and enlarge his scope and spirit. The homiletical precepts are well illustrated by the author's own style, which is muscular, while quivering with nervous life.'— *American Theological Review.*

New Edition,

The Works of Michael Bruce. With a Life of the
Author by Rev. A. B. GROSART, Liverpool. Crown 8vo, toned paper, 3s. 6d.

'It may be safely affirmed that the fame of Bruce as a true poet, and one of our finest hymn writers, is now finally and triumphantly established. We cordially thank Mr. Grosart for what has evidently been a labour of love to him. He has brought to his task the skill and industry of an antiquarian, the keen eye of a logician, the fine enthusiasm of a poet, and, we had almost said, the personal love of a brother.'—*The Freeman,* April 12, 1865.

In crown 8vo, price 5s.,

The Life of John Kitto, D.D. By John Eadie, D.D.,
LL.D. With Illustrations. Cheap Edition, 2s. 6d. In cloth, gilt edges, 3s. 6d.

'Dr. Eadie has done for Kitto what Southey did for Nelson. He has given us a book over which, in the curious incidents and noble struggles it records, age and childhood alike may hang in wonder, and gather a higher lesson than is suggested even by the renowned career of the hero of Trafalgar.'—*News of the Churches.*

Second Edition,

The History of Moses and his Times : Viewed in
connection with Egyptian Antiquities. By the Rev. THORNLEY SMITH, author of 'The History of Joseph.' Beautifully Illustrated, crown 8vo, 3s. 6d.

'Presents the results of careful and extensive reading in a pleasant and interesting form.'—*Evangelical Magazine.*

'Forms an admirable companion to the "Pentateuch."'—*Literary Churchman.*

2

Second Edition,

The History of Joshua : Viewed in connection with
the Topography of Canaan and the Customs of the Times. By the Rev. THORNLEY SMITH. Crown 8vo, 3s. 6d.

' It is practically a commentary, and a very intelligently illustrative one, on the whole Book of Joshua ; and, as being designed for popular use, is more attractive in form than a direct exposition could have been.' —*Nonconformist.*

A Book for Governesses. By One of Them. In fcap.
8vo, price 2s. 6d.

' We recommend this little book for governesses to all whom it may concern. It is a healthy, sensible, and invigorating work,--likely to strengthen the hands and inspire the hearts of young governesses with a cheerful view of their labour, and a respect for themselves, which is a wholesome element in all work.'—*Athenæum.*

William Farel, and the Story of the Swiss Reforma-
tion. By the Rev. WM. M. BLACKBURN, author of ' Young Calvin in Paris,' etc. Crown 8vo, with Frontispiece, price 3s. 6d.

' This book is almost a model of what popular biographies should be. " It ought to be put into the hands of our young people, that they may learn how the Reformation was won, and how great a godly consecrated man " may be.'—*English Independent.*

' Its facts are grouped so skilfully, and its scenes portrayed so vividly, that it equals in interest any romance.'—*Literary World.*

' We have read it with intense satisfaction, and commend it with all possible earnestness to young and old.'—*Christian Witness.*

The Family Circle. By the Rev. A. Morton, Edin-
burgh. Fourth Edition. Crown 8vo, price 3s. 6d.

CONTENTS.—*Part I.*—1. Home. 2. The Husband. 3. The Wife. 4. The Father. 5. The Mother. 6. The Child. *Part II.*—1. The Family Circle in Prosperity. 2. The Family Circle in Adversity. 3. The Family Circle Dispersed. 4. The Family Circle in the Grave. 5. The Family Circle in Eternity.

' The reverend writer of this volume explains in a very wise and tender manner the relative duties and rights of the members of families. The essentials of a real home are clearly and feelingly defined.'—*Critic.*

' This is a volume of unquestionable merit. We have rarely perused a work upon the subject so full of deeply important truth, expressed in language of mingled power and pathos.'—*Glasgow Herald.*

Clifford Castle : A Tale of the English Reformation.
By Mrs. MACKAY, author of ' The Family at Heatherdale,' etc. Crown 8vo, price 3s. 6d.

' A very superior work, full of graphic touches and interesting episodes.'—*Bible Class Magazine.*

www.ingramcontent.com/pod-product-compliance
Lightning Source LLC
Chambersburg PA
CBHW032004120726
47898CB00005BA/1563